The Simpkins Plot

by

George A. Birmingham

The Simpkins Plot
by George A. Birmingham

Copyright © 2024

All Rights reserved.

ISBN: 978-93-64285-26-1

Published by

DOUBLE 9 BOOKS

2/13-B, Ansari Road
Daryaganj, New Delhi – 110002
info@double9books.com
www.double9books.com
Tel. 011-40042856

This book is under public domain

ABOUT THE AUTHOR

George A. Birmingham (1865-1950) was an Irish author and playwright known for his contributions to early 20th-century literature, particularly in the genre of **satirical fiction.** His works often explore themes of **political intrigue, social dynamics,** and **village life,** reflecting his keen observational skills and wit. **Notable Work, The Simpkins Plot (1927):** A satirical novel set in a fictional village, exploring political and social intrigue with a humorous touch. **The Mysterious Mr. Balfour (1929):** A novel combining elements of mystery and social satire. **The Leper of Saint Giles (1931):** Another example of his work that combines social commentary with engaging storytelling. George A. Birmingham's contributions to literature are notable for their **satirical** and **character-driven** approach. His novels offer a humorous and insightful look at the political and social issues of his time, and his ability to blend comedy with social commentary has left a lasting impact on readers and critics alike. Although not as widely known today, his work remains a significant example of early 20th-century satirical fiction, reflecting his unique perspective on Irish and British society. Birmingham passed away on February 15, 1950, but his work continues to be appreciated for its clever narrative style and insightful observations on human nature and societal norms.

CONTENTS

CHAPTER I

The platform at Euston was crowded, and the porters' barrows piled high with luggage. During the last week in July the Irish mail carries a heavy load of passengers, and for the twenty minutes before its departure people are busy endeavouring to secure their own comfort and the safety of their belongings. There are schoolboys, with portmanteaux, play-boxes, and hand-bags, escaping home for the summer holidays. There are sportsmen, eager members of the Stock Exchange or keen lawyers, on their way to Donegal or Clare for fishing. There are tourists, the holders of tickets which promise them a round of visits to famous beauty spots. There are members of the House of Lords, who have accomplished their labours as legislators—and their wives, peeresses, who have done their duty by the London season—on their way back to stately mansions in the land from which they draw their incomes. Great people these in drawing-rooms or clubs; greater still in the remote Irish villages which their names still dominate; but not particularly great on the Euston platform, for there is little respect of persons there as the time of the train's departure draws near. A porter pushed his barrow, heavy with trunks and crowned with gun-cases, against the legs of an earl, who swore. A burly man, red faced and broad shouldered, elbowed a marchioness who, not knowing how to swear effectively, tried to wither him with a glance. She failed. The man who had jostled her had small reverence for rank or title. He was, besides, in a hurry, and had no time to spend in apologising to great ladies.

Sir Gilbert Hawkesby was one of his Majesty's judges. He had won his position by sheer hard work and commanding ability. He had not stopped in his career to soothe the outraged dignity of those whom he pushed aside; and he had no intention now of delaying his progress along the railway platform to explain to a marchioness why he had jostled her. It was only by a vigorous use of his elbows that he could make his way; and it ought to have been evident, even to a peeress, that he meant to go from one end of the train to the other. His eyes glanced sharply right and left as he pushed on. He peered through the windows of the carriages. He scanned each figure in the crowd. At last he caught sight of a lady standing beside the bookstall. She wore a long grey cloak and a dark travelling-hat. She stooped over the books and papers on the stall before her; and her face, in profile as Sir Gilbert saw it, was lit by the flaring gas above her head. Having caught sight of her, the judge pushed on even more vigorously than before.

"Here I am, Milly," he said. "I said I'd be in time to see you off, and I am; but owing to—"

The lady at the bookstall turned and looked at him. She flushed suddenly, and then as suddenly grew pale. She raised her hand hurriedly and pulled her veil over her face. Sir Gilbert stared at her in amazement. Then his face, too, changed colour.

"I—I beg your pardon," he said; "I mistook you for my niece. It's quite inconceivable to me how I—a most remarkable likeness. I'm astonished that I didn't notice it before. The fact is—under the circumstances—"

Sir Gilbert was acutely uncomfortable. Never in the course of a long career at the bar had he felt so hopelessly embarrassed. On no occasion in his life, so far as he could remember, had he been reduced to stammering incoherences. It had not occurred to him to apologise to the jostled marchioness a few minutes before. He was now anxious to abase himself before the lady at the bookstall.

"I sincerely beg your pardon," he said. "I should not have dreamed for a moment of intruding myself on you if I had known. I ought to have recognised you. I can't understand—"

The lady laid down the book she held in her hand, and turned her back on Sir Gilbert. She crossed the platform, and entered a carriage without looking back. Sir Gilbert stood stiff and awkward beside the bookstall.

"It's a most extraordinary likeness," he muttered. "I can't understand why I didn't notice it before. I can't have ever really looked at her."

Then, avoiding the carriage which the lady had entered, he walked further along the platform. He was much less self-assertive in his progress. He threaded his way instead of elbowing it through the crowd. The most fragile peeress might have jostled him, and he would not have resented it.

"Uncle Gilbert! Is that you? I was afraid you were going to be late."

The judge turned quickly. A lady, another lady, leaned out of the window of a first-class compartment and greeted him. He stared at her. The likeness was less striking now when he looked at his niece's full face; but it was there, quite unmistakable; a sufficient excuse for the blunder he had made.

"Ah, Milly," he said; "you really are Milly, aren't you? I've just had a most extraordinary encounter with your double. It's a most remarkable coincidence; quite the thing for one of your novels. By the way, how's the new one getting on?"

"Which one? I'm just correcting a set of proofs, and I'm deep in the plot of another. That's what's taking me over to Ireland. I thought I'd told you."

"Yes, yes; local colour you said in your letter. Studying the wild Hibernian on his native soil; but really, Milly, when you've heard my story you won't want to go to Ireland for wild improbabilities. But I can't tell you now. There isn't time. We'll meet in Bally-what-do-you-call-it next week."

"And you'll stay with me, Uncle Gilbert, won't you? The house I've taken appears to be a perfect barrack. According to the agent, there are any amount of spare bedrooms."

"No," said the judge; "I've taken rooms at the hotel. The fact is, Milly, when I'm fishing I like to rough it a bit. Besides, I should only be in your way. You'll be working tremendously hard."

Neither excuse expressed Sir Gilbert's real reason for refusing his niece's invitation. He did not like roughing it, and he did not think it the least likely that his presence in the house would interfere with her work. On the contrary, her work was likely to interfere with his comfort. He was fond of his niece, but he disliked her habit of reading passages from her MSS. aloud in the evenings. She was very much absorbed in her novel-writing, and took her work with a seriousness which struck the judge as ridiculous.

"I'll dine with you occasionally," he said, "but I shall put up at the hotel. By the way, Milly, am I your tenant or are you mine? I left all the arrangements in your hands."

"I took the house and the fishing," she said. "The agent man wouldn't let one without the other; but you have to pay most of the rent. The salmon are the really valuable part of the property, it appears."

"All right," said Sir Gilbert; "so long as the fishing is good I won't quarrel with you over my share of the rent. The house would only have been a nuisance to me. I should have had to bring over servants, and that would have worried your aunt. Ah! Your time's up, I see. Good-bye, Milly, good-bye. Take care of yourself, and don't get mixed up with shady people in your search for originality. I'll start this day week as soon as ever I get your aunt settled down at Bournemouth."

Millicent King, Sir Gilbert Hawkesby's niece, was a young woman of some little importance in the world. The patrons of the circulating libraries knew her as Ena Dunkeld, and shook their heads over her. The gentlemen who add to the meagre salaries they earn in Government offices by writing reviews knew her under both her names, for no literary secrets are hid from them. They praised her novels publicly, and in private yawned over her morality. Many people, her aunt Lady Hawkesby among them, very strongly disapproved of her novels. Certain problems, so these ladies maintained, ought to be discussed only in scientific books, labelled "poison" for the safety of the public, and ought never to be discussed at all by young women. Millicent King, rendered obstinate by these criticisms, plunged deeper and deeper into a kind of mire which, after a time, she began to dislike very much. She had in reality simple tastes of a domestic kind, and might have been very happy sewing baby clothes if she had married a peaceable man and kept out of literary society. Fortunately, or unfortunately—the choice of the adverb depends upon the views taken of the value of detailed analysis of marriage problems—Miss King had not come across any man of a suitable kind who wanted to marry her. She had, on the other hand, met a large number of people who praised, and a few who abused her. She liked the flattery, and was pleased to be pointed out as a person of importance. She regarded the abuse as a tribute to the value of her work, knowing that all true prophets suffer under the evil speaking of a censorious world. Latterly she had begun to consider whether she might not secure the praise, without incurring the blame, by writing novels of a different kind. With a view to perfecting a new story of adventure and perfectly respectable love, she determined to isolate herself for a couple of months. As certain Irishmen played a part in her story, she fixed upon Connacht as the place of her retirement, intending to study the romantic Celt on his native soil. A house advertised in the columns of *The Field* seemed to offer her the opportunity she desired. She took it and the fishing attached to it; having bargained with her uncle, Sir Gilbert Hawkesby, that she was to be relieved of the duty of catching salmon, and that he should pay a considerable part of the heavy rent demanded by the local agent.

CHAPTER II

These are a few things better managed in Ireland than in England, and one of them is the starting of important railway trains. The departure, for instance, of the morning mail from the Dublin terminus of the Midland and Great Western Railway is carried through, day after day, with dignity. The hour is an early one, 7 a.m.; but all the chief officiate of the company are present, tastefully dressed. There is no fuss. Passengers know that it is their duty to be at the station not later than a quarter to seven. If they have any luggage they arrive still earlier, for the porters must not be hustled. At ten minutes to seven the proper officials conduct the passengers to their carriages and pen them in. Lest any one of independent and rebellious spirit should escape, and insist on loitering about the platform, the doors of the compartments are all locked. No Irishman resents this treatment. Members of a conquered race, they are meek, and have long ago given up the hope of being able to resist the mandates of official people.

Strangers, Englishmen on tour, are easily recognised by their self-assertive demeanour and ill-bred offences against the solemn etiquette of the railway company. Since it is impossible to teach these people manners or meekness, the guards and porters treat them, as far as possible, with patient forbearance. They must, of course, be got into the train, but the doors of their compartments are not locked. It has been found by experience that English travellers object to being imprisoned without trial, and quote regulations of the Board of Trade forbidding the locking of both doors of a railway carriage. There is nothing to be gained by a public wrangle with an angry Englishman. He cannot be got to understand that laws, those of the Board of Trade or any other, are not binding on Irish officials. There is only one way of treating him without loss of dignity, and that is to give in to him at once, with a shrug of the shoulders.

Thus, Miss King, entering upon the final stage of her journey to Ballymoy, reaped the benefit of belonging to a conquering and imperial race. She was, indeed, put into her compartment, a first-class one, ten minutes before the train started; but her door, alone of all the doors, was left unlocked. The last solemn minutes before the departure of the train passed slowly. Grave men in uniform paraded the platform, glancing occasionally at their watches.

The engine-driver watched from his cabin for the waving of the green flag which would authorise him to push over his levers and start the train. The great moment had almost arrived. The guard held his whistle to his lips, and had the green flag ready to be unfurled, in his left hand. Then a totally unexpected, almost an unprecedented, thing occurred. A passenger walked into the station and approached the train with the evident intention of getting into it. He was a clergyman, shabbily dressed, imperfectly shaved, red-haired, and wearing a red moustache. He carried a battered Gladstone bag in one hand. The guard glanced at him and then distended his cheeks with air, meaning to blow his whistle.

"Hold on a minute," said the clergyman. "I'm thinking of travelling by this train."

The audacity of this statement shook the self-possession of the guard.

"Can't wait," he said. "Time's up. You ought to have been here sooner."

To say this he was obliged to take the whistle from his lips; and the engine-driver, who had a strict sense of duty, was unable to start.

"As a matter of fact," said the clergyman, "I'm not only here soon enough, I'm an hour and a half too soon. The train I intended to catch is the next one."

The guard put his whistle to his lips again.

"If you blow that thing," said the clergyman, "before I'm in the train, I'll take an action against the company for assault and battery."

The guard hesitated. He did not see how such an action could be sustained in court; but he felt the necessity of thinking over his position carefully before running any risks. The law, especially in Ireland, is a curious thing, and no wise man entangles himself with it if he can help it. Railway guards are all wise men, otherwise they would not have risen to their high positions.

"Now that I am here," said the clergyman, "I may as well go by this train. Excuse me one moment; I want to get a few newspapers."

This was gross impertinence, and the guard was in no mood to stand it. He blew his whistle. The engine shrieked excitedly, and the train started with a violent jerk.

The clergyman seized a handful of newspapers from the bookstall. Clinging to them and his bag he ran across the platform. He tried the doors of two third-class compartments as they passed him, and found them locked. He happened next upon that which was occupied by Miss King, opened the door, and tumbled in.

"I've only got a third-class ticket," he said cheerfully; "but I shall travel first class the whole way now, and I shan't pay a penny of excess fare."

"Won't they make you?" said Miss King.

She realised that she had found an unexpectedly early opportunity of studying the peculiarities of the Irish character, and determined to make the most of it.

"Certainly not," said the clergyman. "The position is this. I have a through ticket—I bought it yesterday—which entitles me to travel on this railway to Donard. If the doors of all the third-class carriages are locked when I arrive at the station, I take it that the company means me to travel first class. Their own action is a clear indication of their intention. There isn't a jury in Ireland would give it against me, even if the case came into court, which, of course, it won't."

"I'm going to Donard, too," said Miss King.

"Are you? It's a wretched hole of a place. I don't advise you to stop there long."

"I'm not staying there at all. I'm driving straight on to Ballymoy."

"If you're at all familiar with Ballymoy, I expect you've heard of me. My name's Meldon, the Reverend J. J. Meldon, B.A. I was curate of Ballymoy once, and everybody who was there in my time will be talking about me still. I'm going back there now for a holiday."

"But I'm quite a stranger," said Miss King. "I've never been in Ballymoy."

Meldon glanced at the bag which lay on the seat before her. There was no label on it, but it bore the initials M. K. in gold letters on its side.

"I suppose," he said, "that you're not by any chance a sister or a niece of Major Kent's?"

"No. I'm not. I don't even know Major Kent. My name is King. Millicent King."

A clergyman is, necessarily, more or less educated. Mr. Meldon had proclaimed himself a bachelor of arts. It was natural to suppose that he would have known the name, even the real name, of a famous living novelist. Apparently he did not. Miss King felt a little disappointed.

"I daresay," said Meldon, without showing any signs of being impressed, "that you're going to stop with the Resident Magistrate."

"No," said Miss King decisively.

"You don't look like the sort of person who'd be going on a visit to the rectory."

Miss King was handsomely dressed. She appeared to be a lady of high fashion; not at all likely to be an inmate of the shabby little rectory at Ballymoy. She shook her head. Then, because she did not like being cross-questioned, she put an end to the conversation by opening her bag and taking out a bundle of typewritten papers. She was quite prepared to study Mr. Meldon as a type, but she saw no reason why Mr. Meldon should study her. He appeared to be filled with an ill-bred curiosity which she determined not to satisfy.

Meldon did not seem to resent her silence in the least. He leaned back in his seat and unfolded one of the papers he had snatched from the bookstall. It was a London evening paper of the day before, and contained a full account of the last scene of a sensational trial which had occupied the attention of the public for some time. A Mrs. Lorimer was charged with the murder of her husband. Her methods, if she had done the deed, were cold-blooded and abominable; but she was a young and good-looking woman, and the public was very anxious that she should be acquitted. The judge, Sir Gilbert Hawkesby, summed up very strongly against her; but the jury, after a prolonged absence from court, found her "not guilty." The paper published a portrait of Mrs. Lorimer, at which Meldon glanced. Suddenly his face assumed an expression of great interest. He studied the portrait carefully, and then looked at Miss King. She sat at the other end of the carriage, and he saw her face in profile as she bent over her papers. Mrs. Lorimer's side face was represented in the picture; and she, too, was bending over something. Meldon laid down the paper and took up another, this time an Irish morning paper. It contained an interview with Mrs. Lorimer, secured by an enterprising reporter after the trial. Meldon read this, and then turned to the magazine page and studied the picture of the lady which appeared there. In it Mrs. Lorimer wore a hat, and it was again her side face which was represented. Meldon looked from it to Miss King. The likeness was quite unmistakable. He took up a third paper, a profusely illustrated penny daily. He found, as he expected, a picture of Mrs. Lorimer. This was a full-length portrait, but the face came out clearly. Meldon took up the Irish paper again, and re-read very carefully the interview with the reporter on the evening of the trial. Then he folded up all three papers and leaned over towards Miss King.

"You must excuse me," he said, "if I didn't recognise you just now. You put me out by giving your name as Miss King. I'm much more familiar with your other name. Everybody is, you know."

Miss King was mollified by the apology. She looked up from her papers and smiled.

"How did you find me out?" she asked.

"By your picture in the papers," he said. "If you'll allow me to say so, it's a particularly good likeness and well reproduced. Of course, in your case, they'd take particular care not to print the usual kind of smudge."

Miss King was strongly inclined to ask for the papers. Her portrait had, she knew, appeared in the *Illustrated London News* and in two literary journals. She did not know that it had been reproduced in the daily press. The news excited and pleased her greatly. She had a short struggle with herself, in which self-respect triumphed. She did not ask for the papers, but assumed an air of bored indifference.

"They're always publishing my photograph," she said. "I can't imagine why they do it."

"I quite understand now," said Meldon, "why you're going down to Ballymoy. You couldn't go to a better place for privacy and quiet; complete quiet. I'm sure you want it."

"Yes," said Miss King. "I feel that I do. Now that you know who I am, you will understand. I chose Ballymoy because it seemed so very remote from everywhere."

She did not think it necessary to mention that she wanted to study the Irish character. Now that Meldon was talking in an interesting way she felt inclined to encourage him to reveal himself.

"Quite right. It is. I don't know a remoter place. Nobody will know you there, and if anybody guesses, I'll make it my business to put them off the scent at once. But there'll be no necessity for that. There isn't a man in the place will connect Miss King with the other lady. All the same, I don't think I'd stop too long at Doyle's hotel if I were you. Doyle is frightfully curious about people."

"I'm not stopping there," said Miss King. "I have taken a house."

"What house? I know Ballymoy pretty well, and there isn't a house in it you could take furnished, except the place that belonged to old Sir Giles Buckley."

"I've taken that for two months," said Miss King.

Meldon whistled softly. He was surprised. Ballymoy House, even if let at a low rent, is an expensive place to live in.

"My servants went down there yesterday," said Miss King. She opened her bag and groped among the contents as she spoke.

"Would you be very much shocked if I smoked a cigarette?" she asked.

"Not in the least," said Meldon. "I smoke myself."

"I was afraid—being a clergyman—you are a clergyman, aren't you? Some people are so prejudiced against ladies smoking."

"I'm not," said Meldon. "I'm remarkably free from prejudices of any kind. I pride myself on being open-minded. My wife doesn't smoke, but that's merely because she doesn't like it. If she did, I shouldn't make the slightest objection. All the same, you oughtn't to go puffing cigarettes about the streets of Ballymoy. The Major's a bit old-fashioned in some ways, and I don't expect Doyle is accustomed to see ladies smoking. You'll have to be very careful. If you start people talking they may find out who you are, and then there will certainly be unpleasantness."

"Would they disapprove of me?"

"Almost sure to. We Irish have the name of being a wild lot, I know; but—well, if you don't mind my saying so, most of us would be rather shy of you. I don't mind you myself in the least, of course. I'm not that kind of man. Still, your reputation! You've been a good deal in the papers, haven't you?"

Miss King, curiously enough, seemed pleased at this account of her reputation. It is gratifying to a novelist to be famous, and even notoriety is pleasant. She felt that, having braved the censure of Lady Hawkesby, she could afford to despise the morality of the people of Ballymoy.

"The Major?" she said. "You've mentioned him once or twice. What sort of man is he? Does my work shock him?"

"I expect it does," said Meldon. "I haven't seen him for some time, and so we haven't discussed you. But from what I know of him I should say that your work, as you call it, will shock him frightfully. You can't altogether blame him. He's a bachelor, and has very strict ideas about a wife's duty to her husband."

Miss King was moved by a desire to startle Meldon. She was really engaged on quite an innocent novel, but she chose to pretend that she was going on in her old way.

"What will he say," she said, "when he finds out that I'm going on with my work under his very eyes, so to speak, in Ballymoy?"

Meldon sat up suddenly.

"You don't mean that? Surely you can't intend—"

"Now you're shocked," said Miss King, "and you said you wouldn't be."

"I am a little. I didn't think I could be. But I am. I never imagined—"

"But that's exactly what I'm going to Ballymoy for. I want complete quiet in a lonely place where I shan't be disturbed."

"Of course, it's no business of mine," said Meldon. "But don't you think that perhaps you've done enough?"

"No. I have a great deal to do yet. If it were simply a question of earning money—"

Meldon looked at her. She was very well dressed. The bag which lay open at her side was fitted with silver-topped bottles. Her cigarette case appeared to be of gold. She was travelling first class. She had taken Ballymoy House for two months. He was quite ready to believe that she did not want money.

"Do you mean to say that you're doing it simply for amusement?" he asked.

"No. Not amusement." Her voice dropped to a kind of solemn whisper. "For the love of my art."

Miss King took herself very seriously indeed, and was accustomed to talk a good deal about her art. Literary people who might have known better, and critics who certainly did know better, encouraged her. They also talked about her art.

"Of course, if you look at it that way," said Meldon, "there's no more to be said; but you mustn't expect me to help you."

"You!"

"No. As a clergyman I can't possibly do it. Nor will the Major, unless he's greatly changed. I don't expect Doyle will either. He's president of the local branch of the League, but I'm sure he draws the line at—"

"But I don't want any of you to help me. Why should I?"

"I'm glad to hear that, at all events," said Meldon. "For, unless under very exceptional circumstances, I couldn't conscientiously assist you in any way."

"You said just now," said Miss King, "that you had no prejudices, and that nothing shocked you."

"Very few things do," said Meldon. "In fact I can't recollect ever having been shocked before; but this idea is a little new to me. I candidly confess that I never—hullo! We're slowing down into a station. Now I expect there'll be trouble about my ticket."

There was—considerable trouble. But Meldon emerged from it victoriously. He flatly refused to move from the carriage in which he sat. The guard, the station-master, a ticket-collector, and four porters gathered round the door and argued with him. Meldon argued fluently with them. In the end they took his name and address, threatening him with prosecution. Then, because the train was a mail train and obliged to go on, the guard blew his whistle and Meldon was left in peace.

"It's a nuisance," he said to Miss King, "being worried by those men. I wanted to send a telegram, but I couldn't. If I'd ventured out of the carriage they'd never have let me back again. The Major won't be expecting me till the next train. I only caught this one by accident."

"By accident?"

"Yes. The fact is I was up early this morning, wakened by my little daughter, a baby not quite two years old yet. I told you I was married, didn't I? The poor child was upset by the journey from England, and didn't sleep properly. When she had me wakened I thought I might as well get up. I intended to stroll up towards the station quietly. I walked rather faster than I meant to, and when I got within about three hundred yards of the station I discovered that I might just catch this train by running; so, of course, I ran. I'm very glad I did now. If I hadn't I shouldn't have met you."

"What did you do with the baby?"

"I didn't drop her on the way, if that's what you're thinking of. I'm not that kind of man at all, and I am particularly fond of the child. I scarcely ever complain when she keeps me awake at night, though many men I know would want to smother her. She and my wife are stopping with my mother-in-law in Rathmines. I'm going down for a fortnight's yachting with the Major. I might persuade him to give you a day's sailing, perhaps, if he doesn't find out who you are, and we succeed in keeping it dark about your going on with your work. I daresay it would cheer you up to go out on the bay. I expect you find your work pretty trying."

"It is very trying. I often feel completely exhausted at the end of the day."

"Nerve strain," said Meldon. "I don't wonder. It's a marvel how you stand it."

"Then I can't sleep," said Miss King. "Often I can't sleep for two or three nights together."

"It surprises me to hear that you ever sleep at all. Don't they haunt you? I've always heard—"

"My people?"

"Yes, your people, if that's what you call them. I'd have thought they'd never have let you alone."

"Some of them do haunt me. I often cry when I think of them. It's very foolish, of course; but in spite of myself I cry."

"Then why on earth do you go on with it?"

"It's my art," said Miss King.

"I'm not an artist myself," said Meldon, "in any sense of the word, so I can't exactly enter into your feelings; but I should say, speaking as a complete outsider, that the proper thing for you would be to drop the whole thing, take to smoking a pipe instead of those horrid scented cigarettes, drink a bottle of porter before you go to bed, and then sleep sound."

Miss King sighed. There was something in the ideal which Meldon set before her which was very attractive. The details she ignored. Bottled porter was not a drink she cared for, and no woman, however emancipated, likes a pipe. In spite of the satisfaction she found in her literary success, there was in her a desire for quiet and restful ways of life. There was no doubt that she would sleep sounder at night if she lived simply, somewhere in the country, and forgot the excitements of the novelist's art. Meldon, indeed, did not seem to enjoy absolutely unbroken rest at night; but Miss King's imagination, although she wrote improper novels, did not insist on representing a baby as an inevitable part of domesticated life. She got no further than the dream of a peaceful house, with the figure of an inoffensive husband somewhere in the background.

CHAPTER III

Meldon stretched himself in a deep chair and lit his pipe. He had dined to his own satisfaction, eating with an appetite whetted by the long drive from the railway station. He had before him a clear fortnight's holiday, and intended to enjoy it to the full. Major Kent's house was comfortable; his tobacco, which Meldon smoked, was good; his yacht, the *Spindrift*, lay ready for a cruise.

"To-morrow," he said, "I shall stroll round and see my old friends. I'm bound to do that; and, in point of fact, I want to. It's three years since I left, and I'm longing for a look at Doyle and the rest of them. The next day, if the weather is any way moderate, we can go sailing. I suppose Ballymoy isn't much changed. I shall find every one exactly as I left them. Things don't alter much in places like this where you take life easy."

"The place is changed," said Major Kent; "changed for the worse. You'd hardly know it."

"Nothing has happened to Doyle, I hope. I'd be sorry if poor Doyle had taken to drink, or gone bankrupt, or got married, or anything of that sort. I always liked Doyle."

"Doyle," said the Major sadly, "is suffering like everybody else."

"New priest?"

"No. Father Morony's alive still."

"They're not piling on the rates under the pretence of getting a water supply, or running schemes of technical education, or giving scholarships in the new university, are they? Doyle would have more sense than to allow them to break out into any reckless waste of public money."

"No."

"Then what's the matter with you? I've noticed that you're looking pretty glum ever since I arrived. Let's have the trouble, whatever it is. I have a fortnight before me, and I need scarcely say, Major, that if I can set things right in the place, I don't mind sacrificing my holiday in the least. I'm quite prepared to turn to and straighten out any tangle that may have arisen since I left."

"I'm sure you'd do your best, J. J."—the Major dropped naturally into his old way of addressing his friend by his initials—"but I don't think you can help us this time."

Major Kent sighed heavily and struck a match. His pipe had gone out.

"I certainly can't," said Meldon, "if you won't tell me what it is that troubles you."

"It's that damned Simpkins," said the Major.

"Simpkins may or may not be damned hereafter," said Meldon. "I offer no opinion on that point until I hear who he is and what he's done. He can't be damned yet, assuming him to be still alive. That's an elementary theological truth which you ought to know; and, in fact, must know. It will be a great deal more satisfactory to me if you use language accurately. Say that 'damnable Simpkins' if you're quite sure he deserves it; but don't call him damned until he is."

"He does deserve it."

"If he does," said Meldon—"I'm not, of course, certain yet that he does—but if he does, I'll do my best to see that he gets it; but I won't act in the dark. I have a sense of justice and a conscience, and I absolutely decline to persecute and harry a man simply because you don't like him. Who is this Simpkins? Is he any kind of government inspector?"

"He's an agent that they've sent down here to manage the Buckley estates."

"Well, I don't see anything wrong about that. I suppose there must be an agent. I could understand Doyle objecting to him on the ground of his profession. Doyle is the President of the League, and, of course, he's *ex officio* obliged to dislike land agents passionately; but I didn't expect you to take that line, Major. You're a loyalist. At least you used to be when I was here, and it's just as plainly your duty to support agents as it is Doyle's to abuse them."

"I don't object to him because he's an agent," said Major Kent. "I object to him because he's a meddlesome ass, and keeps the whole place in continual hot water."

"Very well. That's a distinct and definite charge. If you can prove it, I'll take the matter up and deal with the man. Pass the tobacco."

Meldon filled and lit his pipe. Then he got up and walked across to Major Kent's writing-table. He chose out a pen, took a quantity of notepaper and a bottle of ink. With them he returned to his armchair and sat down. He put the ink-bottle on the arm of the chair and, crossing his legs, propped the paper on his knee.

"Do be careful, J. J.," said the Major. "You'll certainly upset that ink-bottle, and this is a new carpet."

"We are engaged now," said Meldon, "on a serious investigation. You have demanded that a certain man should be punished in a perfectly frightful manner. I've agreed to carry out your wishes, if—mark my words—if he deserves it. You ought not to be thinking of carpets or ink-bottles. Your mind ought to be concentrated on a single effort to tell the truth. It's not such an easy thing to tell the truth as you think. Lots of men try to and fail. In fact, I'm not sure that any man could tell the truth unless he's had some training in metaphysics and theology. When I was in college I took honours in logic—"

"You've often mentioned that to me before," said the Major. "It's one of the things about you that I have most firmly fixed in my mind."

"And I won a prize for proving the accuracy of the Thirty-nine Articles. Consequently, I may say, without boasting, that I'm more or less of an expert in the matter of truth. My mind is trained. Yours, of course, isn't. That's why I'm trying to help you to tell the truth. But I won't—in fact, I can't—go on helping you if you wander off on to side issues about ink-bottles and carpets."

He waved his hand oratorically as he spoke, and tipped the ink-bottle off the arm of the chair.

"There," said the Major, "I knew you'd do that."

"Never mind," said Meldon. "I have a pencil in my pocket. I'll work with it."

The Major seized the blotting-paper from his writing-table and went down on his knees on the carpet.

"When you've finished making that mess worse than it is," said Meldon, "and covering your own fingers all over with ink in such a way that it will take days of careful rubbing with pumice-stone to get them clean, perhaps you'll go on telling me why you call this fellow Simpkins a meddlesome ass. I was up early this morning, owing to the baby's being restless during the night. Did I mention to you that she's got whooping-cough? Well, she has, and it takes her in the form of a rapid succession of fits, beginning at 10 p.m. and lasting till eight the next morning. That was what happened last night, so, as you'll readily understand, I want to get to bed in good time to-night. It may, it probably will, take hours to drag your grievance out of you, and I don't see any use in wasting time at the start."

"I paid twenty guineas for that carpet," said the Major. "It's a Persian one."

"Has that anything to do with Simpkins? Did he force you to buy the carpet, or did he try to prevent you?"

"No, he didn't. I wouldn't let the beast inside this house."

"Very well then. Don't go on about the carpet. Tell me plainly and straightforwardly why you call Simpkins a meddlesome ass."

"Because he pokes his nose into everybody's business," said the Major, "and won't let people alone."

Meldon took a note on a sheet of paper.

"Good," he said. "Simpkins—meddlesome ass—pokes his nose into everybody's business. Now, who is everybody?"

"Who is what, J. J.?"

"Who is everybody? That's plain enough, isn't it? For instance, are you everybody?"

"No, I'm not. How could I be?"

"Then I take it that Simpkins has not poked his nose into your business. Is Doyle everybody?"

"He *has* poked his nose into my business."

"Be careful now, Major. You're beginning to contradict yourself. What business of yours has he poked his nose into? Was it the carpet?"

"No. I told you he had nothing to do with the carpet. He made a beastly fuss about my fishing in the river above the bridge. He threatened to prosecute me."

"He may have been perfectly justified in that," said Meldon. "What right have you to fish in the upper part of the river?"

"I always fished there. I've fished there for thirty years and more."

"These questions of fishing rights," said Meldon, "are often extremely complicated. There may very well be something to be said on both sides. I don't think I can proceed to deal with Simpkins in the way you suggest, unless he has done something worse than interfere with your fishing. What else have you got against him?"

"He tried to stir up the dispensary doctor to prosecute Doyle on account of the insanitary condition of some of his houses."

"I expect he was perfectly right there," said Meldon. "From what I recollect of those houses that Doyle lets I should say that he richly deserves prosecution."

"Nobody was ever ill in the houses," said the Major. "There hasn't been a case of typhoid in the town as long as I can remember."

"That's not the point," said Meldon. "You're looking at the matter in the wrong way altogether. There never is typhoid anywhere until you begin to be sanitary. The absence of typhoid simply goes to show that sanitation has been entirely neglected. That's probably one of Simpkins' strongest points."

"If that's so, we'd be better without sanitation."

"Certainly not," said Meldon. "You might just as well say that we'd be better without matches because children never died of eating the heads off them before they were invented. Which reminds me that I caught the baby in the act of trying to swallow a black-headed pin the other day; and that, of course, would have been a great deal worse than getting whooping-cough. The thing had been stuck into the head of a woolly bear by way of an eye. She pulled it out, which I think shows intelligence, and—"

"I thought you said, J. J., that you wanted to get through with this enquiry and go to bed."

"I do," said Meldon. "But I naturally expected you'd take some interest in the mental development of my baby. After all, she's your godchild. You wouldn't have liked it if she'd swallowed that pin. However, if you don't care to hear about her, I won't force her on your attention. Go on about Doyle and the drains. What happened?"

"The doctor refused to act, of course," said the Major.

"Naturally," said Meldon; "he didn't care about bringing typhoid into the town."

"You'd have thought Simpkins would have dropped it then, but he didn't. He reported the doctor to the Board of Guardians for neglect of duty."

"We're getting on," said Meldon, taking a note on a fresh sheet of paper. "You started out to prove that Simpkins is a meddlesome ass. You've got half way. He's certainly an ass. Didn't he know that Doyle was chairman of the Board of Guardians?"

"He must have known that, of course."

"Then he's an ass. No one who wasn't an ass could possibly expect Doyle to pass a vote of censure on the doctor for not prosecuting him about his drains. You needn't elaborate that point further. I admit it. But I don't see yet that you've proved any actual malice. Lots of quite good men are asses, and mean to do what's right. Simpkins may have been acting from a mistaken sense of duty."

"He wasn't. He was acting from a fiendish delight in worrying peaceable people."

"Prove that," said Meldon, "and I'll make the man sorry for himself. There's no crime I know more detestable than nagging and worrying with the intention of making other people uncomfortable. In a properly civilised society men who do that would be hanged."

"I wish Simpkins was hanged."

"Prove your point," said Meldon, "and I'll see that he is hanged, or at all events killed in some other way."

"There's no use talking that way, J. J. You can't go out and murder the man."

"It won't be murder in this case," said Meldon. "It will be a perfectly just execution, and I shan't do it myself. I'm a clergyman, and not an executioner. But I'll see that it's done once I'm perfectly satisfied that he deserves it."

"He had a row with the rector at a vestry meeting," said the Major, "about the heating of the church."

"That settles it," said Meldon. "I ask for nothing more. The man who's capable of annoying the poor old rector, who has chronic bronchitis and must keep the church up to a pretty fair temperature—"

"What Simpkins said was that the church wasn't hot enough."

"It's all the same," said Meldon. "The point is that he worried the rector, who's not physically strong enough to bear it, and who certainly does not deserve it. I didn't mind his attacking you or Doyle. You can both hit back, and if you were any good would have hit back long ago in a way which Simpkins would have disliked intensely. But a clergyman is different. He can't defend himself. He is obliged, by the mere fact of being a clergyman, to sit down under every species of insult which any ill-conditioned corner-boy chooses to sling at him. There was a fellow in my parish, when I first went there, who thought he'd be perfectly safe in ragging me because he knew I was a parson. No later than this morning a horrid rabble of railway porters, and people of that sort, tried to bully me, because, owing to their own ridiculous officiousness, I was forced to travel first class on a third-class ticket. They thought they could do what they liked with impunity when they saw I was a clergyman. You don't know how common that kind of anti-clerical spirit is. Simpkins is evidently swelled out with it. It's going now, like an epidemic. Look at France and Italy. The one chance we have of keeping Ireland free from it is to isolate each case the moment it appears. By far the wisest thing we can do is to have Simpkins killed at once."

"I don't quite see how you are going to manage it, J. J., without being hanged yourself."

"Is he a married man?"

"No, he isn't."

"Then the matter's perfectly simple. I don't think I mentioned to you, Major, that I travelled down in the train to-day with a professional murderess."

"Do try to talk sense, J. J."

"Her speciality is husbands," said Meldon. "I don't know exactly how many she has done for in her time, but there must be several. She said their ghosts haunted her at night, and that sometimes she couldn't sleep on account of them."

"I suppose," said Major Kent, "that it amuses you to babble like an idiot in an asylum."

"It doesn't amuse me in the least. I feel desperately depressed when I think of those poor fellows lying in their graves with ounces and ounces of strychnine in their stomachs. That's not the kind of thing I consider amusing, though you may. Miss King doesn't consider it amusing either. She said she often cries when she thinks of her victims, and very often she can't sleep at night."

"Miss King!" said the Major. "That's the name of the lady who has taken Ballymoy House for the summer."

"Exactly. The lady whom I propose to marry to your friend Simpkins."

"Good Lord! J. J. Why? What has the poor woman done?"

"It's not so much what she has done," said Meldon, "that makes me think she'd be a suitable match for Simpkins. It's what she will do. She'll murder him."

"Nonsense."

"It's not nonsense. She will. She told me herself that she has come to Ballymoy for the express purpose of murdering another husband. She said she wanted quiet and security from interruption in order to go on with her work."

"You're going mad, J. J.; stark mad. I'm sorry for you."

"I got into the carriage with her this morning by the merest accident," said Meldon. "If the baby hadn't got whooping-cough a fortnight ago, and kept me awake all night, I shouldn't have caught the early train. I didn't mean to catch it. Directly I looked at her I saw that she was a remarkable woman. You've not seen her yet?"

"No," said the Major, "I haven't, and I don't particularly want to."

"Her face seemed more or less familiar to me," said Meldon. "You'll recognise it, too, when you see it. Or more probably you won't. I suppose you still read nothing but *The Times*, and it doesn't publish the portraits of celebrities."

"Is Miss King a celebrity? I never heard of her."

"Not under that name; but when I mention that her real name is Mrs. Lorimer, you'll remember all about her."

"The woman who was tried the other day for murdering her husband, and got off."

"Precisely," said Meldon. "I happened, by the merest chance, to have five portraits of her in three different papers. I compared them carefully with Miss King, and I haven't the slightest doubt that she's the same woman."

"You're probably quite mistaken," said the Major. "Those pictures in the daily papers are never the least like the person they're supposed to represent."

"I might have been mistaken, though I very seldom am; but in this case I certainly was not. She seemed quite pleased when I said I recognised her, and told me frankly that she had murdered several husbands, and hoped to live to murder many more. I urged her to give it up. Being a clergyman I was bound to do that. But it wasn't the least use. She said it was her art; and you know, Major, when people start talking about art, it simply means that they are dead to all sense of morality. It doesn't in the least matter what the art is. The effect is always the same. That's the reason I've made up my mind not to allow my daughter to learn drawing. I won't have her moral sense blunted while she's young. I don't deny that pictures and books and music are great things in their way, but a simple sense of right and wrong, of truth and falsehood, are much more important. I'm sure you agree with me in that."

"I wish to goodness you had some sense of right and wrong yourself."

"I have," said Meldon, "If I hadn't I should simply enjoy myself during this holiday, as I'm quite entitled to do. Instead of which I mean to devote my time to the troublesome task of marrying Simpkins, whom I don't know at all, to a lady whom I have only seen once. If I hadn't a remarkably pushing sort of a conscience I wouldn't sacrifice myself in that way."

"She won't marry Simpkins," said the Major.

"Oh yes, she will. I don't anticipate any difficulty about that part of the programme."

"Wait till you've seen Simpkins. Wait till you've talked to him. No woman would marry Simpkins."

"Miss King will," said Meldon. "She wants a man on whom to practise her art, and she'll be all the better pleased if he's a particularly undesirable kind of beast. She won't find herself regretting him afterwards. Now that we have that settled, Major, I think I'll dodge off to bed. I don't mind confessing to you that I'm just as glad that I shan't have the baby in her little cot beside me. I'm extremely fond of the child, but she's a little trying at night; the fits of coughing come on at such frequent intervals."

CHAPTER IV

Major Kent, like most men who lead an open-air life, had a healthy appetite at breakfast-time. His table was always well supplied with eggs, bacon, and, when possible, fish. In honour of Meldon's visit, he had a cold ham on the sideboard, and a large dish of oatmeal porridge. He was a man of primitive hospitality, and he surveyed the feast with an air of proud satisfaction while he waited for his guest. He had to wait for a quarter of an hour, and his glow of pleasure was beginning to give way to a feeling of irritation when Meldon burst into the room.

"This place," he said, by way of apology for his unpunctuality, "is certainly the sleepiest in the world. I had forgotten how sleepy it is. I didn't so much as turn round in bed for nine solid hours, and I assure you I never felt less inclined to get up in my life. I daresay I'll get over it in a day or two; but just at present I feel that the night wasn't long enough."

"Have some breakfast," said the Major, "and then you can go to sleep again."

Meldon helped himself to porridge and milk.

"No, I can't," he said. "I've too much to do."

He worked through a helping of bacon and eggs. Then he attacked the cold ham.

"There's nothing," he said, "like a good breakfast when you have a hard day's work before you. I expect to be pretty busy, and I'll hardly be in for lunch. I suppose you've no objection to my making myself a few sandwiches before I start? I may pick up a meal somewhere in the course of the day, but I may not. It's always well to be on the safe side."

"What are you going to do?"

"I'm going to marry Simpkins to Miss King, of course. I thought we settled that last night."

"Don't keep up that joke, J. J. It was all very well pulling my leg last night, and I didn't mind it a bit; but a thing like that gets to be stale the next morning."

"There's no joke that I can see," said Meldon. "If you read the papers with any sort of attention lately, you'd understand that Mrs. Lorimer is the last woman in the world who can be regarded as comic."

"We weren't talking about Mrs. Lorimer."

"Yes, we were. We were talking about Miss King, and she is Mrs. Lorimer; although at present she prefers to be called Miss King. I think she's quite right. It would be extremely bad taste to go on using poor Lorimer's name after what she did to him. He wouldn't like it. You wouldn't like it yourself, Major, if she'd killed you."

"I don't know that she did kill him," said the Major. "Even supposing that you're right in identifying the two women—which of course you're not—you'd still have no earthly right to assume that Mrs. Lorimer is a murderess. The jury found her innocent."

"Of course it did. Any jury would. She's a most attractive-looking woman. You'd have found her innocent yourself if you'd been on that jury."

"I would not."

"Yes, you would. I've seen her, remember. You haven't, so you can't possibly tell what you'd have done."

"I don't see," said the Major, "that her being good-looking proves that she murdered her husband."

"No, it doesn't, but it accounts for the jury letting her off. The evidence was amply sufficient for a conviction, and the judge summed up dead against her. And any way it doesn't matter to us about the evidence, for she owned up to me in the train. I told her I'd keep her secret for her, and I don't intend to tell anybody except you. Apart from her feelings altogether it wouldn't suit us for the story to get out in Ballymoy. Simpkins would be choked off at once if he knew it. Men have such a ridiculous prejudice against marrying a woman with any sort of past."

"I don't think Simpkins would mind," said the Major, "if he thought she had any money. That's the kind of beast he is."

"She has plenty," said Meldon, "Lorimer's, I daresay. At least she looks as if she had plenty, and that's the same thing in this case. If Simpkins marries her, it's extremely unlikely that he'll live long enough to find out whether she really has a large fortune, or is simply spending her capital."

After breakfast Major Kent returned to the subject of Miss King.

"I suppose," he said, "that you're absolutely certain that you've got a hold of the right woman? You couldn't be making any sort of mistake?"

"I told you last night that I was certain, and I gave you my reasons; pretty convincing ones I imagine—the sort of reasons that would be conclusive to any man at all accustomed to criminal investigation. I don't myself see how you can get behind the portrait and the lady's own confession."

"You couldn't possibly have mistaken about that, could you? I mean she couldn't have been confessing anything else which you could have taken up to mean murder?"

"No, she couldn't. In the first place, it isn't at all likely that there would be two attractive-looking lady criminals, travelling about in trains at the same time, both wanting to confess what they had done. In the second place, her crime must have been pretty serious, for she was particularly anxious to find out whether it was likely to shock you."

"Me?"

"Yes, you. She mentioned you by name, and asked particularly whether you'd be likely to be shocked, when you found out who she was. Now, if she had simply been slipping trifling articles off shop counters into her muff, she wouldn't have expected you to be shocked. That's what makes me say her crime was a serious one."

"Still," said the Major, "even supposing she really was afraid of shocking me; though I can't see how she came to consider me at all—"

"She did. You may take that for certain."

"There are other things besides murder that I should strongly disapprove of."

"You're thinking of divorce court proceedings now. But she's not that sort of woman at all. I had every opportunity of studying her character in the train, and I'm certain that she wouldn't mix herself up with anything of a disreputable kind. Whatever poor Lorimer may have had to complain of—and I don't in the least deny that he had a grievance—he'd have been the last man to accuse her of anything of *that* sort. I never met a woman who impressed me more strongly as being thoroughly respectable."

"Come now, J. J. Murder! Surely murder—"

"Not when treated as an art. De Quincey wrote an essay on the subject. If you'd read it, you'd know better than to mix up artistic murder with the commonplace assassinations of the ordinary burglar. You might just as well say that Beethoven is the same sort of person as the Italian organ-grinder who plays abominable tunes under your window, in the hope of your giving him twopence to go away."

"Nothing you've said so far," said the Major, "convinces me in the least that your identification of the lady is certain, or even likely to be right."

"I knew you'd be sceptical. You always are sceptical about anything the least out of the common; so while I was shaving this morning I arranged the evidence in such a way that you can't possibly escape from it. In the first place, there are the portraits. I don't dwell on them because you haven't seen Miss King, and so they won't—for the present—carry much weight with you. In the second place, there is her confession. You choose to consider that I was mistaken about that, and that Miss King was really confessing something of quite a different kind. I say nothing about the improbability of my being mistaken in a perfectly simple matter. I simply leave the confession on one side, and offer you corroborative evidence of a quite unmistakable description. Here's a copy of a Dublin paper. I put it in my pocket on purpose to show it to you. I suppose you'll believe what you see printed in a newspaper?"

"It depends very much what it is. I don't believe everything I see in papers."

"That, if you'll excuse my saying so, seems to me to be carrying your habit of scepticism to the verge of actual mania. I don't think you ought to adopt that kind of attitude, Major. If you had been trained in theology, or even secular metaphysics, it might be excusable; though then, of course, you wouldn't do it. But in a simple and almost entirely uneducated country gentleman like you, it's simply grotesque."

"Go on about the newspaper, J. J."

"Here it is for you; but I don't see that it's much use giving it to you if your mind is made up beforehand to disbelieve every word that's in it."

He took a newspaper from his pocket and handed it to Major Kent, indicating with his thumb a column on the middle page.

"The Lorimer Case. Judge's Charge to the Jury. Acquittal.

"Scene outside the Court. Enthusiasm of the Crowd. A Demonstration."

The Major read aloud the heavily-leaded lines which filled half the column.

"Skip that part," said Meldon. "The cheers don't matter to us, though I daresay Miss King enjoyed them at the time. Go on to the bottom of the next column where you see the words 'An Interview' in large print."

"Our representative," read the Major, "called this evening at Mrs. Lorimer's hotel. He was at once shown up to her sitting-room, where he found her—"

"Go on," said Meldon; "that part about her being cool and unembarrassed, and the next bit about her wearing a well-cut grey travelling-dress, isn't important; though, as a matter of fact, her dress was grey."

The Major skipped a paragraph, and then began to read again.

"'I always felt quite certain,' said Mrs. Lorimer, in reply to a question asked by our representative, 'about what the jury's verdict would be. I have perfect confidence in the commonsense and justice of Englishmen. In fact, I had all my arrangements made, through my solicitors, for my movements after the trial. I have taken a house in a very quiet neighbourhood, where I shall be free from all inquisitive publicity.'"

"There," said Meldon, "those are almost the exact words Miss King used to me in the train."

The Major went on, reading aloud.

"'May I ask,' said our representative, 'in what part of the country—?' 'No,' said Mrs. Lorimer, smiling. 'You may not ask that; or, if you do, I shall not answer you. But you may do this for me, if you like. You may tell the hall porter to order a cab for me, a four-wheeler. I have a good deal of luggage.'"

"She had," said Meldon; "I saw it when we got out at Dunbeg station, and it wasn't all there, for one of her trunks had got lost on the way."

"'Our representative,' read the Major, 'shook hands with Mrs. Lorimer as she entered the cab. The order given to the driver was Euston station. Thus a lady of great personal charm, whose terrible experience has for some weeks focussed the attention of the civilised world upon the affairs of her private life passes—'"

"You needn't go on," said Meldon. "The rest of the article is mere piffle. The essential part is what you've read out, and I imagine it ought to pretty well clinch the matter. She drove to Euston, intending to travel from that station to some very quiet neighbourhood in which she had taken a house beforehand. Now where could you possibly find a quieter neighbourhood than this?"

"I don't see that you've proved your point, J. J. There are a lot of other places for which you might start from Euston."

"Not so many quiet neighbourhoods. Think of where the London and North-Western Railway runs. Lancashire! You wouldn't call Bolton a quiet neighbourhood, I suppose. North Wales! You know what it is at this season of the year, thick with holiday people. No. You may take it for certain that if she left Euston she came to Ireland. Now all English people head straight for the west as soon as they land in this country, especially those who have any kind of a past that they are anxious to keep dark. Dublin and Wicklow are just as thick with people as England is. Nobody ever stops half-way across the country. Besides, there wasn't another woman in the train with me who could possibly have been Mrs. Lorimer."

Major Kent rose from his chair and knocked the ashes out of his pipe.

"I don't suppose, J. J., that it's any use telling you that you're going to make an ass of yourself."

"Not a bit, because it isn't true. I'm going to proceed in the most circumspect and cautious manner. Not that I'm the least afraid of making an ass of myself. I should never do that under any circumstances. But because I have a conscience and I am afraid of doing a grave injustice, I am going to convince myself first of all that this fellow Simpkins really deserves to be killed. I admit the force of all you said about him last night, especially that part about the heating of the church; but it's a serious thing to condemn a man to death. It's a thing that you can't undo again once you've done it. I must see the man myself before I take any further steps."

"You can't have him here, J. J. He's a horrid little cad, and I won't have him inside this house."

"I'm not asking you to, at present. Later on if it becomes necessary in the interests of justice to patch up some appearance of a reconciliation between you and him I shall, of course, ask him here; but in the meanwhile—"

"You may entertain him yourself, if you do."

"I may. But that won't deter me from doing my duty. You haven't had the education in philosophy and literature, Major, that you ought to have had; but the years that you spent in the army ought to have taught you that no amount of unpleasantness should prevent a man doing his duty. I thought that was one of the things which military life impressed on me. Suppose now that it was your duty to stand in a pool of water on a wintry night looking out for the approaching army of a powerful enemy. You wouldn't like doing it because you'd know that you'd have a cold in your head next day which would probably last you for the rest of that particular campaign. But would you allow that fact to interfere with your duty? I'll give you credit, Major, for not even considering your own comfort in the matter. You'd stand in the pool. You wouldn't so much as splash about, and when your feet got wet you'd bear it without grumbling. Why can't you admit that I am actuated by the same sort of motives in doing my duty?"

"But is it your duty? I can't see, really, that there's any need for you to mix yourself up in it at all."

"It is my duty," said Meldon, "for several reasons. In the first place you are my friend, and you've always been kind to me; so it's plainly my duty to do you a good turn when I can. Next, I liked what I saw of Miss King. I'm convinced that she's in earnest about her art, and is really working at it simply for art's sake and not from any selfish motives. Therefore, as an educated man, it's my duty to help her if I can, without outraging my own conscience or acting in any way unsuitable for a clergyman. Assuming Simpkins to be the kind of man you describe, it is a public duty, the duty of every good citizen, to put him out of the world altogether. He's nothing but a nuisance here, and he can't be really happy. I imagine that even for his own sake he'd be a great deal better dead. He may not see that himself, but it's very likely to be true. What's the use of his dragging out a miserable existence in a place where he is getting more and more unpopular every year? He can't like it. Where does he live?"

"He lives," said Major Kent, "in that little house just beyond the police barrack."

"That won't save him," said Meldon. "Miss King would laugh at our police after slipping through the fingers of the Scotland Yard authorities, and any way he'd have to go and live with her once they're married. I'll call there."

"At this time of day," said the Major, "he'll probably be in his office, next to Doyle's hotel."

"I'll leave a card at his house first," said Meldon. "It's only civil. Then I'll go on to the office. I suppose you can send me in, Major? I'll walk back. I wouldn't like to keep your horse in town all day. I shall probably be a long time. I can't scamp the business, you know. I must thoroughly investigate Simpkins. After that, I'll look in and have a chat with Doyle."

CHAPTER V

Mr. Eustace St. Clair Simpkins preferred to have his letters addressed "E. St. Clair-Simpkins, Esq.," as if his second Christian name were part of his surname. He belonged by birth to the *haute aristocratie*, and believed that the use of a hyphen made this fact plain to the members of the middle classes with whom he came in contact. He was a man of thirty-five years of age, but looked slightly older, because his hair was receding rapidly from the left side of his forehead. He had enjoyed, for a time, the education afforded by one of the greatest of the English public schools; but at the age of sixteen, being then classed with boys so small that he looked ridiculous among them, he was removed at the special request of the headmaster. A private tutor, heavily paid, took him in hand, but was no more successful with him than the schoolmasters had been. At the age of eighteen he was found unfit to pass any of the examinations which open the way to gentlemanly employment. Various jobs were found for him by his desponding parents, but on every occasion he was returned to them politely. He drifted at last into an Irish land-agent's office. Mr. Tempest was a successful man of business, and managed estates in various parts of the country from his Dublin office. He was under an obligation to a London solicitor, whose wife was the sister of Mrs. Simpkins, the mother of Eustace St. Clair. He felt that he could not very well refuse to give the young man such a chance as a clerkship afforded. Things went on fairly satisfactorily until Mr. Simpkins conceived the idea of marrying his employer's daughter. He reasoned, quite rightly, that Miss Tempest, being an only child, was likely to have a substantial fortune. Mr. Tempest, unimpressed by the hyphened St. Clair, was unwilling to allow the courtship to proceed. He sent Mr. Simpkins down to Ballymoy, and charged him with the management of such parts of the Buckley estate as were not already sold to tenants.

Mr. Simpkins, for the first time in his life, felt that he had found a position which really suited him. There was very little work to do. He received the ground rents of the town of Ballymoy; saw that Ballymoy House was kept in repair and the grounds in tolerable order; and let the fishing of the river every year by means of advertisements in sporting papers. Many men would have found the life dull, but Mr. Simpkins had a busy and vigorous mind of a sort not uncommon among incompetent people. By temperament he was a reformer of minor abuses, and Ballymoy afforded him an almost unique opportunity for the exercise of his powers. There were, of course, difficulties. The inhabitants of Ballymoy, long unaccustomed to the presence of a reformer amongst them, had drifted into quiet, easy ways of living. Mr. Simpkins, who was not lacking in a certain quality of quiet persistence, troubled every one with fine impartiality, and became exceedingly unpopular in Ballymoy. The Resident Magistrate hated being obliged to enforce unnecessary laws such as that which forbids cyclists to ride on footpaths, and that which ordains the carrying of lighted lanterns on carts at night. The postman, at the other end of the official scale, liked loitering on his rounds, and had adopted a pleasant habit of handing on letters to any wayfarer who might be supposed to be proceeding in the direction of the place to which the letters were addressed. Every one with a public duty of any sort to perform was stimulated by Mr. Simpkins, and consequently came to hate him.

After a while Mr. Doyle, on whom, as chief citizen, the duty naturally devolved, got up a petition to Mr. Tempest. The necessity for removing Mr. Simpkins was presented in the strongest terms. Mr. Tempest, who was a man of wide experience and kindly heart, sympathised with Mr. Doyle and the others who signed the petition, but he did not recall Mr. Simpkins. He knew of no place in Ireland further from Dublin than Ballymoy is; and it appeared to him above all things desirable to keep Mr. Simpkins at a distance. It was better, in his opinion, that Ballymoy should suffer, than that his own house should be haunted on Sundays and his office disorganised on week-days by Mr. Simpkins. He acknowledged the receipt of the Ballymoy petition, and promised, mendaciously, to consider the matter.

Meldon drove into Ballymoy on the first morning of his holiday, and went straight to Mr. Simpkins' house. He left a card there, and then walked on to the office. Mr. Simpkins was in the office, and Meldon greeted him with a warmth which seemed actually affectionate. Mr. Simpkins was surprised, and rubbed his hand, which had been hurt by the hearty way in which Meldon shook it.

"Is there," he asked, in a puzzled tone, "anything that I can do for you?"

"Nothing," said Meldon; "nothing whatever. If there was I'm sure you'd do it, and I shouldn't hesitate to ask you. But there isn't. I simply called in to have a chat. You won't mind if I smoke, will you?"

"I never smoke in my office," said Simpkins. "I dislike free and easy and slipshod ways of doing business."

Meldon filled and lit his pipe.

"You're perfectly right," he said. "There's nothing impresses the intelligent stranger so unfavourably as the smell of tobacco in an office when he comes into it in the hope of doing business with a competent man. I wish you would impress your idea on that subject, and I may say a good many other subjects, on the people of this town. They are lamentably deficient in what I may call the etiquette of commercial life; and yet all these little points count for a lot. You and I know that."

Simpkins hesitated. He was at first inclined to be angry. Meldon was smoking vigorously, and his tobacco was of the kind described as "full-flavoured." But the remarks about the etiquette of business were certainly sound. Mr. Simpkins really believed that he had a mission to teach manners and method to the people of Ballymoy.

"Would you mind telling me," he said at last, "who you are?"

"Not in the least," said Meldon; "I shall be quite pleased. At the same time I think I ought to point out to you that, if you'd been on speaking terms with Major Kent, you'd have heard all about me weeks ago, and very likely would have been asked to dinner to meet me last night. Why have you quarrelled with the poor Major? He's a nice enough sort of man, and most people find him easy enough to get on with."

"It was he who quarrelled with me. I had no intention—"

"So it was. I remember that now; something about fishing, wasn't it? Curious how people will lose their tempers about ridiculous little trifles. That's the worst of places like this. The people who have never lived anywhere else become irritable and take offence about nothing, simply because their minds are cut off from wider interests. You and I, now, know that no fish in the world, however large, is worth fighting about. We wouldn't, either of us, mind a bit if some other fellow came along and hooked the whale which we had marked down as our private prey."

Simpkins was puzzled again. The doctrine about fishing rights struck him as slightly socialistic. It might possibly be applicable in the case of whales, but society could scarcely survive as an organised whole if many men regarded the possession of salmon as of no importance. At the same time he was pleased; it gratified him immensely to be hailed as a fellow citizen of a larger world.

"Would you mind," he said, speaking in quite a friendly tone, "telling me your name?"

"Not in the least," said Meldon. "I said so before. As a matter of fact, so far from having any wish to conceal my name from you, I went round to your house before I called here and left my card on you. You'll find it there when you get back. I always like to be strict in the observance of the rules of civilised society. I particularly dislike the slack ways into which people in places like this are inclined to drift. I must say for the Major, he's not as bad as the rest in that respect. He always dresses for dinner."

"So do I."

"I'm glad to hear it. That ought to be a bond of union between you and the Major. You must be the only two men in Ballymoy who do. By the way, have you met Miss King?"

"No. She arrived yesterday, I hear; but I haven't seen her."

"You ought to go up and call on her at once. You'll like her, I'm sure. She's very good-looking."

He paused for a moment. The announcement did not seem to excite Simpkins' interest. He was, indeed, not of the temperament which is strongly moved by beauty or personal charm.

"She's also very rich," said Meldon.

"I thought she must be pretty well off when she took Ballymoy House."

"She is. And what's more, she's uncommonly well connected. Her uncle is an earl. I forget at this moment what his exact title is; but I know he's an earl, and I have it on very good authority that he's likely to be made a marquis quite soon."

He paused, and was gratified to observe that Simpkins appeared to be greatly interested by this information about Miss King. He pursued his advantage at once.

"I shall call on her myself," he said, "though there's not really much use in my making myself agreeable to her. I'm married already. The Major would have told you that, too, if you'd been on speaking terms with him. You really must make it up with the Major, Simpkins. I hope to see a good deal of you while I'm in Ballymoy, and it will be most inconvenient for me if you won't speak to the Major while I'm staying in his house."

"Did you say that you knew Miss King?"

"Not intimately," said Meldon; "at least not very intimately. I travelled down in the train with her yesterday, and we had a pleasant chat together. If I wasn't married already—but there's no use talking about that. And I don't for a moment suppose that the Major will care about having a try. He's a confirmed old bachelor. Though it would be a right good thing for him if he did. Miss King must have a whole pot of money, and she looks to me the sort of woman whom it would be quite easy to marry. I'm afraid I must be going now. I'm so glad I caught you, Simpkins. I've heard a lot about you during the short time I've been in Ballymoy; and I may say, without the least wish to flatter, that I was most anxious to meet you. Good-bye, and be sure to call on Miss King. It's a pity to think of that poor girl all alone in a great barrack of a place like Ballymoy House, without a civilised creature to speak to."

Meldon left the Office very well satisfied with himself. He went next into the hotel. The day was hot, and there was very little going on in the town. The streets were almost empty, for the country people were busy on their farms. The hotel appeared to be entirely deserted. The waiter had left the coffee room, and gone to visit a friend in the police barrack. The barmaid, after finishing one penny novel, had gone into the shop next door to borrow another from the milliner. Meldon penetrated to the kitchen, and found an untidy maid asleep, very uncomfortably, on an upright chair. She woke with a start when he banged a frying-pan against the front of the oven.

"I hope I haven't startled you," he said politely. "I shall be greatly obliged if you will tell me where Mr. Doyle is to be found."

"He's within in his own room; and what's more, the doctor's along with him, and he did say that nobody was to be let next or nigh him by reason of his being busy."

"If he's busy," said Meldon, "he's the only man in Ballymoy that is, excepting myself; and any way that prohibition doesn't apply to me. I'm an old friend. I'll just step in and see him. You needn't announce me. If you like you can go to sleep again; but if I were you I'd be beginning to get the dinner. It's near twelve o'clock."

"Is it, then?"

"It is. Is your name Bridget or Mary?"

"It's Sabina they call me."

"You're not a bad-looking girl, Sabina; and if you'd attend to your business instead of going to sleep in the middle of the day, you might die a rich woman yet."

"I would not, then. How would the like of me be rich?"

"You certainly won't be," said Meldon, "if you don't do your work."

"The potatoes is in the pot," said Sabina.

"They may be; but Mr. Doyle will be looking for more than potatoes at dinner time. He doesn't look as if he lived entirely on potatoes."

Sabina grinned. Doyle was a portly man.

"It won't take me long to fry a couple of rashers," she said, "once the grease is hot."

"And is fried bacon and potatoes all you're going to give the poor man? What wages does he pay you?"

"Six pounds."

"Very well. Now listen to me, Sabina. You put your back into it and cook the man a decent dinner. Give him soup, and then a nicely done chop with a dish of spinach and some fried potatoes. After that a sweet omelette—"

"Glory be to God!" said Sabina.

"And then a little savoury, tomato and olives, beaten to a cream, with the yolk of a hard-boiled egg served up on toast, cut into dice."

"Arrah, what talk!" said Sabina.

"Get him accustomed to that sort of dinner for three weeks or a month, and then ask him for a rise in your wages. He'll give it to you."

"He would not."

"He would. Any man would. The mistake you make is half-starving him. That makes his temper bad, and—"

"I wouldn't say then that ever I heard a cross word out of his mouth," said Sabina, "unless it might be when he'd be talking of Mr. Simpkins or the like."

"I suppose he swears then," said Meldon.

"He does terrible."

"I don't wonder. I never swear myself. Being a clergyman, I can't, of course. But from what I've seen of Mr. Simpkins, and from what I've heard about him, I should think he'd make most men swear. Do you know him at all intimately, Sabina?"

"I do not; but the girl that's with him beyond in the house is a cousin of my own, and I hear her talking about him. She does be saying that the like of him for nonsensical goings on she never seen. She—"

"Thank you," said Meldon. "I don't want to hear your cousin's views of Mr. Simpkins' domestic arrangements. She's red-haired, if she's the girl that opened the door to me a while ago, and I never knew one of her colour that spoke the truth."

Sabina was loyal to her family. She resented Meldon's remark.

"If you were to put me on my oath," she said, "I wouldn't call the hair that's on your own head black, nor yet yellow."

"My hair," said Meldon, "is what's called auburn; and in any case I have more strength of character than to be driven into untruthfulness by the colour of my hair. Did you say it was Dr. O'Donoghue was inside with Mr. Doyle?"

"It is," said Sabina.

"I suppose, now, he isn't particularly fond of Mr. Simpkins either."

Sabina grinned broadly.

"From the pleasant way in which you're smiling," said Meldon, "I think I may take it for granted that Dr. O'Donoghue wouldn't go far out of his way to find out exactly the kind of medicine that would cure Mr. Simpkins if by any chance he happened to fall sick."

"He would not. But they do say he'd poison him if he got the chance."

"I don't want him to do that. I should be very sorry if he did. All I want to be sure of is that the doctor wouldn't put himself out to cure Mr. Simpkins if anybody else poisoned him."

"The Lord save us!" said Sabina. "Is it murder you're thinking of?"

"It is not," said Meldon. "Don't get any foolish idea of that kind into your head. I'm not a murderer. I'm merely putting what is called a supposititious case, with a view to finding out what Dr. O'Donoghue's real feelings are. I don't suppose you know what a supposititious case is?"

"I do not. It was a backward place where I was reared, and I wasn't kept to school regular; and what's more, the Irish wasn't taught in them times."

"It wouldn't have helped you much if it was," said Meldon. "A supposititious case is the same thing, very nearly, as a hypothetical proposition. It consists of two parts, a protasis and an apodosis. For instance—"

"It's laughing at me you are."

"It is not, but trying to educate you a little. For instance, I should be putting a hypothetical case if I were to say, 'Supposing you cooked the dinner I described every day for Mr. Doyle—'"

"I couldn't do it then, for I wouldn't be fit."

"That's exactly what makes it a supposititious case," said Meldon. "Now perhaps you'll understand that I don't intend to poison Mr. Simpkins myself."

"Nor the doctor won't do it for you," said Sabina.

"You said a minute ago that he would."

"He would not, for he's a nice gentleman, as simple and innocent as a child, only an odd time when his temper would be riz."

"Any way he won't be asked to. Good-bye, Sabina. I'll look in and see you next time I'm passing. Don't let that red-haired cousin of yours be putting phosphorous paste, or any of those patent rat poisons, into Mr. Simpkins' food. She'll get herself into trouble if she does."

CHAPTER VI

Meldon opened the door of Mr. Doyle's private sitting-room without knocking and walked in. The hotel keeper and Dr. O'Donoghue were sitting at opposite ends of the table, with a bottle of whisky and a jug of water between them. Doyle, who was placed with his back to the door, spoke without looking round.

"Didn't I tell you, Sabina Gallagher," he said, "that if you came into this room, interrupting me and the doctor, I'd cut the two ears off you, and send you back to your mother with them in a box in the well of the car? Did I tell you that or did I not? And now nothing will do you but to fling open the door as if the Lord-Lieutenant and the rest of them playboys beyond in Dublin Castle was—"

The expression of Dr. O'Donoghue's face made Mr. Doyle pause. He turned and saw Meldon standing on the threshold.

"Be damn!" he said, "if it isn't Mr. Meldon. The Major was telling me last week he was expecting you. You're looking well, so you are. England agrees with you."

"I can't say as much for you," said Meldon. "You're getting fat. You ought to take more exercise. Why don't you start a golf links? It would do you all the good in the world, and be an attraction to the hotel besides."

"If I'm putting on flesh," said Doyle, "it's a queer thing, for the life's fair tormented out of me."

"Simpkins, I suppose," said Meldon.

"The same," said Doyle. "The like of that man for making trouble in a place I never seen; no, nor nobody else."

"I hear," said Meldon, "that the doctor's thinking of poisoning him."

"Whoever told you that told you a lie," said Dr. O'Donoghue; "not but what—"

"Myself and the doctor," said Doyle, "was making up plans when you come in on us. We was thinking of what you might call an ambuscade, worked so as we'd get the better of him without his being able to take the law of us; and he's mighty fond of the law, that same gentleman—too fond."

"If I can be of any help to you," said Meldon, "you can count on me. I have a good deal of natural talent for ambuscades. Trot out the details of your scheme, and I'll be able to tell you in two words whether it's workable or not."

"They do say," said Doyle, "that he has the fishing let to an English gentleman; and he's mighty particular about preserving it. Now the doctor here has the name of being a good fisherman."

"If he goes poaching," said Meldon, "he'll get the worst of it. The Major appears to have tried that on, and he simply made things unpleasant for himself, without annoying Simpkins in the least."

"It's not poaching we're thinking of," said Doyle; "but—you know I'm a magistrate these times, on account of being the Chairman of the Urban Council."

"I know that; but if you're thinking of dragging up Simpkins before the Petty Sessions on a bogus charge, you may as well put the idea out of your head at once. It won't work. You'll have the Major on the Bench with you, and though he doesn't like the man, I don't think he'd commit him to prison for cruelty to children, or breaking windows while under the influence of drink, or anything of that sort, unless he'd really done it."

"I wouldn't do the like," said Doyle, "and no more would the doctor."

"Our plan," said the doctor, "is to get a salmon, a large salmon."

"Poach it?" said Meldon.

"No; buy it. Doyle would buy it. Then he'd give it to me in the presence of several witnesses—"

"Sabina would do for one," said Meldon, "She's a most intelligent girl, and I'm sure she'd swear anything afterwards that she was wanted to."

"She wouldn't have to swear anything but the truth," said Doyle.

"Of course not," said Meldon. "But lots of people won't do even that."

"I'd go up the river," said Dr. O'Donoghue, "and I'd take my rod and landing-net and the salmon with me, and I'd sit down on the bank and wait."

"Simpkins," said Doyle, "does be walking up along the river every evening, so the doctor wouldn't be there for very long before he'd be caught."

"I see," said Meldon. "The idea would be for Simpkins to prosecute the doctor for poaching that salmon, and then to trot out Sabina in court to prove—"

"Sabina and the rest of the witnesses," said Doyle. "We'd have plenty."

"It's not a bad ambuscade at all," said Meldon.

"The Major," said Doyle, "would talk straight to him off the Bench, the way he'd feel small; and I'd have a word or two myself to say to him after the Major was done. And the police would be standing round smiling like—"

"I can't imagine anything more unpleasant," said Meldon, "than being grinned at by a policeman. All the same, I think it will be better not to catch him in that ambuscade."

"And why not?" said Doyle.

"The fact is," said Meldon, "I'm thinking of dealing with the man myself, and I'd rather he was left entirely in my hands for the present."

"Be damn!" said Doyle, "but I wouldn't ask better than just for yourself to take in hand and hunt him out of the place altogether."

"It's you could do it," said Dr. O'Donoghue.

"It is," said Doyle. "Divil the better man at devising of ambuscades ever I come across, and I've known some in my day that you might call gladiators."

"I'm not precisely a professional gladiator," said Meldon modestly; "but I've studied strategy a little in my time, and I rather think I'll get the better of Mr. Simpkins. I suppose now you would not object to attending his funeral?"

"I would not," said Doyle, "if so be there was no risk of my being hanged for any share I might have in bringing the same about."

"There's not the least chance of that," said Meldon. "You won't have to do anything except refrain from making a public fool of the man with any kind of tricks about salmon for the next fortnight."

"What is it you're thinking of doing?" asked Doyle.

"The doctor," said Meldon, "will of course have to sign the death certificate."

"I'll do that," said Dr. O'Donoghue, "as soon as ever you satisfy me that the man's dead. If there isn't a hole drilled in his skull with a bullet, I'll say it's heart failure that finished him. After the way he behaved to me, I can't be expected to make a *post mortem* of him. I daresay the Major was telling you what he did."

"I hear he wanted you to put some ridiculous sanitary act in force against poor Doyle. That, of course, was quite intolerable."

"There was worse besides that," said Dr. O'Donoghue gloomily.

"He had it put out against the doctor," said Doyle, "that old Biddy Finnegan died for the want of proper medical attendance, and her a woman of near ninety, that was bound to die any way, and would have died sooner, most likely, if the doctor hadn't let her alone the way he did."

"That old woman," said the doctor, "wasn't neglected. She had a bottle by her, when she died, that I sent out to her less than a week before, and she hadn't the half of it drunk. What's more, I wouldn't have minded a bit if Simpkins had had any right to be interfering; but he hadn't. Thady Flanagan—that's married to old Biddy's grand-daughter—was contented enough with the way she died, and asked me civilly would I have any objection to his taking home the half-bottle of medicine for the use of one of his own children. What I say is, that if the woman's own relations had no complaint to make, what business had Simpkins to be putting in his oar? What aggravated me was that kind of gratuitous and unnecessary interfering."

"I quite see your point," said Meldon. "It's—"

"You've only heard the half of it," said Doyle. "The doctor's backward in telling you, and small blame to him; but Simpkins wrote off to the Local Government Board, preferring a lot of charges against the doctor, and against myself as Chairman of the Board of Guardians—things you'd wonder any man would have the face to say."

"What happened?" said Meldon.

"We've quietened them down for the present," said Doyle, "but there was a lot of talk of a sworn enquiry. And what did Simpkins do it for if it wasn't just the delight he takes in destroying the peace of the town? You know very well, Mr. Meldon, the way we all pulled together here, Catholics and Protestants, and never had any bad feeling. And where's the good of bringing in the Local Government Board to be stirring up strife among us? But that's not all he did, nor the half or it. He wrote a letter last October to the Inspector-General of the Police, complaining of the sergeant beyond, that he wasn't doing his duty."

"I wouldn't expect you to be taking the part of the police," said Meldon. "You always went in for being a strong Nationalist."

"And so I am," said Doyle. "And so's the doctor. In a general way there isn't two men in Ireland that hates the police worse than the doctor and myself; but the sergeant was a decent, poor man, with a long family dependent on him, and I never heard tell of his doing any harm to any one."

"Perhaps," said Meldon, "that was the reason Mr. Simpkins complained of him. After all, Doyle, we must be reasonable. What are the police for, if it isn't to do harm to people—objectionable people? A policeman who never injures anybody isn't worth his keep. If what you say about the sergeant is true, or anything like true, Simpkins was evidently perfectly justified in acting as he did."

"You won't say that," said Doyle, "when you hear the way it happened. There's two apple trees in the garden at the back of the house Simpkins lives in."

"I remember them," said Meldon; "but there never were any apples on them in my time."

"There were apples on them last year," said Doyle, "however they came there. Simpkins did be saying it was on account of the way he pruned the trees; but he'd be talking a long time before I'd believe the like of that. Any way, the apples were there, and a good many of them. I didn't see them myself, but they tell me there might have been up to ten stone altogether. Well, one night the half of them was gone. The gossures from about the town had them ate."

"Of course they had," said Meldon. "What would you expect?"

"What nobody would expect," said Doyle, "was the temper Simpkins was in in the morning. He was up and down, in and out of the police barrack, cursing all sorts. Well, the sergeant came out and looked at the trees, and he asked Simpkins did he have the apples counted before they were took, and would he be prepared to swear to them if so be that the police found them for him. You'd think that would have pacified him, but it didn't. So the sergeant, who wanted to do the best he could for the peace of the town, went down to the house again after he had his dinner ate, and two constables along with him, and asked the girl that does be with Mr. Simpkins—"

"Sabina's red-haired cousin," said Meldon.

"Asked her," said Doyle, "was there ever a boy about the place at night; which of course there wasn't, her being a respectable girl that wasn't keeping company with any boy, unless it might be walking out now and then of a Sunday with Jamesy Carroll. Believe you me, it took the sergeant all he knew to quieten down her mother that was over at the barracks asking for the name of the villain that was taking away her daughter's character.

That night the rest of the apples was took, and Simpkins was fit to be put in the asylum in the morning. He said the sergeant was an incompetent jackass.—Wasn't them the words he used, doctor?"

"And others along with them," said Dr. O'Donoghue.

"The sergeant, being a man who'd always kept himself to himself and didn't mix with bad company, wasn't going near the house while the like of that language was going on. But he sent down the whole of the four constables to look at the apple trees; which they did. But Simpkins got worse instead of better. He wrote off a note to the District Inspector complaining of the sergeant. But the D.I. had more sense than to take any notice, knowing well that if there's an apple in the place the gossures will get it, and small blame to them."

"Sensible man," said Meldon.

"When Simpkins got no satisfaction out of him," said Doyle, "he wrote to the County Inspector. I can tell you he took mighty little by that. It was a week after, or maybe more, when he got an answer back. It was Sabina Gallagher told me what was in it, having got it out of her cousin, that's servant to Simpkins and seen the letter, so I know what I'm telling you is the truth. The County Inspector said that if there was boycotting in the place, or cattle driving, or any kind of lawlessness, he'd be quick enough to have extra police drafted in and a baton charge up and down upon the streets of the town; but that he wasn't going to upset the policy of the Government, and maybe have questions asked about him in Parliament, for the sake of a few shillings' worth of apples. You'd think that would have been enough for Simpkins, but it wasn't. He wrote another letter, up to Dublin Castle, to the Inspector-General of Police, no less, and the end of it, was that the sergeant was moved out of this."

"Poor fellow," said Meldon. "Did he mind much?"

"He did not then, for they sent him to a better station. It was only last week they moved him, there being a lot of enquiries to be gone through that occupied them the whole of the winter and the spring. The doctor and myself is thinking of getting up a subscription to present him with an illuminated address on account of the way he conducted himself to the satisfaction of the inhabitants of this town while he was in it, and as a protest against the underhand way that Simpkins went about trying to injure him and take the bread out of the mouth of his children."

"I'll see that the Major subscribes to that," said Meldon.

"Tell Mr. Meldon," said Doyle, "what it was you were saying ought to be on the address."

"It isn't worth speaking about," said the doctor modestly.

"You'd better tell me," said Meldon. "If I'm to be responsible for revenging the wrongs of the community on Simpkins, I ought to be well up in every detail of what's going on."

"It was nothing but just an idea that came across my mind," said the doctor.

"It may be only that," said Meldon, "but it may be more. The proper person to judge of its importance is me. You must have frequently observed, doctor, that the man to whom an idea occurs is not by any means the best judge of its value. Sometimes he thinks too much of it. Take Galileo, for instance. He hit upon the fact that the earth goes round the sun, and it struck him as immensely important. He gassed on about it until everybody got so tired of the subject that the authorities had to put him in prison and keep him there until he said it wasn't true, and that he'd stop writing books to say it was. As a matter of fact it was true, but it didn't matter. We'd all be doing exactly the same things we are doing to-day if he had never made his beastly telescope. On the other hand, men who get a hold of really important ideas often think very little of them. Look, for example, at the case of the man who first thought of collecting a lot of people together and making them pass a unanimous resolution. He didn't even take the trouble to patent the process, and now there's no record left of when and where he hit upon his idea. And yet, where would we all be without unanimous resolutions? Doyle will tell you that government couldn't be carried on and civilisation would practically become extinct. It may be the same with this idea of yours, and I've no doubt that I'll be able to judge if you tell me what it is."

"He was thinking," said Doyle, "of having a picture of an apple tree in the top left-hand corner of the address with apples on it, and the same tree in the top right-hand corner with no apples. He says it would be agreeable to the sergeant."

"I don't think much of that," said Meldon. "It strikes me as a poor idea, for three reasons. In the first place, you'll not be able to get an artist who can draw the apple trees so that any ordinary man could recognise them. I know what I'm talking about, for apple trees necessarily come a good deal into ecclesiastical art, the kind of art I'm most familiar with. I give you my word that the most of them might as well be elms, and I've seen lots that look like Florence Court yews. As a general rule, you wouldn't have a ghost of a notion what they were meant for if it wasn't for Eve and the serpent. In the next place, I don't think the sergeant would care for it. The whole business must be painful to him, and he won't care to be obliged every day of his life to be staring at something that would remind him of Simpkins. In the third place, it would almost certainly irritate Simpkins when he heard of it."

"It's that," said Doyle, "that we were hoping it might do."

"Well, then, you may put the idea out of your heads. I can't have Simpkins irritated at present. It's of the utmost possible importance that he should be lulled into a sense of security. I can't deal with him if his suspicions are aroused in the slightest. I've been with him myself this morning, lulling him."

"Were you, then?" said Doyle.

"I was, and I think I may say that for the immediate present he's lulled."

"And how did you like him?" said Doyle.

"My feelings don't matter," said Meldon. "As a matter of fact, judging from a single interview, I should say he was a pleasant enough, straightforward sort of man who is trying to do what is right."

"If he tried less," said Doyle, "he'd get on better."

"Quite so. And you mustn't think that I'm going to allow my personal feelings to interfere with my action in the matter. The Major is my friend, and I have a great regard for the poor old rector, in spite of his suffering from bronchitis. Also I like the people of Ballymoy, and I'm ready to help them in any way I can. So, whatever opinion I have formed of Simpkins, I'm going to deal with him precisely as if he were my personal enemy."

"What do you mean to do to him?" said the doctor. "You were speaking this minute of a *post mortem*."

"It won't come to that," said Meldon, "unless you boggle over the death certificate. But the precise details of my scheme I must keep to myself for the present, merely saying that I shall be severe with him. I couldn't, in fact, be severer if I caught him throwing stones at my infant daughter."

"Is that the one the Major stood for?" said Doyle. "He was talking to me about her. A fine child she is by all accounts."

"She was a fine child," said Meldon, "until she got the whooping-cough. Since then she's been wakeful at night.—By the way, doctor, what do you think is the proper way to feed a child that has the whooping-cough? At the present time she's living chiefly on a kind of yellow drink made up out of a powdery stuff out of a tin which tastes like biscuits when it's dry. Would you say now that was a good food for her?"

"You can rear a child," said the doctor, "whether it has the whooping-cough or not, on pretty near anything, so long as you give it enough of whatever it is you do give it."

"I'm glad to hear you say that," said Meldon; "for my wife has a notion that food ought to be weighed out by ounces, so that the child wouldn't get too much at a time."

"Did she get that out of a book?"

"She did—a little book with a pink cover on it. Do you know it?"

"I do not; but if I were you I'd burn it."

"I did," said Meldon. "I burned it before it was a week in the house. If I hadn't been a good-tempered man, I'd have burned the baby along with it. She spent the whole of four nights crying, and that was before she got the whooping-cough, so there was no excuse for her."

"It was hunger ailed her then," said the doctor.

"It was," said Meldon. "I found that out afterwards, for she stopped crying as soon as ever she got enough to eat. If I'd allowed her to be brought up on the principles laid down in that book her temper would have been ruined for life, and she'd have been a nuisance to every one she came across."

"I wouldn't wonder," said Doyle, "but it might be according to that book that Simpkins was reared. It would be hard to account for the kind of man he is any other way."

"It might be that," said the doctor; "but I'd say myself it's more likely to be the want of beating when he was young that's the matter with him."

"Will you stay and have a bit of dinner now you're here, Mr. Meldon?" said Doyle. "I wouldn't like your temper would be destroyed for the want of what I'd be glad to give you."

Meldon looked at his watch.

"Thank you," he said, "I will. It's one o'clock, and Sabina ought to have the bacon ready by now if she started cooking it the time I told her."

CHAPTER VII

Ballymoy House, save for the occasional presence of a fishing tenant, has been unoccupied for years. Two men are employed to keep the grounds tidy, and Mr. Simpkins does his best to see that the work is done. But in spite of his exertions the place is in a condition of disorder. There is long grass where there ought to be trim lawns; wild growths of brambles in nooks originally dedicated to rose gardening; and a general air of exuberance about the trees and shrubs. Miss King found all this very charming. She took a walk round the pleasure grounds on the evening of her arrival, and felt that she had happened upon the Irish demesne of her dreams—a region of spacious dilapidation, exquisite natural beauty, romantic possibilities, and an inexhaustible supply of local colour; a place very different indeed from the trim Thames-side villas in which she generally spent her summer holidays. Her maid unpacked a large box of requisites for the country life supplied by the Stores, and came, at the bottom of it, upon a very gay hammock made of green and scarlet strings. Miss King was delighted with its appearance, and the promise it gave of luxurious rest. After breakfast next morning she summoned the two gardeners to her presence, and gave orders that the hammock should be securely hung in a shady place. The men were unaccustomed to hammocks, but with the help of some advice from the maid, they tied it to two trees in a corner of what had once been a tennis court. They were so pleased with it that they stood looking at it with great appreciation until Miss King came out at about twelve o'clock. She brought with her a bundle of manuscript and a fountain pen, intending to work into her new novel a description of Ballymoy House and the demesne.

The men watched her settle herself, and then came forward cautiously and asked if there was anything they could do for her. Miss King suggested that they should go away and do their work. They went obediently, but returned in a few minutes with two scythes.

"If it's pleasing to your ladyship," said the elder of the two, "I was thinking of cutting the grass beyond, while the weather's fine, and we'd have a chance of getting the hay saved without rain."

Miss King was not very well pleased. She would have preferred to be left alone, in order that she might enjoy thoroughly the picturesque dilapidation she wished to describe. But she did not see her way to forbid the cutting of the grass. The two men sharpened their scythes noisily and mowed down several swathes of long grass. Miss King watched them, mildly interested. At the end of five minutes they stopped mowing and whetted their scythes again. Then they sat down, lit their pipes, and looked at Miss King. She busied herself with her papers, and made some corrections with the fountain pen. When their pipes were about half smoked, the men rose, whetted their scythes for the third time, and mowed again. Miss King stopped writing and watched them. The day grew hotter, and the spells of mowing became shorter. Miss King gave up the attempt to write, and lay dreamily gazing at the men, roused to active consciousness now and then by the rasp of the hones against the scythe blades. At one o'clock the men, guessing it to be dinnertime, stopped pretending to work and went away. A few minutes later Miss King, feeling the need of luncheon, disentangled herself from the hammock, bundled her papers together, and went into the house.

At two o'clock the men, carrying their scythes, returned to the tennis court, which was nearly half mowed. At half-past two Miss King joined them, and climbed as gracefully as she could into the hammock. She brought a book with her this time instead of her manuscript. The afternoon was hotter than the morning had been, and there was a very soothing sound of bees among the branches of the trees. Miss King, who had eaten her luncheon with a good appetite, went to sleep. The two gardeners, after a short consultation, sat down under a tree and smoked. At half-past three Meldon arrived.

"You seem," he said to the men, "to be taking things pretty easy. Are you supposed to be mowing that lawn, or is Mr. Simpkins paying you to cut the legs off any tiger or other wild beast that comes up with the idea of devouring Miss King in her sleep?"

The men grinned pleasantly, and put their pipes in their pockets.

"It's how we didn't like to be disturbing the young lady," said the elder of the two men, "and her lying there quiet and innocent, maybe tired out, the creature, with the way she's been travelling to and fro."

"Isn't it Callaghan your name is?" said Meldon.

"It is. Glory be to God! but it's wonderful the way you'd know me, Mr. Meldon, and you out of the place these three years."

"Send that other man away," said Meldon, "and listen to me while I speak to you."

"Mickey," said Callaghan to his fellow-labourer, "let you be off with you and get the potatoes earthed up beyond in the garden. It's wonderful, so it is, the way you'd take a delight in sitting there all day and not doing a hand's turn."

Mickey went off, still grinning. He had no intention of earthing up the potatoes. Digging is hard work, not to be lightly undertaken on a hot afternoon. Meldon watched him out of sight, and then turned to Callaghan.

"I'm speaking confidentially to you," he said, "and I hope that nothing I say will—"

"Take care," said Callaghan, "that you wouldn't wake herself, talking so loud and all."

Meldon looked at Miss King.

"She seems pretty sound," he said, speaking more softly.

"It's tired she is, the creature,", said Callaghan. "It would be a shame to wake her, though I wouldn't care myself for the notion of sleeping in one of them new-fashioned beds."

"What I want to say to you is this," said Meldon. "You know Mr. Simpkins, of course?"

"I do."

"Is he a particular friend of yours?"

"He is not," said Callaghan. "The Lord forgive me for saying the like! but I hate him worse than I do the devil."

"I thought you probably would," said Meldon, "and I don't wonder at it. Any man who works the sort of way you were working when I arrived would be pretty sure to hate Simpkins."

"Since ever he come to the place," said Callaghan, "there's been neither peace nor quiet in it. There doesn't a day pass but he's up here asking why this isn't done, and what's the matter with the other thing, and whether I couldn't manage to settle up some contraption or other. Many's the time I've said to myself it would be better for me to starve out on the bog beyond than to have the life plagued out of me listening to the way he does be talking."

"I expect," said Meldon, "that he's simply trying to make you do your work, and a hard job he has of it."

"Any way, it's what I'm not accustomed to; and what's more, won't stand."

"You'll have to stand it for a while more, any way. That's what I want to impress on your mind. I can't have a word said against Mr. Simpkins, in the presence of Miss King."

"The young lady there?"

"Yes, that exact young lady. She's a stranger in these parts, and you're more or less responsible for the opinions she forms of the people she comes across. It's to you she'll be looking for guidance when she's in a difficulty and wants information about any one."

"She will, of course. Why wouldn't she? Amn't I old enough to be her father and the father of a dozen more like her?"

"Exactly," said Meldon. "So when she consults you about Mr. Simpkins you'll say all the good you can of him, and you'll praise him up to the servants in the house in such a way that they'll repeat what you've said to her."

"Would you have me tell what isn't true?"

"I would."

"Well, then, I'll not do it. I've more respect for myself, let alone the young lady, than to do the like."

"Don't take that tone with me," said Meldon, "for I'll not stand it. There isn't a man in Ireland this minute that has a greater respect for the truth than I have. It's a good thing—one of the best things there is—in its proper place. But there's no bigger mistake than to suppose that because a thing is good in one place at one time, it must necessarily be good everywhere and always. Take the case of bottled porter. You're not a teetotaller, are you?"

"I was one time," said Callaghan, "after the mission there did be going round the country last spring. They had me pledged before I rightly understood what it was they were doing; but, thanks be to God, I'm through with it now, and can take a drop of drink as well as another."

"Very well. Then you'll appreciate what I say about bottled porter. It's a good thing when you have it in a tumbler, and the tumbler in your hand, and you thirsty."

"It is." Callaghan spoke with conviction. He was thirsty at the moment, and he had some hope that Meldon might possibly have the bottle of which he spoke in his pocket. He was disappointed when Meldon went on with his speech.

"But it's not a good thing when somebody jogs your elbow and spills the whole of it over the legs of your trousers. Now it's exactly the same with truth. It's all right under certain circumstances. It's one of the worst things going when it's told to the wrong man at the wrong time. You follow me so far, I hope. Very well. Now I want to make it plain to you that the truth about Mr. Simpkins must not be told to Miss King. I expect he'll be up to call on her tomorrow or next day, and it's most important that she should not be prejudiced against him."

"Have you a match made up between them?" asked Callaghan.

"I have."

"And why couldn't you have said so before? If that's the way of it, it isn't likely I'd be saying a word that would turn her against the man that's laid down for her to marry. There was a friend of my own one time that had a match made up for his son with a girl that had a good fortune. But there was only one leg on her, and he was terrible feared that the boy'd never take her if he found it out. There wasn't one in the place, only myself, that knew the way the girl was on account of her father living away beyond the bog. Do you think I said the word? I did not. And the boy was well enough pleased at the latter end."

"In this particular case," said Meldon, "you'll have to do rather more than keep your mouth shut. Simpkins' legs are all right, of course, but—"

"He has the divil of a long tongue."

"Well, don't dwell on his tongue when you're talking about him to Miss King."

"Beyond saying an odd time that he's a pleasant-spoken gentleman, I will not."

"That's right," said Meldon. "I shall rely absolutely on you. And you are to let me know from time to time how they get on together when he comes up here to visit her."

"If there's any impropriety of conduct between them," said Callaghan, "I'll speak to your reverence."

"Don't misunderstand me," said Meldon. "I don't want to interfere with their love-making. The more of that they do, the better I'll be pleased. Even if they run rather into extremes—"

"It's what I won't be a party to," said Callaghan; "I don't hold with them ways, and the clergy is against them, all but yourself; and you ought to be ashamed to be encouraging the like."

"You don't in the least understand the situation," said Meldon. "Mr. Simpkins and Miss King are both English, and in England they manage these things quite differently from the way we do here."

"Well, it's yourself ought to know about that, seeing that you're a Protestant."

"It's not so much a question of religion," said Meldon. "It's temperament. I don't suppose you understand what that means; but the fact is, that an Englishwoman wouldn't marry a man who hadn't been making love to her off and on for at least a week. If he hadn't got her thoroughly accustomed to his occasionally squeezing her hand, and offering to pick flowers for her, and picking up anything she dropped about, and— But I needn't go into details. The fact is, that if he hadn't made love to her pretty violently, she wouldn't consider it decent to marry him. That's the sort of people the English are."

"They're queer," said Callaghan, "and that's a fact."

"They are," said Meldon. "But we've simply got to take them as we find them. There's no use our trying to teach them better ways, for they wouldn't listen to us. I'm telling you all this so that you won't be shocked if you happen to see Simpkins kissing Miss King. It's no affair of yours, to start with; and, in the second place, there's no point in comparative ethnology so firmly established as the fact that morality is quite a different thing among different peoples. What would be wrong for you and me may be, and is, perfectly right for Miss King and Simpkins. I needn't go into that more fully. All you have to do is to crack up Simpkins as a first-rate sort of man that any girl would be lucky if she married; and then let me know how they hit it off together when they meet."

"I'll do it. I'd do more than that to oblige your reverence in the matter of making a match for any boy about the place; for I'm not one to spoil his chances on a boy, not if I hated him worse than I do Simpkins."

"Very well. Now I want to speak a few words to Miss King, but it won't do for me to wake her up. She wouldn't like it; and what's more, she might suspect that we'd been talking together about her. I'll go back to the house and walk over here across the lawn. I'll signal to you as soon as I'm ready to start, and then you go over and wake Miss King."

"I wouldn't like to do it. I'd be ashamed, for fear she might think I was taking a liberty."

"I don't want you to go and shake her," said Meldon, "or pour cold water over her, or anything of that sort. Just take your scythe over close to where she is, and as soon as ever I give the signal, you begin to scrape the blade of it with your stone and whistle a tune at the same time as loud as you can."

"'The Wearing of the Green,' or the like?"

"Not 'The Wearing of the Green.' It's a melancholy, soothing sort of tune which would probably only make her sleep sounder. Whistle a good lively jig."

"I will," said Callaghan.

Meldon walked away. When he reached the house he stood on the top step of the flight which leads to the hall door and waved his pocket handkerchief. Callaghan picked up his scythe cautiously, and went on tip-toe across to Miss King's hammock. He did not wish to disturb her prematurely. Then, his hone in one hand and his scythe in the other, he stood and watched Meldon, The handkerchief waved again, and Meldon started walking briskly across the lawn. The hone rasped harshly against the scythe blade, and "The Irish Washerwoman" rang out shrilly. Miss King woke with a start. Callaghan turned away from her, and still whistling vigorously, began to mow. Meldon hurried forward.

"How do you do, Miss King?" he said. "I happened to be passing the gate and I just called in to see how you are getting on, and to see whether there is anything I can do for you."

Miss King blinked, got her feet out of the hammock, sat up, and shook hands with Meldon.

"It's very kind of you. Won't you come inside and have some tea, or shall I get them to bring it out here?"

"No, thanks. No tea for me. I haven't time to stay; and besides, I've had luncheon with Mr. Doyle. You know what that means."

"No," said Miss King. "I don't."

"Well, I needn't go into details," said Meldon; "but as a matter of fact when you've lunched with Mr. Doyle you don't want anything more to drink for a long time. By the way, you're not looking out for a cook just at present, are you?"

"No, I'm not. What made you think I was?"

"People generally are," said Meldon. "In fact, I've hardly ever met any one who wasn't. I happen just now to know of a really excellent girl, called Sabina. With a little training she'd make a first-rate cook. She's first cousin to the red-haired girl who's with Mr. Simpkins. That's a recommendation in itself."

"Is it? Who is Mr. Simpkins? Oh, of course, he's the man from whom I took the house."

"A capital fellow," said Meldon; "young, strong, and vigorous. The sort of man," he sank his voice impressively, "that it would take a lot to kill."

Miss King seemed moderately interested.

"But why do you think," she said, "that his servant's first cousin—"

"Sabina is her name," said Meldon. "It's a very attractive name, isn't it?"

"Yes. But why do you think it likely that Mr. Simpkins' servant's first cousin can cook?"

"He's a most particular man," said Meldon; "fidgety to a degree about having everything quite right, always worrying the life out of his servants, which is excellent for them, of course; but, well, if he was married"—he sank his voice again—"I expect his wife would consider herself quite justified in killing him. I daresay he'll be up to call on you this afternoon."

"If he's as bad as that," said Miss King, "I had better go in and tidy my hair before he comes."

"Perhaps you had," said Meldon.

"You're very rude," said Miss King.

She smiled as she spoke, blushed slightly, and then looking at Meldon from under her eyelashes, said,—

"Come now, tell me the truth. Am I an absolute fright?"

Most men would have attempted a pretty speech of some sort. Many men would have responded to Miss King's eyes with a glance of admiration. She had very fine eyes, and a singularly attractive way of looking out of the corners of them. Miss King was, in fact, a little tired of her own company, and would have liked to hear Meldon say something pleasant about her appearance. She would have enjoyed herself very well if he had attempted some slight flirtation with her. But he snubbed her severely.

"I told you yesterday," he said, "that I'm a married man. I have a daughter two years old, and I'm a clergyman. I really can't allow you—"

The soft look vanished in an instant from Miss King's eyes. They flashed fiercely. Her face became suddenly crimson.

"You are outrageous," she said. "How dare you suggest—? How dare you even think—?"

She sprang to her feet and started at a rapid pace towards the house. Her head was poised defiantly. Meldon, though he could only see her back, felt certain that her chin was in the air. Callaghan, who had retired with his scythe to the middle of the lawn, stopped mowing and stared after Miss King. Then he laid down his scythe and approached Meldon.

"Were you telling her," he asked, "of the match you had laid out for her?"

"No," said Meldon, with a broad smile, "I wasn't."

"From the look of her," said Callaghan, "I thought maybe you might."

"Well, I wasn't. All I was trying to make plain to her was that she couldn't marry me."

"I'd say," said Callaghan, "that she seen that plain enough, however it was that you put it to her."

"I thought it better to make it quite clear at once," said Meldon. "She was looking at me in a kind of way you'd hardly understand."

"I might, then," said Callaghan, still grinning.

"You would not," said Meldon. "You told me a moment ago that the priests wouldn't let you!"

"There's many a thing," said Callaghan, "that the clergy might not approve of, but—"

"Any how," said Meldon, "it was that kind of way she looked at me, and I thought it better to put a stop to it at once."

"You're right there; and it's no more than what I'd expect of you."

"I don't think you quite grasp my point yet," said Meldon. "In a general way I shouldn't mind her looking at me any way she liked. I might have enjoyed it, if she'd done it well, as I expect she could. But under the existing circumstances I had to stop her; because, if she took to looking at me like that, she'd look quite another way at Mr. Simpkins, and then he wouldn't be inclined to marry her."

"You're dead set on that match," said Callaghan.

"I am. It's most important that it should come off."

"She's a fine girl," said Callaghan. "She's too good for the like of Simpkins. He'll be tormenting her the way he does be tormenting everybody about the place."

"Believe you me," said Meldon, "she'll know how to manage him."

"She might," said Callaghan. "By the looks of her, when she left you this minute, I wouldn't say but she might."

CHAPTER VIII

It was eight o'clock, and the evening was deliciously warm. Major Kent and Meldon sat in hammock chairs on the gravel outside Portsmouth Lodge. They had dined comfortably, and their pipes were lit. For a time neither of them spoke. Below them, beyond the wall which bounded the lawn, lay the waters of the bay, where the *Spindrift*, Major Kent's yacht, hung motionless over her mooring-buoy. The eyes of both men were fixed on her.

"I feel," said Meldon at last, "like the village blacksmith."

"There are four in Ballymoy," said the Major. "Reilly is the man who works for me. If you feel like him, I'm sorry for you. He's generally drunk at this hour."

"I refer," said Meldon, "to Longfellow's village blacksmith. You're not a highly-educated man, I know, but I thought you'd have heard of him.

"'The muscles of his brawny arms
Were strong as iron bands.'

It's a poem which most people learn while at school. I am sometimes tempted to think that you never were at school."

"I don't see, J. J., that your muscles are anything particular to swagger about."

"I wasn't referring to my muscles," said Meldon. "The resemblance I speak of lies in the fact that I've 'earned my night's repose.' The village blacksmith felt that he deserved his after listening to his daughter singing in the local church choir. I've undergone an even severer nerve strain. I've practically arranged the marriage between Simpkins and the murderess."

"I wish very much that I knew exactly what you've been doing all day, J. J. I always feel nervous when you go out alone. I never know—"

"I'll give you an exact account of my proceedings, if you like. First, I had a personal interview with Simpkins; and I may as well say at once that I was on the whole favourably impressed by him. I don't mean to say that he ought not to be killed, but merely that if left to myself I would not go out of my way to kill him. I next talked the matter over with Doyle and Dr. O'Donoghue. I found that they quite agreed with you; and the doctor is prepared to sign the death certificate as soon as Miss King—who will then, of course, be Mrs. Simpkins—has finished him off. I then called at Ballymoy House and arranged with Callaghan, the gardener, to keep me informed of the progress of events. Finally, I interviewed Miss King herself. I was unfortunately obliged to offend her a little, and I expect she won't care about talking to me for the next few days."

"Did you allude to the trial?"

"No. And she wouldn't have minded in the least if I had. She's quite frank with me in talking about her art. The fact is, she wanted to flirt with me, and of course I couldn't have that."

"Are you sure of that, J. J.? It seems to me very unlikely that a lady of that sort would want to flirt with a clergyman."

"I'm not exactly an ordinary clergyman," said Meldon, "and she certainly did want to flirt with me. I could see it by the expression of her eye. Any man who knows anything about women gets into the way of judging them very largely by the expression of their eyes. You find after a little practice that you are able to tell with almost absolute certainty what their intentions are; and there was no mistake about Miss King's this afternoon."

"I'm glad," said the Major, "that you went away at once."

"I didn't," said Meldon. "It was she who went away. I hurt her feelings by telling her plainly that I was a married man. She flew into a temper and pranced off."

"She must be a very—"

"No, she's not—not in the least. It was simply a case of what Virgil calls 'spretae injuria formae.'"

"Talk English," said Major Kent. "You know I don't understand Latin."

"Never mind," said Meldon; "you wouldn't understand it a bit better if I put it into English. You haven't the necessary experience. And in any case it doesn't in the least matter. The important thing for you to get a hold of is that the marriage is arranged, and unless something quite unforeseen turns up it will come off. I told Simpkins that she had a large fortune and was the niece of an earl. Those facts, in addition to her personal charm, will, I imagine, bring him rapidly up to the scratch. I can do no more for the present. That's why I said I was like the blacksmith and had earned my night's repose."

"It's early yet," said the Major. "I seldom turn in before eleven. But, of course, you can go off at once if you like."

"When I quoted that line about the night's repose," said Meldon, "I was speaking figuratively. I haven't the least intention of going to bed at this hour. I don't suppose the original blacksmith did either, even if he was feeling a bit upset about the choir. What I really meant was that I am quite entitled now to have a couple of days off in the *Spindrift*."

"I'm glad to hear you say that," said the Major. "I was afraid you were going to spend your whole holiday running backwards and forwards between this and Ballymoy."

"I can't take a regular cruise," said Meldon. "I absolutely must be back here the day after to-morrow. No matter how carefully you arrange things, there's always a risk of something going wrong. Quite a trifling accident might upset the entire plan, and I ought to be on the spot to straighten things out directly they begin to get into a tangle."

Major Kent made no answer. He sat smoking until his pipe went out. Then for a while he sat with the empty pipe in his mouth, sucking at it as if it were still alight. He was thinking deeply. The evening darkened slowly, and a faint breeze stole in from the sea.

"Every prospect of a fine day to-morrow," said Meldon.

The Major took no notice of the remark. Meldon filled a fresh pipe, and watched the *Spindrift* tugging at her moorings as the breeze freshened or died and the tide caught her.

"J. J.," said the Major at last, speaking very solemnly, "I'd rather you didn't."

"Didn't what?"

"I know you enjoy this sort of thing, and I don't want to spoil your holiday. I'd like you to have a really good time, but I wish you'd hit on some other amusement."

"Try and be a little more explicit, Major. I'm a quick-witted man, and I can generally guess at your meaning, no matter how you wrap it up in paraphrases, but this time I really can't. The only amusement I've proposed so far is a short trip in your yacht. I suppose you don't grudge me that?"

"You know very well I don't, J. J. But I wish you wouldn't play these tricks with Simpkins. He's a man I don't like."

"You told me that last night," said Meldon, "and I agreed at once to have him murdered."

"Of course I know that you like talking in that sort of way, and I don't mind it a bit. It's your way of making jokes, and you don't mean any harm by what you say; but I'd really rather not be mixed up with Simpkins even by way of a joke. I don't like the man at all."

"Don't repeat that again," said Meldon. "I quite believe you. And as for the murder of Simpkins being a joke, I assure you it's nothing of the sort. I may be flippant—several people have called me flippant—but I draw the line at making jokes about murder. It's a serious subject. In fact I've more than once hesitated about going into this business at all. It's mainly for your sake that I'm doing it."

"Then don't do it," said the Major. "I know quite well that you don't mean a word you say, but—"

"I mean it all. Am I the kind of man who says what he doesn't mean? Come now, Major; you've known me a good many years, and we've been in some tight places together. Have you ever heard me say a thing I didn't mean?"

"To be quite candid," said the Major, "I have, once or twice."

"You're entirely mistaken. You have not. And in any case I mean what I say now. Do you really suppose that I'd have spent the whole of this hot day fagging up and down the roads about Ballymoy if I wasn't in earnest about what I was at?"

"But you don't. You can't think that this lady—Miss King or whatever her name is—will really murder Simpkins?"

"She'll try to if she marries him. I can't be absolutely certain that she'll succeed, but I think it's very likely that she will. She's had a lot of practice, and by her own account she's been unusually successful."

"That's all rot, of course," said the Major. "Murder isn't committed in that sort of way. No woman would deliberately with her eyes open—"

"Did Mrs. Lorimer murder her husband by accident, or did she intend to do it and plan the whole thing out beforehand?"

"I don't know."

"You do know. You read the evidence and you read the judge's charge, and you know as well as I do that she proceeded in the most deliberate way possible."

"It looked like it," said the Major. "I must say it looked like it."

"Very well. Is Miss King Mrs. Lorimer, or is she not?"

"I don't know."

"I proved to you yesterday evening that she is. I proved it in a way that left no possible room for doubt in your mind, if you are honest with yourself and look facts plainly in the face. I am not going into the proof again, because it's a very exhausting thing and I've had a hard day. Besides, if it didn't convince you the first time, it wouldn't the second. Trains of reasoning aren't like advertisements. You come to believe that a certain kind of pill will prevent your going bald because you've seen statements to that effect ten thousand times. It's the cumulative weight of repeated assertion which compels belief in that case. But the kind of belief which depends on reasoning is quite different. If you've the sort of intellect which cannot grasp the proof which Euclid gives of one of his propositions, no number of repetitions of it will help you in the least. That's a curious psychological law, but it is a law. Therefore it would be the merest waste of time for me to demonstrate to you again that Mrs. Lorimer and Miss King are the same person. I pass on to the next stage in our enquiry. Will Miss King murder her next husband?"

"If she's Mrs. Lorimer," said the Major, "and if Mrs. Lorimer murdered—"

"There are no 'ifs' about the matter," said Meldon; "she unquestionably will. She told me so herself, and whatever else she is she's a woman of her word. There remains now only one question, Who is her next husband to be? And the answer to that may be given in two syllables—Simpkins."

"If you really believe all that," said the Major, "and—"

"I do," said Meldon.

"Then you're going to commit a horrible crime, and I insist on your stopping at once."

"I can't stop it now. I've set the thing going, and it can't be stopped. You might have stopped it yesterday, but you're too late now. I'm sorry for poor Simpkins myself. I thought him a decent enough sort of man."

"He's a cad."

"There you are again. In one breath you try to stop me, and in the very next breath you urge me strongly to go on. Which do you mean? Not that it matters, for the thing is as good as done now. Still you ought to try and cultivate the habit of definitely making up your mind, and then sticking to it. You said yesterday distinctly, and so far I could judge sincerely, that you wished Simpkins was dead. Now you pretend that it's a shock to you to hear that he's going to be killed. That's what I call vacillation, and you ought to be ashamed of it."

Major Kent sighed heavily.

"There's no use my talking," he said, "but you'll get yourself into trouble some day with these jokes of yours."

"Major," said Meldon, "I've absolutely no patience with you. You're back again at that joke theory of yours, after I've spent half the evening explaining to you that this isn't a joking matter at all. I must decline to discuss the matter any further. We'll talk of something else. I was speaking to O'Donoghue to-day about the proper way of feeding the child when it has whoping-cough. He says it ought to be given as much as it wants to eat of any ordinary kind of food. I'm inclined to agree with him. Now what is your opinion?"

"I suppose you're thinking of your own child?"

"Yes, I am. And don't forget that she's not merely my child. She's also your god-child."

"Well, I gave her a silver mug. Didn't I?"

"You did. A capital mug, large and heavy. She'll be very grateful to you for that mug some day; though, up to the present, all she has done to it is to dint its side one day by dropping it against the corner of the fender when it was given her to play with. You did your duty in the matter of a mug, and I'm not suggesting for a moment that you should give her another. When I reminded you that you are her god-father, I merely wanted to suggest that you ought to take some little interest in her health and education."

"But I don't know what babies ought to eat."

"What you really mean is that you don't care. You're so wrapped up in this miserable local squabble with Simpkins about a salmon that you've lost all interest in the wider subjects which are occupying the attention of the world."

"Come now, J. J. Your baby—she's a very nice baby and all that. But really—"

"I won't talk about her any more if she bores you. I thought, and hoped, that she might interest you. That's the reason I started her as a topic of conversation. As she doesn't, I'll drop her again, at once. But what am I to do? I began this evening with a literary allusion, and found that you'd never heard of Longfellow's 'Village Blacksmith.' That wasn't a very encouraging start, you'll admit. Last night I tried you with art, and all you did was to mix it up with morality, which, as everybody knows, is a perfectly hopeless thing to do. The ancient Hebrews had more sense. They were specialists in morality, and they absolutely forbade art. Whereas the Greeks, who were artists, went in for a thoroughly immoral kind of life. Finding that you were totally indifferent to the metaphysics of the aesthetic, I offered you an interesting chain of abstract reasoning. What was the result? You were absolutely unable to follow me. I then threw out some hints which might have led to an interesting psychological discussion, but you didn't know what I meant. This evening I touched on one of the great principles which must guide us in the consideration of the whole feminist question—"

"That was when you talked about judging Miss King's intentions by the look of her eyes," said the Major.

"Yes; it was. And so far as I can recollect, all you did was to grin in a futile and somewhat vulgar way. Finally, I tried to talk to you about child culture, which is one of the most important problems of our day; a problem which is occupying the attention of statesmen, philanthropists, philosophers, doctors, and teachers of every kind, from kindergarten mistresses to university professors. I began in quite a simple way with a question about the food of an infant. We might, if you had taken the subject up at all warmly, have got on to the endowment of motherhood, nature study, medical examination of schools, the boarding-out of workhouse children, religious education, boy scouts, eugenics, and a lot of other perfectly fascinating topics. But what do you do? You say frankly and shamelessly that you know nothing at all about the matter."

"But I really do not know how to feed babies. What was the use of pretending that I do?"

"Is there—to get back to the point from which I started—is there any subject that you do know anything about besides politics and polo ponies?"

"I'm afraid not, J. J., except the yacht. I do know something about her."

"Then," said Meldon, "we'll discuss her. I expect we'll come to an end of her soon, but we can at all events decide where we'll go to-morrow."

The yacht turned out to be a more fruitful subject than Meldon expected. The Major had made some alterations in her trim, which led to an animated discussion. He also had a plan for changing her from a cutter into a yawl, and Meldon was quite ready to argue out the points of advantage and disadvantage in each rig. It was half-past eleven o'clock before they parted for the night, and even then they had not decided where to go next day.

CHAPTER IX

It was the evening of the second day of the *Spindrift's* cruise. The wind, which had come fresh from the east in the morning, followed the sun round in its course, blowing gently from the south at mid-day, and breathing very faintly from the west in the evening. After sunset it died away completely. The whole surface of the bay lay calm, save here and there where some chance movement of the air ruffled a tiny patch of water; or where, at the corners of the islands and in very narrow channels, the inward drawing of the tide marked long, curved lines and illusive circles on the oily sea. The *Spindrift* was poised motionless on the surface of the water, borne slowly, almost imperceptibly, forward by the sweep of the tide. Her mainsail, boomed out, hung in loose folds. The sheet, freed from all strain, was borne down by its own weight, until the slack of it dipped in the water. Terns and gulls, at lazy rest, floated close to the yacht's side. Long rows of dark cormorants, perched on rocky points, strained their necks and peered at her. Innumerable jelly-fish spread and sucked together again their transparent bodies, reaching down and round about them with purple feelers. Now and then some almost imperceptible breath of wind swayed the yacht's boom slowly forward against the loose runner and the stay, lifted the dripping sheet from the water, and half bellied the sail. Then the *Spindrift* would press forward, her spars creaking slightly, tiny ripples playing round her bows, a double line of oily bubbles in her wake. Again the impulse would fail her, and she would lie still among the palpitating jellyfish, perfectly reflected in the water beneath her; but carried steadily on by the silent shoreward swelling of the tide.

Major Kent sat at the tiller smoking. He was in that mood of vacant obliviousness of the ordinary affairs of life which long drifting on calm seas induces. The helplessness of man in a sailing-ship, when the wind fails him, begets a kind of fatalistic acceptance of the inevitable, which is the nearest thing to peace that any of us ever attain. Indeed to drift along the tide is peace, and no conviction of the inevitableness of the worries which lurk in ambush for us on the land has any power to break the spell.

Meldon lay stretched on the deck outside the combing of the cockpit. Nirvana had no attraction for him. He resented forced inactivity as an unendurable wrong. Instead of smoking with half-closed eyes, he peered eagerly forward under the sail. He noted everything—the floating gulls and puffins, the stiff, wild-eyed cormorants, the jelly-fish, the whirling eddies of the tide. As the yacht drifted on, or was driven forward by the occasional faint puffs of air, he hissed through his teeth in the way known to sailors as whistling for a breeze. He gazed long and steadily at the beach beyond the *Spindrift's* moorings.

"I think," he said at last, "that there is a man on the shore, and he looks to me very much as if he was waiting for us."

Major Kent made no answer. His feeling was that the man who waited might be left to wait without speculation about his purpose. Guessing at the possible business of an unknown and distant man is a form of mental exertion very distasteful to any one who has entered into the calm joy of drifting home after sunset. But Meldon was a man of incurably active mind. He was deeply interested in the solitary figure on the beach. The yacht was borne very slowly on, and it became possible at last to distinguish the figure of the waiter more clearly.

"He looks to me," said Meldon a few minutes later, "very like that fellow Callaghan, the Ballymoy House gardener."

There was another pause. A puff of wind, the last vital rally of the expiring breeze, carried the *Spindrift* forward till the punt at her moorings lay almost under her bow.

"It is Callaghan," said Meldon, "and there's only one thing which can possibly bring him here at this hour. Something of real importance must have happened between Simpkins and Miss King. I wonder what it is."

"Catch the punt, J. J., and haul her aft till you get a hold of the buoy. If we drift past we'll never get back again. There's barely steerage way on the boat this minute."

Meldon stepped forward. There was a noise of straining ropes and splashing. Then he stood upright and pulled the buoy on board.

"Unless something exceptionally interesting has occurred," said Meldon, "I can't understand Callaghan waiting for us like this. Perhaps they've got engaged."

"Nonsense," said the Major; "how could they in two days? Let go the peak halyards, and take a pull on the topping lift."

The sail came slowly down. Major Kent and Meldon leaned across the gaff and dragged at the folds of it. Callaghan hailed the yacht from the shore.

"Hold on," said Meldon. "Keep what you've got to say till I come to you. I can't have the details of an interesting love affair shouted across a stretch of water."

The sails were made up and the yacht safely moored. Meldon hustled Major Kent into the punt, and pulled rapidly for the beach. The punt's keel grated on the gravel. Meldon seized the painter in his hand and leaped ashore.

"Now," he said to Callaghan, "trot out your news. Have they got engaged?"

"They have not," said Callaghan.

"Then I suppose there must have been what you call impropriety of conduct. If so—"

"There has not," said Callaghan.

"That's just as well; for if there had been, I should have had to ask you to wait before giving me details until the Major had gone a good bit of the way home. He's an unmarried man, and I don't think it would be good for him to—"

"There was no impropriety of conduct that I seen," said Callaghan.

"Well, it can't be helped. I should have been glad, of course, to hear that Simpkins had been pushing his way on a bit, holding her hand or something of that kind. I suppose, now, if anything of the sort occurred you'd be sure to have seen it."

"Don't I tell you there wasn't," said Callaghan; "nor there couldn't have been, for Simpkins wasn't near the place since the afternoon you was in it yourself."

"What! Do you mean to say—?"

"He was in it the once," said Callaghan, "not long after you leaving, and barring that she gave him a cup of tea there was nothing passed between them, and I wouldn't say he was there half an hour."

"Do you hear that, Major? That silly ass Simpkins has actually flung away a priceless opportunity. He hasn't been near her."

"I'm glad to hear it," said Major Kent. "Perhaps now you'll stop your foolish games."

"Could she have gone out to meet him anywhere?" said Meldon to Callaghan.

"She could not. It wouldn't be possible for her to do the like unbeknown to me, for I had my eye on her."

"All day?"

"After what your reverence was saying to me I'd have been afraid to let her out of my sight."

"Very well, Callaghan, you can go home. I shall have to think the matter over. I don't deny that I'm disappointed. I thought when I saw you standing there on the shore that you'd have had some definite news for me."

"I was up at the Major's house searching for you," said Callaghan, "and when you weren't within I took a look round and I seen the yacht coming in on the tide, so I thought it would save me a journey to-morrow if I waited for you."

"Quite right," said Meldon. "It's not your fault nothing has happened, and I don't blame you in the least. Good-night."

Callaghan shambled off along the beach. The Major and Meldon, who carried the punt's oars, struck across the fields towards Portsmouth Lodge.

"I can't understand it at all," said Meldon. "After what I said to Simpkins I simply can't understand his neglecting his opportunities like this. You'd think from the way he's behaving that he doesn't want to be married at all."

"Perhaps he doesn't," said the Major. "Any way, you can do no more than you've done. You may as well drop it now, and have the rest of your holiday in peace."

"The fact is," said Meldon, "I ought not to have gone away and left them. I had no business to take that cruise in the *Spindrift*. If I'd been here—"

"I don't see what you could have done. If the fellow doesn't want the girl, how could you force him to go and marry her? Any way, it's a good job for Miss King that he hasn't."

"If I'd been here—" said Meldon, and then paused.

"What would you have done?"

"I'd have done what I'm going to do now that I'm back."

"And what's that?"

"Throw them together," said Meldon. "Insist on his being constantly with her until he begins to appreciate her charm. I defy any one, any one who's not already married, to resist Miss King if she looks at him out of the corners of her eyes as she did at me the other day."

"She won't do that," said the Major. "No woman would, once she had seen Simpkins."

"Oh, she'll do it all right. Don't you fret about that. All I have to do is to give her a proper opportunity by throwing them together a bit."

"I don't quite see how you're going to do that if Simpkins won't go near her."

"You wouldn't see, of course. Indeed you couldn't, because I don't quite know myself yet how it is to be managed. I shall have to think it all over very carefully. I may have to spend the greater part of the night considering the matter; but one thing you may be quite confident about, Major, and that is that when I say they are to be thrown together, they will be thrown together. I shall make such arrangements that Simpkins simply won't be able to escape, however hard he tries."

Meldon was not obliged to spend a sleepless night devising meetings between Simpkins and Miss King. He put the oars into the coach-house as soon as he reached Portsmouth Lodge, and then settled down with a pipe on a hammock-chair outside the door. He was ready with a practical suggestion by the time Major Kent had finished dressing for dinner. Being too wise to propose a difficult matter to a hungry man, he waited until the meal was nearly over before he said anything to his friend.

"Major," he said, "to-morrow is Sunday, and I think it would be a capital thing if you introduced yourself to Miss King after church. You could waylay her just outside the porch, and tell her who you are. I've talked to her a good deal about you, so she'll know you directly she hears your name."

"I don't think I'll do that, J. J.," said the Major. "From what you've told me about her I don't think she's the kind of woman I'd care about. I think I'll keep clear of her as much as I can."

"I told you," said Meldon, "that she was good-looking and had pleasant manners when not irritated. I don't see what objection you can have to her."

"I wasn't thinking about her appearance or her manners. They may be all right, but if what you said is true and she really—"

"Don't be narrow-minded, Major. I hate that kind of pharisaical bigotry. The fact that Mrs. Lorimer behaved as she did is no reason in the world why you should cut the poor woman. It's a well-known fact that people who are really much worse than she is are freely received into the best society; and, in any case, the latest systems of morality are quite changing the view that we used to take about murder. Take Nietzsche, for instance—"

"Who's Nietzsche?"

"He's a philosopher," said Meldon, "or rather he was, for he's dead now. He divided all morality into two kinds—slave morality, which he regards as despicable, and master morality, which is of the most superior possible kind."

"Still—I don't know anything about the man you mention, but I suppose even he would have drawn the line at murder."

"Not at all. Master morality, which, according to his system, is the best kind, consists entirely of being the sort of man who is able to get into a position to bully other people. Slave morality, on the other hand, consists in having the kind of temperament which submits to being bullied, and pretends to think it a fine thing to suffer. Now murder, as any one can see, is simply an extreme form of bullying; and therefore a successful murderer, according to Nietzsche's philosophy, is the finest kind of man there is. Whereas his victims, the late Lorimer, for instance, are mere slaves, and therefore thoroughly despicable. You follow me so far, I suppose?"

"No, I don't. If any man says what you say that fellow says—"

"Nietzsche doesn't actually say all that," said Meldon. "He hadn't a sufficiently logical mind to work out his philosophy to its ultimate practical conclusions, but you may take my word for it that I've given you the gist of his system."

"Then he ought to have been hanged."

"I daresay he ought," said Meldon. "I need scarcely say I don't agree with him. But that's not the point. As a matter of fact, so far from being hanged or incurring any kind of odium, his system is quite the most popular there is at present. London is full of young men in large, round spectacles, and scraggy women who haven't succeeded in getting married—the leaders of modern thought, you'll observe, Major—every one of whom is deeply attached to Nietzsche. You can't, without labelling yourself a hopeless reactionary, fly right in the face of cultured society by refusing to associate with Miss King."

"I won't mix myself up with—"

"Come now, Major, that sort of attitude would have been all very well fifty years ago, but it won't do now. You simply can't shut yourself up and say that you won't speak to any one who doesn't agree with you in every opinion you have. As a matter of fact, you associate freely with lots of people who differ from you in religion and politics far more fundamentally than poor Miss King does. You can't refuse to know her simply because she accepts a system of philosophy which you never heard of till this minute, and even now don't thoroughly understand in spite of all I've told you about it."

"In any case," said the Major, "I don't like women who flirt. And you told me yourself that she tried to flirt with you."

"Ah," said Meldon, "now we're getting at your real reasons. I thought you couldn't be in earnest about the Nietzschean philosophy. That was merely an excuse. What you're really afraid of is that Miss King might marry you. I don't blame you for being a little cautious about that, knowing what you do about the fate of her former husbands. At the same time I may point out—"

"I'm not the least afraid of her marrying me. She won't get the chance."

"Then why do you say you object to her flirting?"

"Because I do object to it. I don't like that kind of woman."

"Do you mean to say, Major, that a girl isn't to be allowed to make eyes at the man she's going to marry?"

"I don't say anything of the sort. Of course, if she's going to marry a man—but really, J. J., I don't know anything about these things."

"Then don't talk about them. You may take my word for it, Major, that Miss King is perfectly justified in being as nice as ever she can to Simpkins."

"I never said anything about Simpkins. As far as I can make out she isn't particularly nice to Simpkins."

"No, she isn't, so far; but that's only because she hasn't had a fair chance. When we get them out together in the *Spindrift*—"

"What?"

"When we get the two of them out together in the *Spindrift*," said Meldon, speaking slowly and distinctly, "you'll see that she'll make herself perfectly fascinating—not to you or me, but to Simpkins."

"Leaving Miss King out of the question," said the Major, "I'd like you to be perfectly clear about this. I won't—"

"Before we go on to Simpkins," said Meldon, "we must settle definitely about Miss King. Is it understood that you catch her after church tomorrow and invite her out for a sail with us in the *Spindrift*?"

"No; I won't. I wouldn't in any case; but if Simpkins—"

"I'm not going on to Simpkins yet. I must finish Miss King first. You've given your reasons for not making her acquaintance, and I've shown you that they are utterly feeble and won't hold water for a minute. If you've no other objection, then I think, as a straightforward man, you are bound to admit you are in the wrong and do what you ought to have been ready to do without all this arguing."

"To oblige you," said the Major, "and because I want you to have a pleasant holiday now you're here, I will ask Miss King out with us once. But I won't ask Simpkins. The man is a horrid bounder, who makes himself objectionable to everybody, and I won't ask him."

"Nobody wants you to ask him. I'll ask him."

"That will be just the same thing. Once for all, J. J., I won't have that man on board my boat."

"I don't think," said Meldon, "that you are behaving with quite your usual fairness, Major. You don't like Simpkins. I am not going into the reasons for your dislike. They may be sound, or they may be the reverse. I simply state the fact that you don't get on with the man. Very well. I don't get on with Miss King. I told you the other day that I offended her, and she was what I should call extremely rude to me afterwards. But do I bring that up as a reason why you should not take her for a sail in the *Spindrift*? Certainly not. It won't, as a matter of fact, be particularly pleasant for me having to sit in the same boat all day with a young woman who won't speak to me; but I'm prepared to sacrifice myself and do it. And you ought to be ready to do the same thing in the case of Simpkins."

"I'm not," said the Major. "I can't and won't have Simpkins."

"My dear Major, don't you see that your quarrel with Simpkins is one of the strongest points in the whole plan? He won't speak to you when he sees that you dislike him. Miss King won't speak to me. What will the consequence be? Why, of course, they'll be thrown together. They must talk to each other, and that's exactly what we want them to do. If Simpkins was a friend of yours, and if Miss King was particularly fond of me, there'd be no use our taking them out at all. They wouldn't be obliged to talk to each other."

"If you've finished your dinner, J. J., we may as well go into the next room and smoke. I don't see that there's any use going on with this conversation."

"There isn't; not the least. But you'll do me the justice, Major, to admit that it wasn't I who insisted on it. I could perfectly well have arranged the matter in two sentences, but you would argue with me about every single thing I said."

Major Kent rose and opened the door for his friend. They went together into the study and sat down. The Major, after a few preliminary excuses, took the two copies of *The Times*, which had arrived by post whilst he was out in the *Spindrift*. He settled down to the leading articles with a comfortable sense that he was doing his duty. Meldon wandered round the room looking for something to read. He found a new book on boat-building which promised to be interesting. Unfortunately it turned out to be highly technical, and therefore dull. It dropped from his knees. He nodded, took the pipe from his mouth, lay back comfortably, and went to sleep. Major Kent satisfied himself that the English navy, though in some ways the best in the world, was in other respects inefficient and utterly useless as a national defence. Then, at about ten o'clock, he too went asleep. A few minutes later he began to snore, and the noise he made woke Meldon. He felt for his pipe, filled and lit it. He sat gazing at Major Kent for a quarter of an hour, then he coughed loudly. The Major woke with a start.

"It's a remarkable thing," said Meldon, "how sleepy two days on the sea make one. I had a nap myself. You were sound and snoring."

"It's early yet," said the Major, glancing at the clock. "I seldom turn in before eleven."

"I'm going to turn in now," said Meldon. "I'd be better in bed, for I can't sleep here with the way you're snoring. I just woke you up to say that I'll get a hold of Simpkins some time to-morrow and settle things with him. I daresay, after the way he has behaved to the poor old rector, that he'll be ashamed to come to church, but I'll look him up afterwards. You'll be responsible for Miss King."

"I can't argue any more to-night," said the Major, yawning; "but don't you go to bed under the impression that I'm going to have Simpkins in the yacht, for I'm not."

"I don't want to argue either, but I'll just say one word to you before I go: one word that I'd like to have imprinted on your mind during the night. You won't mind listening to one word, will you?"

"Not if it's only one."

"It is literally and simply one. Duty."

"Duty!" said the Major, sitting up.

"Yes, duty. You're an Englishman, Major, at least by descent, and you know that there's one appeal which is never made in vain to Englishmen, and that is the appeal to duty. Wasn't that the meaning of the signal Nelson hoisted just before he asked Hardy to kiss him! And what did Hardy do? Kissed him at once, though he can't possibly have liked it."

"I think you've got the story wrong somewhere, J. J. As well as I recollect—"

"I may be inaccurate in some of the details," said Meldon, "but the broad principle is as I state it; and I put it to you now, Major, before I say good-night, will you or will you not respond to the appeal? Remember Trafalgar and the old *Victory*. You're a military man, of course, but you must have some respect for Nelson."

"I have. But I don't see how duty comes in in this case. Oh, J. J.! I wish you'd go to bed and stop talking."

"I will. I want to. I'm absolutely dropping off to sleep, but I can't go till I've explained to you where your duty lies. Here is the town of Ballymoy groaning under an intolerable tyranny. Doyle's life is a burden to him. O'Donoghue can't sleep at night for fear of a Local Government Board enquiry. The police are harried in the discharge of their duties. The rector's bronchitis is intensified to a dangerous extent. Sabina Gallagher's red-haired cousin, whose name I've not yet been able to discover, is perfectly miserable. Poor old Callaghan, who means well, though he has a most puritanical dread of impropriety, is worn to a shadow. It rests with you whether this state of things is to continue or not. You and, so far as I can see at present, you alone, are in a position to arrange for the downfall of Simpkins. Is it or is it not your duty, your simple duty, to do what you can, even at the cost of some little temporary inconvenience to yourself?"

"If I thought all that—" said the Major. "But I'm much too sleepy to think."

"You're not asked to think," said Meldon. "Whatever thinking has to be done I'll do myself. You have to act, or rather in this case to permit me to act."

"I expect you'll act, as you call it, whether I permit you or not."

"Of course I will," said Meldon. "But I'd rather have your permission. I'd rather you didn't shatter the ideal I've always had of you as a duty-loving Englishman."

"All right," said the Major wearily. "Do what you like, but for goodness' sake go to bed and stop talking."

"Good-night," said Meldon. "If you find yourself inclined to change your mind before morning, just murmur over to yourself, 'England expects every man to do his duty.' That will stiffen your back."

CHAPTER X

Major Kent came down to breakfast next morning in a frock coat and a white waistcoat. His silk hat, carefully brushed and glossy, lay on the hall table with a pair of pale grey kid gloves beside it. Meldon, who was a little late for breakfast, paused in the hall and looked at the hat. Entering the dining-room he took a long stare at his friend.

"Major," he said, "you're a wonderful man. I had forgotten how wonderful you are. Now that I am getting to know you again I am struck dumb with absolute amazement."

The Major was uneasily conscious that his attire was in strong contrast to Meldon's shabby jacket and wrinkled trousers.

"I don't suppose," said Meldon, "that there's another man in the whole world who could go on dressing himself up like that Sunday after Sunday in a place like Ballymoy. However, the habit will turn out beneficial for once. I expect you'll produce an excellent effect on Miss King."

"I was thinking over that plan of yours last night," said the Major, "and—"

"I was under the impression that I distinctly told you not to think. There's not the slightest necessity for you to exert yourself in that way; and besides, so far as I know, you invariably think wrong. However, if you really have thought, you'd better get the result off your chest at once."

"It occurred to me—" said the Major.

"That's not quite the same thing as thinking. I don't blame you so much, now that I know that the thing, whatever it is, merely occurred to you. No man can be held responsible for the things that occur to him. There was one of the ancient Egyptian hermits who made a very sensible remark on that subject. You'll find it in Migne's 'Patrologia Latina,' in the volume which contains the 'Verba Seniorum.' I can't quote the exact words at the moment, but they are to this effect: 'If you can't stop the wind from blowing, neither can you prevent evil thoughts from entering your mind.' I daresay the thing that occurred to you wasn't actually evil in the sense which the hermit meant, but it is pretty sure to have been foolish; and that, for all practical purposes, is the same thing. By the way, this is excellent bacon; quite the best I've tasted for a long time. Does Doyle supply it?"

"No; I get it down from Dublin. But about that plan of yours. It occurs to me that Miss King is not likely to be in church."

"Of course she'll be in church. Why shouldn't she?"

"Well, if she's a disciple of that man you were speaking about last night, she can hardly be what's generally called a Christian, can she?"

"Of course not. But she'll come to church just the same."

"But surely— Not if she doesn't believe in Christianity?"

"My dear Major! your ideas in some respects are extraordinarily primitive. The less anybody likes Christianity for himself, the more sure he is that it's an excellent religion for other people. That's the reason you find statesmen all over the world supporting whatever Church is uppermost at the moment in the particular country they happen to be dealing with. Look at the history of Ireland, for instance. For a century and a half British statesmen steadily fatted up our church. Now they are dropping any plums that they can spare—Congested Districts Boards and such things—into the mouths of the Roman Catholic bishops. Do you suppose they care a pin for either? Not they. All they want is to strengthen up some form of religion which will keep the people quiet. They think that Christianity is an excellent thing for everybody they have to govern, though they take jolly good care not to act on it themselves. In just the same way you'll see that Miss King will be in church to-day. As a follower of Nietzsche she doesn't herself accept the ethics of Christianity, but she'll consider it her duty to encourage everybody else to accept them, and the only practical way she has of doing that is to attend church regularly."

"You're preaching to-day, aren't you, J. J.?"

"Yes, I am. I promised the poor old rector that I would do all I could to help him while I'm here. Why do you ask?"

"I was wondering," said the Major, "if you were going to give us that doctrine out of the pulpit."

"Well, I'm not. You ought to know, Major, that my sermons are always strictly practical, and deal entirely with matters of pressing local importance: the ordinary difficulties and dangers of the people I'm preaching to. There won't be any statesmen in church to-day, so there'd be no point in my explaining that theory. If I'm ever asked to preach before the House of Commons I shall give it to them."

This account of Meldon's theory of sermons made the Major a little nervous. He asked his next question anxiously.

"Are you going to be personal, J. J.? I hope not."

"I can't preach the whole sermon to you beforehand, Major; but I don't mind telling you that it will deal with the vice of squabbling which I find rampant in small communities. I shan't, of course, mention you and Simpkins; or, for the matter of that, Doyle and O'Donoghue, though it wouldn't matter much if I did mention them. Being Roman Catholics, they won't be there to object."

"The sermon will be personal, then?"

"No, it won't. I shan't even allude to the subject of fishing. I shall preach in such a way as to get at everybody who has ever quarrelled with anybody else. After listening to what I say, you will be much more inclined to take Simpkins out in the *Spindrift*."

Meldon's sermon was all that he boasted. He chose as his text a verse out of the Book of Proverbs which compares any one who meddles unnecessarily with strife to a man who takes a dog by the ears. He spoke feelingly, from what appeared to be the recollection of unpleasant experience, of the way in which spirited dogs behave when any one takes them forcibly by the ears. He explained in a short parenthesis the best way of dealing with dog-fights. He also described in simple language the consequences which result from being bitten—consequences which range from hydrophobia and tetanus down to simple blood-poisoning. Then he passed on to show that human bites, inflicted, so he said, oftener with the tongue than with the teeth, were far more dangerous than those of dogs. The congregation became greatly interested at this point, and allowed themselves to be swept forward by a violent sophism which carried the preacher far beyond the original statement of Solomon. All quarrelling, not merely interfering with existing quarrels of long standing, was denounced in forcible language. Major Kent felt uncomfortable; then, as the preacher worked himself up, resentful. Finally, he was cowed. Meldon seized the psychological moment and closed his discourse with a quotation from the poetry of Dr. Watts. He made a remarkably apposite citation of the well-known lines which exonerate dogs, bears, and lions from any blame when they bark, bite, growl, or fight, and emphasised the entirely different position of the human race.

Major Kent, bruised by the vigour of his friend's eloquence, accosted Miss King in the church porch after service; apologised for not having formally called on her; and invited her to go yachting with him next day in the *Spindrift*. Miss King accepted the invitation, and then, worked up perhaps to an unusual pitch of friendliness by the sermon, asked the Major to go back to Ballymoy House with her for luncheon. Meldon appeared from the door of the vestry room and urged the Major to accept the invitation.

"As I expected," he said, "Simpkins wasn't in church.—How do you do, Miss King? I'm glad you and the Major have made friends. You're sure to like each other.—So I shall have to go round to his house and look him up. I daresay he'll give me a bite to eat; and if he doesn't, Doyle will. You will of course accept"—he appeared to be addressing Major Kent—"Miss King's invitation. I'll call round for you at about four. I daresay Miss King will give us both a cup of tea. You drive her home in your trap, Major. I can walk down to Simpkins' house quite easily."

Meldon, carrying his hat in one hand, strode off in the direction of Mr. Simpkins' house. Miss King looked at Major Kent.

"You see it's all settled for you," she said. "You'll have to come back with me."

"I suppose I had better," said the Major. Then after a pause he added, "Of course I'm delighted to, and it's very kind of you to ask me."

Simpkins was stretched in a hammock chair reading a novel when Meldon found him. He received a severe lecture for not attending church, which seemed to surprise him a good deal, especially as his absence was attributed by Meldon to shame and a consciousness of guilt, feelings from which Simpkins had never in his life suffered. Then—and this seemed to astonish him still more—he was warmly invited to go for a day's yachting in the *Spindrift*.

"I didn't hear," he said doubtfully, "that Major Kent was going away."

"He isn't," said Meldon. "Don't I tell you he's giving a picnic in his yacht?"

"Are you sure he wants me?"

"Certain. He sent you an invitation, which is a plain proof that he wants you. He would have delivered it himself, only that Miss King caught him after church and carried him off to luncheon. But I have one of his cards with me, and if you insist on everything being done in the most accurate and correct possible manner, I'll leave it on the umbrella stand in your hall as I go out."

Meldon had provided himself with a few of the Major's visiting cards before leaving Portsmouth Lodge in the morning. He was a man who prided himself on leaving nothing to chance. Since it was just possible that the cards might turn out to be useful, he had put a few in his pocket.

"In fact," he went on, "to prevent any possible mistake or misunderstanding I may as well hand it over to you at once." He produced a card, slightly crumpled and a good deal soiled, from his waistcoat pocket, and laid it on Simpkins' knee. Simpkins looked at it doubtfully, took it up in his hand, and examined both sides of it. Then he spoke slowly.

"I think you know," he said; "in fact, I've told you myself, that the Major and I aren't on very good terms. I was obliged to speak to him rather strongly about the way he used to fish in a part of the river—"

"I know all about that; you needn't go into it again. It's entirely over and done with. An era of peace is beginning to dawn. After listening to my sermon this morning—it's a great pity for your own sake that you weren't in church, Simpkins—the Major finds himself in a position to forget the past and to start fresh. His attitude now—very largely owing to my sermon—is that of the dove which came to the ark with an olive leaf plucked off in its mouth."

Simpkins was not apparently prepared to accept the olive leaf. He asked Meldon whether that dove was the text of his sermon.

"No, it wasn't. I might have alluded to it, but I didn't. I might have explained, if I'd thought of it at the time—in fact, I will explain to you now. The dove is of all birds the most peaceful and the least inclined to quarrel with other birds. You'd know that by the soothing way it coos, and also by the colour of its breast. Tennyson, the poet, notes the fact that the peculiar bluey shade of its feathers arouses feelings of affection in people who weren't thinking of anything of the sort before they saw it. I'm not prepared to assert that positively myself, but I shouldn't wonder if there was something in the idea. Then the olive branch is the regular, recognised symbol of peace. The reason of that is that oil is got out of olives, and oil is one of the most soothing things there is. Of course, you get oil from other sources too—from whales, for instance; but the olive branch is chosen as a symbol because it's such a much more convenient thing to carry about than a whale is. No explorer, when meeting a savage tribe with which he doesn't want to fight, could possibly wave a whale, even if he had one with him— and he wouldn't be likely to, unless he was exploring the polar regions— whereas he can wave an olive branch, and always does. That's the reason the olive branch and not the whale is chosen as the symbol of peace. You'll be able to realise now how extraordinarily peaceable the Major is when I compare him to a dove with an olive leaf in his mouth."

"If," said Simpkins, who had only partially followed the reasoning about the dove and the olive—"if the Major apologises for the way he spoke, I'm quite ready—"

"He doesn't actually apologise," said Meldon. "You can hardly expect that of him. I think myself he's going as far as can reasonably be expected of him when he asks you out for a day's yachting. Very few men would do as much; and I may say to you, Simpkins, that if you'd been in church to-day and heard my sermon, you wouldn't be inclined now to stand out for an apology. You would, in fact, most likely be looking out for an olive leaf and a dove of your own to carry to the Major."

"But he was entirely in the wrong about the fishing. I admitted all along that he was perfectly entitled to fish below the bridge, but he insisted—-"

"Quite so," said Meldon. "That's my exact point. Any fool can apologise when he's been in the right. That gives him such a comfortable sense of superiority that he doesn't a bit mind grovelling before the other fellow. What is totally impossible is to apologise when you're in the wrong. You must be able to realise that."

"I'm not at all sure," said Simpkins, "that I ought to accept the invitation. Major Kent's hostility to me has been most marked. Everybody about the place has noticed it."

"Unless you're perfectly sure that you ought not to accept the invitation," said Meldon, "I think you'd better give yourself the benefit of the doubt. It will be a most enjoyable expedition. Miss King is coming. By the way, I hope you haven't quarrelled with Miss King in any way?"

"No, I haven't. Why should I?"

"I'm glad to hear it, I was afraid perhaps you and she might have fallen out over something. But if you haven't, why didn't you go near her for the last two days?"

"I was there on Thursday afternoon. I can't with any decency call on her every day in the week."

"Oh yes, you can; and, if you mean to marry her, you ought to. Believe me, there's nothing estranges a woman's affection so rapidly as that kind of studied neglect. She can't call on you, you know, without putting herself in a wholly false position."

"I haven't quite made up my mind about marrying her."

"Oh, well, the day in the *Spindrift* will do that for you. There's something very exhilarating, Simpkins, about a fresh sea breeze. It simply sweeps away all hesitation, and renders you capable of marrying almost any one. That's the reason why sailors are famous for having a wife in every port they call at, and why nobody blames them for it. Exposed, as they necessarily are, to the sea air at its purest, they simply can't help themselves. They become exaggeratedly uxorious without in the least meaning to."

"Besides," said Simpkins, "I've no reason to suppose that Miss King would marry me."

"Have you any reason to suppose she won't?"

"No. I've only seen her once, you know."

"Then I think it extremely likely that she will. Everybody knows that most people do things not so much because they want to as because they haven't any reason for refusing. Take the average party, for instance—tea party, tennis party, garden party, or dinner party. How many men go to parties because they want to? Not one in a hundred. The other ninety-nine go simply because there's no available reason for not going. It's just the same with marrying. Unless you give Miss King some good reason for refusing you, she'll marry you as soon as ever you ask her. And if I were you I'd ask her to-morrow. We'll land on an island for luncheon. The Major and I will slip off by ourselves and give you your opportunity."

"I'm not sure—"

"Come now, Simpkins, have you anything against the girl? Has anybody been circulating stories about her of any sort? I know this is a gossipy sort of place, and—"

"Oh no; it's simply that I don't know her."

"If that's all," said Meldon, "a day in the *Spindrift* will set it right. You'll be surprised how intimate you become with a person when you're sitting for hours crammed up against him or her in the cockpit of a five-ton yacht. By the time you've disentangled her twice from the mainsheet, with the Major swearing all the time, and been obliged to haul her up to windward whenever the boat goes about and she gets left with her head down on the lee side, you get to feel as if you'd known her intimately for years. By the way, what time do you lunch?"

"Half-past one," said Simpkins. "Will you—"

"Thanks," said Meldon; "I will, if you're quite sure there's enough for two. I'm due at Miss King's at four. The Major's there. Miss King asked him to luncheon with her. But you needn't mind. He hasn't the least notion of marrying her or anybody else. You can come with me in the afternoon if you like. In fact, I think it would be a very good plan if you did. I'll clear the Major out of the way at once, and then you can have a good innings. If you play your cards properly to-day, you'll certainly be in a position to propose to her to-morrow."

At four o'clock Meldon led the rather embarrassed Simpkins up to Ballymoy House. Miss King and Major Kent were sitting together on the lawn, and were apparently getting on very well indeed. The greeting between Mr. Simpkins and the Major was constrained and cold. Miss King seemed to feel that the situation demanded tact. She suggested ordering tea at once, and having it out of doors.

"Not for us, thanks," said Meldon. "The Major and I must be off at once. We haven't a moment to delay."

Major Kent looked surprised, and seemed inclined to ask questions. He resented the arrival of Simpkins, but he did not want to leave Miss King so soon.

"I said this morning," said Meldon, "that we'd stop for tea; but since then I find that I'm tied—in fact, we're both tied—to a most important engagement, and must absolutely run if we are to be in time. Come along, Major." He seized him by the arm as he spoke. "Good-bye, Miss King. Good-bye, Simpkins. We'll see you both at Portsmouth Lodge at ten to-morrow morning."

"I suppose, J. J.," said the Major, when Meldon, reaching the highroad, slackened his pace—"I suppose that I'm being hustled about like this so that Simpkins can have Miss King all to himself, but—"

"Exactly," said Meldon. "I may tell you, Major, that I now look upon Simpkins as practically a dead man. I don't see how he can possibly escape."

"What I was going to say," said the Major, "is that I think you are mistaken about Miss King. She doesn't seem to me the least like a criminal."

"Of course not. She wouldn't be the successful murderess she is if she hadn't the manners and appearance of a very gentle and gracious lady. That's what gives her the pull she has when it comes to the verdict of a jury. You ought to know, Major, that the old Bill Sykes sort of criminal, the brutalised-looking man with a huge jaw and a low forehead, is quite out of date now. No one gets himself up in that style who means to go in for serious crime. In a book published the other day there was a composite photograph made up of the faces of fifty or sixty criminals of the most extreme kind. I assure you that the net result was an uncommonly good-looking man. That shows you the truth of what I'm saying."

"In any case, J. J., setting aside her personal appearance and manner—"

"Your impression of her personal appearance. I wasn't taken in by it."

"She isn't the sort of woman you said she was. She'd never heard of that philosopher of yours."

"Do you mean to say that she denied ever having heard the name of Nietzsche?"

"Not exactly. The fact is that I couldn't recollect his name, but I gave her a sketch of his doctrines—"

"I don't expect she recognised your sketch. You were probably grossly inaccurate."

"I gave her almost word for word what you said last night about murder being a very virtuous thing and bullying being the highest form of morality."

"Even so I don't expect she recognised it. You see I had to paraphrase the whole thing to bring it down to the level of your understanding. If you'd been in a position to quote a phrase or two, like Herren Morale, for instance, she'd have recognised the system at once, even without the name of Nietzsche."

"I couldn't do that, of course."

"Now I come to think of it, I don't suppose she'd have owned up to Nietzsche in any case. She'd have been bound to deny any knowledge of the system. You see she doesn't know that I've told you who she really is. She probably distrusts you as a magistrate. After the brutal way in which Sir Gilbert Hawkesby summed up against her, she would naturally be a bit shy of any one occupying any sort of judicial position. Of course if she knew that you were keenly interested in the death of Simpkins it would have been different. She'd have spoken quite openly to you then."

"I don't believe she'll kill Simpkins."

"She will if she marries him. Not that Simpkins is a particularly objectionable man in my opinion. I rather like him myself. But Miss King lives for her art, and once Simpkins proposes to her his fate is sealed."

"She did mention her art once or twice," said the Major. "Now that you remind me of it, I distinctly recollect her saying that it was the great thing in her life."

"There you are then. Perhaps now you'll believe me for the future, and not be starting miserable, sceptical objections to every word I say. What did you say when she talked to you about her art? Did you cross-question her about what it was?"

"No, I didn't. I wasn't thinking of your absurd theories when I was talking to her. I thought she meant painting, or something of that sort. I felt sorry for her, J. J. She seems to me to have a very lonely kind of life."

"Of course she does—in the intervals."

"What?"

"There are intervals, of course. Miss King isn't the sort of woman to form an intimacy with another man until she is really a widow. It's quite natural that she should feel lonely just now, for instance. The mere absence of the excitement she's been accustomed to for so long would have a depressing effect on her."

CHAPTER XI

Meldon was a man who liked to get the full possible measure of enjoyment out of his holidays. He counted the hours of daylight which he spent in bed as wasted, and although always late for breakfast, was generally up and active before any other member of the Major's household. On Monday morning he got out of bed at half-past five and went down to the sea to bathe. He wore nothing except his pyjamas and an old pair of canvas shoes, and so was obliged to go back to his bedroom again after his swim. As he passed Major Kent's door he hammered vigorously on it with his fist. When he thought he had made noise enough to awaken his friend, he turned the handle of the door, put his head into the room, and shouted,—

"Splendid day. Absolutely the best possible; first-rate sailing breeze, and no prospect of rain."

Major Kent growled in reply.

"What's that you say?"

"Confound you, J. J. Get out of that. What's the good of waking me at this hour?"

Meldon opened the door a little wider and stepped into the room.

"I thought you'd like to know about the weather," he said. "It's extremely important for us to secure a really first-rate day. If it turned out that we could do nothing but lollop about half a mile from the shore in a dead calm, poor Simpkins wouldn't have a chance; or if—"

"Go away, J. J."

"And if it were to come on a downpour of rain, his spirits would be so damped that he'd never get himself worked up to the pitch of—"

"I suppose I may as well get up," said the Major despairingly.

"Not the least necessity for that," said Meldon. "You can sleep for another hour and a half at least. It can't be more than half-past six, and allowing time for the most elaborate toilet you can possibly want to make, you needn't get up till eight. I should say myself that you'd sleep much more comfortably now you know that the day is going to be fine. Nothing interferes with slumber more radically than any anxiety of mind."

The weather was all that Meldon said it was; but his satisfaction with it turned out to be ill-founded. It was based on a miscalculation. What seemed to him a desirable sailing breeze was a cause of grave discomfort to half the party.

Simpkins began to give way in less than an hour. He yawned, pulled himself together, and then yawned again. After that he ceased to take any active part in the conversation. Then Miss King began to lose colour. Meldon, who was sitting forward with his legs dangling over the combing of the cockpit, winked at Major Kent. The Major, uncomfortably aware of the feelings of his guests, scowled at Meldon. The nearest island on which it was possible to land was still some way off. He foresaw a period of extreme unpleasantness. Meldon winked again, and mouthed the word "Ilaun More" silently. It was the name of the nearest island, and he meant to suggest to the Major that it would be very desirable to go no further. He might, without giving offence, have said all he wanted to say out loud. Simpkins had reached a stage of his malady in which it was impossible for him to listen intelligently to anything, and Miss King would have rejoiced to hear of a prospect of firm land.

The *Spindrift*, which had been thrashing her way into the teeth of the wind, was allowed to go free, and reached swiftly towards Ilaun More. The change of motion completely finished Simpkins, but the period of his extreme misery was short. The yacht rounded up into the wind in a sheltered bay, and Meldon let go the anchor. The boom, swinging rapidly from side to side, swept Simpkins' hat (a stiff-brimmed straw hat) into the sea. He made no effort to save it; but the Major, grabbing the boat-hook, got hold of it just before it floated beyond reach, and drew it, waterlogged and limp, into the boat. Simpkins expressed no gratitude. Meldon hauled the punt alongside, and asked Miss King if she would like to go ashore. She assented with a feeble smile. There was no use consulting Simpkins. His wishes were taken for granted, and he was deposited, with great difficulty, in the bow of the punt. Meldon rowed them ashore. He gave his arm to Miss King and led her up to a dry rock, on which she sat down. He went back to the punt again, straightened out Simpkins, hauled him up, and set him down beside Miss King. Then he rowed back to the *Spindrift* in the punt.

"This," said the Major angrily, "is a nice kind of party. You might have had more sense, J. J., than to invite people of that sort out in the *Spindrift*."

"You're very unreasonable," said Meldon. "I thought you'd have found the keenest delight in watching the sufferings of Simpkins. If I had an enemy in the world—I'm thankful to say I haven't—but if I had, there's nothing would give me greater pleasure than to see him enduring the agony that Simpkins has just been through. But that's the worst of you. I arrange these little surprises for you, hoping to see your face light up with a smile of gratification, and all I get in return is growls and grumbles."

Major Kent grinned.

"That's better," said Meldon. "I'm glad to see that you're capable of getting some good out of an innocent pleasure, even if you have to wait till somebody points out to you what it is you ought to enjoy."

"Any way, J. J., this will put a stopper on your plan. There'll be no love-making to-day."

"On the contrary," said Meldon, "I expect we've laid the foundation of a deep and enduring affection. There's nothing draws people together more than a common misfortune."

"But you can't expect a woman to take to a man when she sees him in the state Simpkins was in when we were on the reach towards the island."

"Not if she's all right herself," said Meldon; "but when she's in the state Miss King was in she's past noticing anybody's complexion. The only emotion Miss King could possibly have felt, the only emotion of a spiritual kind, was a bitter hatred of you and me; and that, of course, would make her feel a strong affection for Simpkins. On the whole, Major, we may congratulate ourselves on our success so far. Just put the luncheon basket into the punt, will you? They'll be as hungry as wolves in another half-hour. Simpkins is beginning to buck up already. Look at him."

Simpkins was staggering towards his hat, which Meldon had left lying at the place where the punt landed.

"I expect," said the Major, "that he feels as if the sun on the back of his head would upset him again. It must be pretty hot in there where they're sheltered from the wind."

"We'll give him a drop of whisky," said Meldon, "and set him on his feet properly. Get in, Major."

"I'm not at all sure that I'm going ashore. I think I'd be more comfortable where I am. Simpkins is bad enough when he's healthy, but in the condition he's in now I simply couldn't stand him at all. Besides, I don't think Miss King would like us to land. It doesn't seem to me quite fair to go spying on a woman when she's sick. She'd rather be left alone for a while, till she recovers her ordinary colour. I felt very sorry for her on the boat, and if I could have done anything—"

"That sort of sympathy and delicacy of feeling is all very fine, Major; but I tell you plainly that if it leads to your refusing to give the poor girl any lunch she won't appreciate it."

"Couldn't you land the luncheon basket and then come back here?"

"Certainly not. Then I should get no luncheon. I don't shrink from sacrifice in a good cause, Major, whenever sacrifice is necessary; but I see no point in starving myself merely to satisfy your ridiculous ideas of chivalry."

"Well, then, you go and give them their lunch, and leave me here."

"That's the worst plan you've suggested yet," said Meldon. "If I go without you I shall be a damper on the whole proceedings. A third person on these occasions always finds the greatest difficulty in not being in the way, whereas if you come we can stroll off together after lunch under pretext of searching for lobsters or something of that kind, and leave the happy couple together."

"Happy couple!" said the Major. "They look it."

"Get into the punt at once," said Meldon, "and don't try to be sarcastic. Nothing is less becoming to you. Your proper part in life is that of the sober, well-intentioned, somewhat thick-headed, bachelor uncle. You do that excellently; but the moment you try to be clever you give yourself away piteously."

"Your own part, I suppose, J. J., is that of irresponsible buffoon."

"No; it's not. What I do best is just what I'm doing—arranging things for other people, so that difficulties and unpleasantness disappear, and life looks bright again."

Major Kent had provided an excellent luncheon for the party, and Miss King had revived rapidly since she landed. She allowed herself to be persuaded to drink some weak whisky and water. Afterwards she ate cold chicken with a good appetite. Poor Simpkins was less fortunate. He insisted on wearing his damp hat, and could not be persuaded to eat anything except biscuits. Meldon, who was most anxious to restore him to a condition of vigour, pressed a tomato on him; but the result was unfortunate. After eating half of it, Simpkins turned his back even on the biscuit tin. He refused to smoke after lunch, although the Major and Meldon lit their pipes in an encouraging way quite close to him, and Miss King appeared to find pleasure in a cigarette. The situation was not promising; but Meldon was a man of unquenchable hope. Seizing a moment when Miss King was looking in another direction, he winked violently at Major Kent. The Major was extremely comfortably seated with his back against a rock, and was enjoying himself. The *Spindrift* lay secure at her anchor. The sun shone pleasantly. An after luncheon pipe is a particularly enjoyable one, and Miss King was talking in a very charming way, besides looking pretty. The Major was disinclined to move, and although he guessed at the meaning of Meldon's wink, he deliberately ignored it. Meldon winked again. Then he rose to his feet, shook himself, and looked round him.

"I think, Major," he said, "that if we mean to catch any lobsters to-day, we ought to be starting."

The Major grunted.

"Lobsters! Can we catch lobsters here?" said Miss King. "I should like to help. I have never caught a lobster."

"It's not exactly a sport for ladies," said Meldon. "The lobster is an ugly fish to tackle unless you are accustomed to him. Besides, we shall have to take off our shoes and stockings."

"But I only mean to look on. I shouldn't run any risks."

She had in her mind at the moment a scene in her new novel into which lobster fishing, as practised in the west of Ireland, might be introduced with great effect. The idea that there was some risk about the sport added to its value for her purpose. She foresaw the possibility of vividly picturesque descriptions of bare-limbed, sun-tanned muscular folk plunging among weedy rocks, or spattered with yellow spume, staggering shorewards under a load of captured lobsters. But Meldon was most unsympathetic.

"Besides," he said, "the chief haunt of the lobsters is at the other side of the island, quite a long way off."

"I should like the walk," said Miss King, "and I'm sure there's a charming view."

"It's very rough," said Meldon, "and you'd get your feet wet."

He nudged the Major as he spoke. It did not seem fair that the making of all the excuses should be left to him.

"I really believe," said Miss King, "that you don't want me to go with you, Mr. Meldon. It's most unkind of you. I'm beginning to think that you don't like me. You said something quite rude to me the other day, and I don't believe half you're saying to me now.—It's not dangerous to catch lobsters, is it, Major Kent?"

The Major felt Meldon's eye on him. He was also aware that Miss King was looking at him appealingly.

"No," he said; "at least, not very; not if you're careful about the way you take hold of them."

"And I shouldn't get my feet wet, should I? not very wet?"

"No," said the Major, "or you might, of course. There's a sort of pool at the other side of the island, and if you walked through it—; but then you could go round it."

"There now," said Miss King. "I knew you were only making excuses, Mr. Meldon."

"I was," said Meldon. "I may as well own up to it that I was. My real reason for not wishing you to come with us—"

He edged over to where Simpkins was sitting, and kicked him sharply in the ribs. It was, after all, Simpkins' business to make some effort to retain Miss King.

"My real reason," he said, "though I didn't like to mention it before, is that there's a dead sheep on the other side of the island, just above the lobster bed. It's a good deal decayed, and the sea-gulls have been picking at it."

Miss King shuddered.

"Is there a dead sheep, Major Kent?" she asked.

"I don't know," said the Major. "I haven't been on this island for years; and I don't believe you have either, J. J."

"Dr. O'Donoghue told me about it yesterday," said Meldon. "He said it was a most disgusting sight. I don't think you'd like it, Miss King. I don't like telling you about it. I'm sure a glance at it would upset you again—after this morning, you know."

Miss King was evidently annoyed by this allusion to her sea sickness, but she was not inclined to give up her walk.

"Couldn't we go somewhere else for lobsters," she said; "somewhere a good way off from the dead sheep?"

"No," said Meldon decisively. "We shouldn't catch any if we did. All the lobsters, as you can easily understand, will have collected near the dead sheep. It's a great find for them, you know, as well as for the sea-gulls."

"In any case," said Miss King, who felt that she could not with decency press her company on Meldon any more, "I'd rather stay where I am. I don't think I care for crossing the island after all."

Meldon kicked Simpkins again. Then he took Major Kent by the arm, dragged him to his feet, and set off at a rapid pace across the island.

"J. J.," said the Major, "these plans of yours are all very well, and of course I'm not going to interfere with them, but I don't see any necessity for being actually rude to Miss King. She strikes me as being a very nice girl."

"I am disappointed in Miss King," said Meldon. "I thought better of her before. She's not what I call womanly, and I hate these unsexed females."

"What do you mean? I suppose you think she had no right to try and force herself on us, but I thought—"

"I'm not complaining of that in the least," said Meldon. "That was quite natural, and not at all what I call unwomanly. In fact, most women would have acted just as she did in that respect. What I was thinking of was those famous lines of Sir Walter Scott's. You recollect the ones I mean, I suppose?"

"No; I don't."

"'Oh woman,'" said Meldon, "'in our hours of ease'—that's now, Major, so far as we're concerned—'uncertain, coy, and hard to please.' That's what Miss King ought to have been, but wasn't. Nobody can say she was coy about the lobsters. 'When pain and anguish wring the brow.' That's the position in which Simpkins finds himself. 'A ministering angel thou.' That's what Miss King should be if she's what I call a true woman, a womanly woman. But she evidently isn't. She hasn't the maternal instinct at all strongly developed. If she had, her heart would bleed for a helpless, unprotected creature like Simpkins, whose brow is being wrung with the most pitiable anguish."

"Do you mean to say," said the Major, "that you think she ought to take a pleasure in holding that beast Simpkins' head?"

"That, though you put it coarsely, is exactly what I do mean. Any true woman would. Sir Walter Scott distinctly says so."

"Considering what you believe about her—I mean all that about her and Mrs. Lorimer being the same person, and her wanting to kill Simpkins—I don't see how you can expect her to be what you call womanly."

"There you're wrong, Major; quite wrong, as usual. There's no reason in the world why a woman shouldn't be womanly just because she happens to hold rather advanced opinions on some ethical subjects. As a matter of fact, it came out in the trial that Mrs. Lorimer was devotedly attentive to her husband, her last husband, during his illness. She watched him day and night, and wouldn't allow any one else to bring him his medicine. I naturally thought she'd display the same spirit with regard to Simpkins. I hope she will after they're married; but I'm disappointed in her just at present."

"What are you going to do about the lobsters, J. J.?" said the Major, dropping the subject of Miss King's character. "You know very well that there are none on the island, and after all you said about their swarming about in a lobster bed, Miss King will naturally expect us to bring her back a few."

"No, she won't. Not when she knows that they've been feeding on the disgusting and half-decayed dead sheep. She'd hate to see one."

"What made you think of saying there was a dead sheep, J. J.?"

"I had to think of something," said Meldon, "or else she'd have come with us. You contradicted every word I said, and gave the show away, although you knew very well the extreme importance of giving Simpkins his chance."

"I don't think he looked much like taking it when we left."

"No, he didn't. A more helpless, incompetent idiot than Simpkins I never came across. He won't do a single thing to help himself. I suppose he expects me to— I'll tell you what it is, Major; I had some regard for Simpkins before to-day, but I'm beginning to agree with you and Doyle about him now."

"Then perhaps you'll stop trying to get him to marry Miss King."

"No, I won't. My coming round to your way of thinking is all the more reason for marrying him. As long as I had any regard for him I felt it was rather a pity to have him killed, and I was only doing it to please you. Now that I see he really doesn't deserve to live I can go on with a perfectly clear conscience."

"Any way," said the Major, "I don't believe that he'll do much love-making to-day."

"Don't be too sure of that. If Miss King is behaving now as she ought to be; if she has taken that wet hat off his head and stopped it wringing his brow; if, as I confidently expect, she is showing herself a ministering angel, we shall most likely find them sitting in a most affectionate attitude when we get back."

Miss King did not do her duty. When Meldon and Major Kent returned, lobsterless, after half an hour's absence, they found Mr. Simpkins sitting on a stone by himself with the wet hat still on his head. Miss King was a long way off, stumbling about among the stones at the water's edge. She may, perhaps, have been trying to catch lobsters.

The voyage home was most unpleasant for every one except Meldon. The wind had risen slightly since morning, and the motion of the yacht in running before it was very trying. Mr. Simpkins collapsed at once and was dragged by Meldon into the cabin, where he lay in speechless misery. Miss King held out bravely for some time, and then gave way suddenly. Major Kent, watching her, was very unhappy, and did not dare to smoke lest he should make her worse. He attempted at one time to wrap her in an oilskin coat, thinking that additional warmth might be good for her; but the smell of the garment brought on a violent spasm, and he was obliged to take it away from her shoulders.

In the evening, after Miss King and Mr. Simpkins had been sent home on a car, Meldon reviewed the day's proceedings.

"As a pleasure party," he said, "it wasn't exactly a success; but then we didn't go out for pleasure. Considered as a step in advance towards the marriage of Miss King and the death of Simpkins, it hasn't turned out all we hoped. Still I think something is accomplished. Miss King must, I think, have felt some pity for Simpkins when she saw me dragging him into the cabin by his leg, and we all know that pity is akin to—"

"If she thinks of him in that sort of way," said the Major, "she won't kill him."

"I've told you before," said Meldon—"in fact, I'm tired telling you— that she hasn't got to kill him until after she's married him. You don't surely want her to be guilty of one of those cold-blooded, loveless marriages which are the curse of modern society and end in the divorce court. She ought to have some feeling of affection for him before she marries him, and I think it is probably aroused in her now. No woman could possibly see a man treated as I treated Simpkins this afternoon without feeling a little sorry for him. I bumped his head in the most frightful manner when I was dragging him down. No; I think it's all right now as far as Miss King is concerned. I'll go in and see Simpkins to-morrow and spur him on a bit. I'll tell him—"

"Some lie or other—" said the Major.

"Only for his own good," said Meldon. "I saw quite plainly on Sunday that he wanted to marry Miss King, and whatever I say to-morrow will be calculated to help and encourage him. You can't call that kind of thing telling lies. It's exactly the same in principle as why a good doctor tries to cheer up a patient by saying that he'll be perfectly well in the inside of a week after a trifling operation. Everybody admits that that's perfectly right, and nobody but a fool would call it a lie."

CHAPTER XII

Meldon was even more energetic than usual on the morning after the boating picnic. By getting up very early indeed he was able to shoot four rabbits, members of a large family which lived by destroying Major Kent's lettuces. He also bagged two wood-pigeons which had flown all the way from the Ballymoy House trees for the purpose of gorging themselves on half-ripe gooseberries in the Major's garden. He then rowed out in the boat about a mile from the shore, and had the satisfaction of bathing in absolute solitude and diving as far as he could into deep water. He had, as was natural, a fine appetite for breakfast, and ate in a way which gratified Major Kent and afterwards startled his housekeeper. But nature takes her revenges even on those who seem best able to defy her. After breakfast Meldon settled himself in a comfortable chair on the lawn, and was disinclined to move from it. The Major went into his study to make up some accounts, and the day being fine and warm, sat beside an open window. Meldon's chair was only a short distance from the window, so that he was in a position to carry on a conversation without raising his voice. For some time he did not speak, for his morning pipe was particularly enjoyable. Then he felt it necessary to make some excuse for his idleness.

"There's no use," he said, "my starting before eleven. Simpkins won't be out of bed until late to-day. He'll be thoroughly exhausted after all he went through on the *Spindrift*."

"Start any time you like," said the Major.

Meldon's remark interrupted him in the middle of adding up a long column of pence. He failed to recollect where he had got to and was obliged to begin over again.

"I can have the trap, I suppose," said Meldon, a couple of minutes later.

Major Kent had got to the shillings column.

"Yes. But do stop talking."

"Why?" said Meldon. "Without conversation we might as well be living in total solitude; and Bacon says, in one of his essays, that solitude is only fit for a god or a beast. You may like being a beast, Major, but I don't. You'll hardly set up, I suppose, to be a god."

"Hang it all, J. J.! I've forgotten how many shillings I had to carry, and now I shall have to begin the whole tot over again."

"Hand it out to me," said Meldon, "and I'll settle the whole thing for you in two minutes."

"Certainly not," said the Major. "I know your way of dealing with account books. I may be slow, but I do like to be tidy."

"Very well," said Meldon, "if you choose to be unsociable, merely in order to give yourself a lot of quite unnecessary trouble, of course you can. I won't speak again."

Ten minutes later he did speak again, to the great annoyance of Major Kent, who was estimating the total cost of the hay eaten by his polo ponies during the year—a most intricate business, for hay varied a good deal in price.

"Doyle's coming along the road in his trap," said Meldon, "and he looks to me very much as if he was coming here. He must want to see you about something. He can't possibly have any business with me."

"Hang Doyle!"

"If you like," said Meldon, "I'll deal with him and keep him off you. I should rather enjoy a chat with Doyle."

"Thanks. I wish you would. It can't be anything important."

"I expect he has come for your subscription for the illuminated address he and Dr. O'Donoghue are getting up for the police sergeant. I promised the other day that you'd give something. If you sign a cheque and stick it out on the window-sill, I'll fill up the amount and hand it on to Doyle. I should say that one pound would be a handsome contribution, and I may get you off with ten shillings. It'll all depend on how the money is coming in. He's turning in at the gate now, so you'd better hurry up.—Ah! Good morning, Doyle. Lovely day, isn't it? Seen anything of our friend Simpkins this morning?"

"I have not," said Doyle, "and I don't want to. I wouldn't care if I never set eyes on that fellow again."

"You'd have liked to have seen him yesterday," said Meldon.

"I would not."

"You would. The Major had him out for a day in the *Spindrift*, and—" Meldon winked.

Doyle got down from his trap and stood at the horse's head.

"A sicker man," said Meldon, "you never saw."

"Sick!"

"As a dog. Beastly sick. I don't care to enter into details; but, considering the small amount he ate during the day, the way he kept at it would have surprised you."

"Sick! What's the good of being sick? Why didn't you drown him?"

"We had Miss King out too," said Meldon, "and we didn't want to drown her. Besides, it wasn't the kind of day in which you could very well drown any one."

"What brought me over here this morning," said Doyle, "was—"

"I know," said Meldon. "You want to gather in the Major's subscription to the illuminated address with the apple trees in the corners. You shall have it. He's signing the cheque this minute."

"I'll take it, of course," said Doyle, "if it's quite convenient to the Major; but it wasn't it I came for."

"What was it, then? If you have any idea of dragging the Major into that salmon ambuscade of O'Donoghue's, I tell you plainly I won't have it."

"It's nothing of the kind," said Doyle. "After what you said on Friday we gave that notion up. What brought me here to-day was to see if the Major would lend me a set of car cushions. The rats got in on the ones I have of my own, and they've holes ate in them so as you'd be ashamed to put them on a car."

"You shall have them with the greatest possible pleasure," said Meldon.

"Not the new ones," said the Major through the window.

"I thought," said Meldon; "that you didn't want to be disturbed, and that I was carrying on this negotiation with Mr. Doyle. You must do one thing or the other, Major. Either come out and manage your own affairs, or else leave them entirely in my hands.—You can't," he said, turning to Doyle, "have the new cushions unless for some very special purpose. Is Miss King thinking of going for a drive on your car? If she is, the Major will lend the new cushions."

"She is not," said Doyle; "not that I heard of any way, though she might take the notion later."

"Then what do you want the cushions for?"

"It's an English gentleman," said Doyle; "a high-up man by all accounts, that has the fishing took from Simpkins. He'll be stopping in the hotel, and he'll want the car to take him up the river in the morning. The kind of man he is, I wouldn't like to be putting him off with my old cushions. They're terrible bad, the way the rats has them ate on me."

"If he really is a man of eminence in any walk of life," said Meldon—"a bishop, for instance, or a member of the House of Lords, or a captain of industry, you can have the cushions. If he's simply a second-rate man of the ordinary tourist type, you can't."

"He's a judge," said Doyle, "and what's more, an English judge."

"I'm surprised to hear you saying a thing like that. As a Nationalist you ought to be the last to admit that an English judge is in any way superior to an Irish one. He may be better paid—I daresay he is better paid, for we never get our fair share of what's going—but in the things that really matter—in legal acumen, for instance, which is the great thing we look for in judges—I don't expect the Irishman is a bit behind. However, English or Irish, the mere fact of his being a judge doesn't prove that he's a man of what I call real eminence. I don't think the Major will let you have his best car cushions for some sleepy old gentleman who sits on a bench and makes silly jokes. There are lots of judges knocking about that rat-eaten car cushions would be too good for. What's your man's name?"

"Hawkesby," said Doyle. "Sir Gilbert Hawkesby, no less."

Meldon started from his chair.

"Are you sure of that?" he asked, "absolutely dead certain? This is a business over which it won't do to make mistakes."

"It's what was in his letter, any way," said Doyle, "when he wrote engaging rooms in the hotel."

"When does he arrive?"

"To-morrow," said Doyle; "to-morrow afternoon, and I told Sabina to kill a chicken to-day, for it's likely he'll be wanting a bit of dinner after the drive over from Donard. I thought if he had a chicken and a bit of boiled bacon, with a custard pudding after that—"

"Go into the coach-house at once," said Meldon, "and take any cushions you want. I can't talk any more to you this morning. I'm going to be frightfully busy."

Doyle, grinning broadly, led his horse round to the yard. He did not believe that Meldon was ever busy. Like most people he failed to appreciate the real greatness of the clergyman.

Meldon hurried into the house and flung open the door of the study. Major Kent looked up from his papers with a weary smile.

"Couldn't you and Doyle settle that business of the car cushions between you? I shall never get these accounts done if I'm interrupted every minute."

"We could have settled it," said Meldon. "In fact we have settled it, but a question of vastly greater importance has arisen. We are threatened with something like an actual catastrophe."

"If it's the kind of catastrophe which involves an hour or so of solid talk, J. J., don't you think you could manage to put it off for a little? I shall be quite ready to go into it at any length you like this evening after dinner."

"Major," said Meldon, "if an earthquake came—the kind of earthquake which knocks down houses—and if thunderbolts were falling red-hot out of the sky, and if a large tidal wave was rushing up across the lawn, and if a moving bog was desolating your kitchen garden and engulfing your polo ponies, would you or would you not sit calmly there and go on with your accounts?"

"If all those things were happening I'd move, of course."

"There's no 'of course' about it. Some men wouldn't."

"Nonsense, J. J. The tidal wave alone—"

"Some men," repeated Meldon, "would sit on and finish their accounts. There was a soldier at Pompeii, for instance—they found his body centuries afterwards—who wouldn't stir from his post even when he saw the molten lava flowing down the street. I thought you might be that sort of man."

"I'm not."

"I'm glad to hear it. That sentry has been made a hero of. I've frequently heard him mentioned in sermons as a person to be imitated. In reality he was the worst kind of ass; and I wouldn't like to think of your getting embalmed as he did, and being dug out afterwards by an antiquary with a chisel. For the matter of that I shouldn't care to hear of people writing odes about you on account of your going under while your sword was in its sheath and your fingers held the pen."

"What was he doing with the pen?" said the Major. "If he was on sentry duty—"

"It wasn't that sentry whose fingers held the pen, but brave Kempenfelt, another man of the same sort; though there was more excuse for him, because he seems to have been taken by surprise when the land breeze shook the shrouds."

"I don't in the least know what you're talking about," said the Major. "Is there a moving bog, or a high tide, or anything unusual?"

"There's something a great deal worse," said Meldon. "Did you hear what Doyle said to me a few minutes ago?"

"I heard him asking for the loan of my car cushions. I don't particularly want to lend them, but I shouldn't regard his getting them as a catastrophe at all to be compared to the earthquake and all the other things you were gassing about."

"The cushions in themselves are nothing, and less than nothing, but did you hear who he wants them for?"

"Some judge or other, wasn't it? Salmon fishing."

"Some judge! What judge?"

"Did he mention his name? If he did I have forgotten it."

"He did mention it," said Meldon. "It was Hawkesby—Sir Gilbert Hawkesby. Now do you see why I say that we are threatened with a disaster worse than the eruption of Mount Vesuvius or the fire and brimstone that overwhelmed Sodom and Gomorrah?"

"No, I don't see anything of the sort. What on earth does the judge matter to us?"

"Can you possibly be ignorant of the fact? No, you can't, for I told it to you myself. Can you possibly have forgotten that Sir Gilbert Hawkesby was the judge who tried Mrs. Lorimer for the murder of her husband?"

"Oh!" said the Major, "I had forgotten. I never took the same interest in that case that you did, J.J."

"Well, he was. He was the very judge who summed up so strongly against the poor woman. I suppose now it will hardly be necessary for me to explain how his arrival at Doyle's hotel is likely to affect our plans?"

"Do you want me to invite him out in the *Spindrift*? If so, I hope to goodness he won't be sick. I had enough of that yesterday."

"I sometimes think, Major, that you pretend to be stupid simply to annoy me. Don't you see that sooner or later he's bound to come across Miss King? He'll see her next Sunday in church, if he doesn't meet her sooner. He'll recognise her at once. The trial occupied ten days, and during the whole of that time she was standing opposite to him and he was studying her face. He can't fail to know her again when he sees her. Now, recollect that he believed in her guilt. I pointed out to you at the time that he summed up dead against her—"

"I don't believe she was guilty, J. J."

"Nor, apparently, did the jury," said Meldon. "But the judge did. That's the point to bear in mind. Under the circumstances, what is he likely to do? He finds Mrs. Lorimer here masquerading as Miss King, and—"

"I wish you wouldn't say things like that. Since I have met Miss King I'm less inclined than ever to believe in that identification of yours. She strikes me—"

"We are now considering how she will strike the judge," said Meldon, "and how he's likely to act. It seems to me there's only one thing he can do, and that is warn every marriageable man in the neighbourhood of Miss King's real character and past record, and then what will happen to your plan? Will Simpkins be prepared to marry her? Certainly not."

"Well, I'm extremely glad the judge is coming if he puts a stop to the way you're going on."

"I'm not quite sure yet that he is coming," said Meldon.

"I thought Doyle said—"

"Doyle said he had engaged rooms at the hotel and taken the fishing. It doesn't absolutely follow that he'll occupy the rooms and catch the salmon. Sabina Gallagher is, I understand from Doyle, to kill a chicken, but it's not quite certain yet that the judge will eat the chicken."

"It'll depend a good deal on the way it's cooked, I suppose," said the Major.

"It will also depend upon the judge's reaching Ballymoy. As a matter of fact, I have a plan in my mind which may—which probably will—prevent his getting further than Donard. I intend to ask Dr. O'Donoghue to co-operate with me. I can't be quite certain yet that we'll be successful in heading off the judge and sending him somewhere else for his salmon fishing. But my plan is an extremely good one. It ought to come off all right. If it fails, I shall try another. I shall try two or three more if necessary."

"I wish you wouldn't. These plans of yours always end in involving us all in such frightful complications."

"Do you mean to say, Major, that you wish to give up the idea of Simpkins' marriage and subsequent death?"

"I've always wished to give it up," said the Major. "Since the day you first suggested I never liked it, and I like it much less now that I have got to know Miss King. It seems to me a wicked thing even to think of a girl like that being married to such an utter cad as Simpkins."

"I don't know how you can sit there and confess without a blush that you don't know your own mind for two days together. I'd be ashamed to go back on a thing the way you do. And I'm not going back on this. For one thing, I have a duty to perform to you and Doyle, and O'Donoghue and Sabina Gallagher, and the rector and the police sergeant. In the next place, after all the trouble I've taken to carry this scheme through, I'm not going to give in just at the moment of success. I shall go in this morning and see O'Donoghue. To-morrow he and I will drive over to Donard—"

"I can't give you a horse to-morrow," said the Major.

"You can if you like."

"I won't, then."

"Why not?"

"Because, if you go playing off fools' tricks on a judge, you'll end in getting yourself put in prison. There is such a thing as contempt of court, and judges are just about the most touchy men there are about their dignity. They don't hesitate for an instant to—"

"A judge isn't a court," said Meldon, "when he hasn't got his wig on, and besides an English judge has no jurisdiction in this country. However, I'm not going down on my knees to you for the loan of a horse and trap. If you don't choose to oblige me in the matter of your own free will I won't place myself under any obligation to you. I shall simply borrow a bicycle and ride to Donard. O'Donoghue will have to ride too, though I don't expect he'll like it. It's twenty miles, and O'Donoghue drinks more than is good for him."

"Are you going to tell O'Donoghue the whole cock-and-bull plan about Simpkins and Miss King and the murder?"

"No. O'Donoghue is a reasonable man. He doesn't argue and browbeat me the way you do. When I tell him that the removal of Simpkins, and consequently his own future happiness and comfort, depend very largely on our being able to keep Sir Gilbert Hawkesby out of Ballymoy, he will believe me at once and act in a sensible way."

"What do you mean to do to the judge when you catch him?"

"I don't mean to *do* anything. I suppose you have some wild idea in your head—"

"No ideas could be wilder than yours are, J. J."

"Some wild idea of my maiming the old gentleman, or bribing a man to kidnap him, or sending him a bogus telegram to say that his wife is dying. As a matter of fact, I'm going to do nothing except tell him the simple truth."

"I don't believe you could do that, J. J. You've never had any practice since I knew you."

"If you think that you will get me to reveal the details of my plan by taunting me you're greatly mistaken. I can stand any amount of insults without turning a hair. A man who is in the right, and conscious of his own integrity—you recollect what the Latin poet says about that—"

"No. I don't. You know I don't read Latin poets, so what's the good of quoting bits of them to me?"

"Very well. I won't. But I won't tell you my plan either. I'll say no more than this: what the judge will hear from my lips to-morrow will be the simple truth, the truth as Simpkins or any other unprejudiced observer would tell it. But the truth in this particular case is of such a land that I should be greatly surprised if he doesn't turn straight round and go home again."

"Are you going to tell him that Mrs. Lorimer is here? Not that that is the truth, but I'm really beginning to think you believe it is."

"No. I'm not going to tell him that. When I said I was going to tell the truth, I didn't mean that I was going to sit down opposite that judge and tell him all the truth I know about everything. It would take days and days to do that, and he wouldn't sit it out. No, I'm going to tell him one solid lump of truth which he will listen to—a truth that O'Donoghue will back up; that you'd back up yourself if you were there; that even Doyle would be forced to stand over if he was put into a witness box on his oath. But I can't spend the whole day explaining things to you. I must go in and hustle Simpkins a bit. There's no reason in the world that I can see why he shouldn't go up to Ballymoy House and propose this afternoon. Then I must see O'Donoghue and make arrangements about to-morrow. I shall also, thanks to your churlishness, have to borrow a bicycle for myself. Then I must look up that doddering old ass Callaghan, and tell him to precipitate matters a bit if I succeed in hunting Simpkins up to Ballymoy House. If I fail to head off the judge—I don't expect to fail, but if by any chance I do—we shall have no time to spare, and must have Simpkins definitely committed to the marriage as soon as possible. Not that it will really be much use if the judge gets at him. Simpkins is just the sort of dishonourable beast who'd seize on any excuse to wriggle out of an engagement; particularly as he'll know that Miss King is scarcely in a position to go into court and get damages for breach of promise."

CHAPTER XIII

Sir Gilbert Hawkesby had the reputation of being a just and able judge, a man of fine intellect, great vigour, and immense determination of character. On the bench he looked the part which popular imagination had given him to play. His eyes were described as "steely" by a lady journalist, who had occasion to watch him during the sensational trial of Mrs. Lorimer. His chin she described later on in her article as "characteristic of a strong fighter." His manner in court was exceedingly severe. In private life, especially during his summer holiday, he tried not to look like a judge, and was always pleased when strangers mistook him for a country gentleman, the owner of a landed property. He had a broad figure, and emphasised its breadth by wearing on his holiday loose jackets of rough tweed. He had strong, stout legs which looked well in knickerbockers and shooting stockings. A casual observer, not knowing the man, would have set him down as an ardent sportsman, and would have been perfectly right. The judge loved fishing, and was prepared to go long distances in the hope of catching salmon. He liked yachting, and owned a small cutter which was one of the crack boats of her class. Men who met him for the first time on the banks of a Norwegian river, or at a regatta at Cowes, were more impressed by his physical than his intellectual strength. They would perhaps have suspected him of obstinacy, the obstinacy of the inveterate prejudice of the country gentleman. They would not, unless they knew him, have given him credit for being a man of wide reading, and a judgment in literary matters as sound as his decisions in court.

Sir Gilbert had spent nearly a week in the Bournemouth villa which he had taken for Lady Hawkesby. The place wearied him, and nothing but a chivalrous sense of the duty he owed to his wife kept him there so long. Lady Hawkesby was a little exacting in some ways; and though she recognised that the judge had a right to go fishing, she disliked his running away without spending a few days with her after the busy season was over, and she was able to leave London. The day of the judge's departure had arrived, and he sat with Lady Hawkesby after luncheon, waiting for the carriage which was to take him to the station.

"You'll see Millicent, of course," said Lady Hawkesby. "Be sure to keep her out of mischief if you can."

"I don't suppose," said Sir Gilbert, "that Millicent can get into any mischief in Ballymoy."

Lady Hawkesby sighed. She distrusted her niece, regarding her as a highly dangerous person who might at any moment create a sensation which would amount to a public scandal.

"I understand," she said, "that the place is twenty miles away from the nearest railway station."

She sighed again. She was a little uncertain as to whether she ought to find comfort or fresh cause of anxiety in the remoteness of Ballymoy from civilisation. On the one hand, scandals of a literary kind—and Lady Hawkesby did not suspect Miss King of giving occasion for anything worse—are unlikely in the wilds of Connacht. On the other hand, her distance from all friends and advisers would give Miss King a freedom which was very perilous.

"I can't think," she said, "what takes either of you to such a place."

"I'm going to catch salmon," said Sir Gilbert. "Millicent tells me that she wants rest and quiet. I daresay she does."

"I wish very much," said Lady Hawkesby, "that she was safely married to some quiet sensible man."

There was a good deal of sound common sense and knowledge of human nature in her "safely." Lady Hawkesby was not a brilliant woman. She was in many ways a foolish woman. But she had certain beliefs founded on the experience of many generations of people like herself, and therefore entitled to respect. She believed that a woman is much less likely to wander from the beaten paths of life when her hands are held by a husband, if possible "a quiet sensible man," and her petticoats grasped by several clinging children.

"I'm afraid," said Sir Gilbert, "that she's not likely to meet with any suitable person in Ballymoy, but if she does I'll give her your blessing as well as my own."

The fact that Miss King was not likely to meet an eligible man in Ballymoy set Lady Hawkesby's thoughts working in a fresh direction.

"I am sure," she said, "that Millicent will be very glad to see you. In a place like that where there can't be anybody to talk to—"

"Even I might be welcome. I'll look her up every Sunday. I'll dine with her if she asks me on week-days; but I'm not going to stay with her in the house she has taken. I like to be a free bird of the wild when I'm on my holidays. The local inn, which is called the Imperial Hotel, and owned by a man named Doyle, is the place for me. I've taken rooms in it."

"I'm sure they'll cook abominably. You'll be half-starved."

"Potato cake and bottled porter," said Sir Gilbert. "That's what I always live on when I go to Ireland. In Scotland I have oatcake and whisky. Last summer, in Norway, I throve on smoked salmon."

"I hear the carriage. I hope all your things are properly packed, and that nothing is forgotten."

"As long as I have my rods and my fly book," said Sir Gilbert, "I shall be able to get along. Good-bye, my dear. I shall dine at the club, and catch the night mail from Euston."

"Do write to me, Gilbert."

"I'll write on Sunday, not sooner, unless I find that Milly has got into a scrape."

Sir Gilbert travelled comfortably, and enjoyed his journey. At Euston he got into the carriage with an Irish Member of Parliament, a Unionist, who was returning to his native Dublin after making himself as brilliantly objectionable as possible for six months to a Liberal Chief Secretary. He mistook the judge for an Irish country gentleman, and gave expression to political opinions which Sir Gilbert found extremely amusing. On the steamer he fell in with another Member of Parliament, this time a Nationalist, who had travelled third class in the train, and only emerged into good society at Holyhead. He, getting nearer to the truth than his enemy, thought the judge was an English tourist, and explained the good intentions of the Congested Districts Board at some length. The judge found him amusing too, and sat up talking to him in the smoking-room. In the morning he introduced his two acquaintances to each other at five o'clock, just as the steamer reached Kingstown pier. He was delighted with the result. They both looked round them cautiously, and satisfied themselves that there was no one on the pier who knew them. Then they fell into an animated conversation, and found each other so agreeable that they travelled together in a second-class carriage to Dublin, the Nationalist paying ninepence extra for the privilege, the Unionist sacrificing the advantages conferred by his first-class ticket. The judge, who was going in a different train, put his head into the window of their compartment and urged them to settle their political differences by a similar compromise. He made a habit of being festive and jocular when he was on holiday, and he particularly enjoyed poking fun at the inhabitants of foreign countries.

In the breakfast car of the train which carried him westwards he came into contact with a Local Government Board inspector. This gentleman was extremely reticent for a long time, and was only persuaded to talk in the end when the judge assured him that he was a complete stranger in Ireland, and was not a newspaper correspondent. Then the inspector talked. He told a series of amusing tales which were all of them true, but which Sir Gilbert regarded as inventions. He had to change his carriage at Athlone, and parted from the inspector with great regret. For the rest of his journey he was alone. It was his first visit to the part of Ireland he was travelling through, and he looked with keen interest at the bogs, the scattered cottages, the lean cattle, scanty pasture lands, potato fields, patches of oats, and squalid towns.

At Donard Station, which is the terminus of this branch of the railway, and the nearest station to Ballymoy, he got out. He had telegraphed to the hotel for luncheon, and given orders that a car should be ready to drive him over to Ballymoy, He was accosted on the platform by two strangers. He eyed them with some surprise. The one was a shabby, red-haired clergyman, with a bristling moustache and a strikingly battered hat. He looked about thirty years of age. The other was a slightly older man, dressed in a seedy grey suit and a pair of surprisingly bright yellow gaiters.

"Sir Gilbert Hawkesby, I presume?" said Meldon.

"Yes," said the judge; "I am Sir Gilbert Hawkesby."

"This," said Meldon, "is my friend Dr. O'Donoghue, medical officer of health for the Poor Law Union of Ballymoy, a man greatly respected in the neighbourhood for his scientific attainments and the uncompromising honesty of his character. I need scarcely remind you, Sir Gilbert, that the two things don't always go together."

Dr. O'Donoghue bowed and took off his cap.

"And you?" said the judge. "May I ask who you are?"

"It doesn't really matter who I am," said Meldon. "The important fact for you to grasp is that O'Donoghue is the officer of health of the Union of Ballymoy. That's what you are, isn't it, O'Donoghue?"

"It is," said O'Donoghue.

"I'll make a note of it at once," said the judge.

"A mental note will do," said Meldon. "You needn't bother writing it down. If you happen to forget it in the course of our conversation, you've only got to mention that you have and I'll tell it to you again."

"Thanks," said the judge. "I'm so glad that we are to have a conversation. When shall we begin?"

Sir Gilbert was enjoying Meldon very much so far. He'd never before come across any one exactly like this clergyman, and he wanted to see more of him.

"Perhaps," said Meldon, "as what we have to say is of a strictly private kind, and may turn out to be actually libellous, we'd better go down to the hotel."

"Certainly," said the judge. "I've ordered luncheon there. If you and the medical officer of health will join me I shall be delighted. After luncheon I shall have to leave you, I'm afraid. I have a long drive before me. I'm on my way to Ballymoy."

"When you've heard what we have to say," said Meldon, "you won't go to Ballymoy."

"I expect I shall," said the judge. "But of course I don't know yet what form your libel is going to take. Still, I can hardly imagine that the defamation of any one's character will keep me out of Ballymoy. I have a car waiting for me outside the station, but I'm afraid I cannot offer to drive you down to the hotel. I have a good deal of luggage."

"As far as the luggage is concerned," said Meldon, "you may just as well leave it here. There's no point in dragging a lot of trunks and fishing-rods down to the hotel when you'll simply have to drag them all back again. When you've heard what we have to say you'll take the next train home."

"I don't expect I shall. In fact, I feel tolerably certain I shall go on. I'll take the luggage with me any how, in case I do."

"You mustn't think," said Meldon, "that I'm suggesting your leaving the luggage behind simply in order to get a seat on your car."

"I assure you," said the judge, "that such a suspicion never crossed my mind."

"O'Donoghue and I both have bicycles, so we don't want to drive. He has his own, a capital machine, and I borrowed Doyle's this morning, which is quite sound except for the left pedal. It's a bit groggy, and came off twice on the way here."

"That makes me all the more sorry I can't drive you down," said the judge, "but you see what a lot of things I have. I needn't say good-bye: we shall meet again at the hotel."

Luncheon—chops and boiled potatoes—was served in the commercial room of the hotel. When the maid had gone away after supplying the three men with whisky and soda, Meldon laid down his knife and fork.

"I may introduce my subject," he said, "by saying that I have a high respect for you. So has O'Donoghue. Haven't you, O'Donoghue?"

"I have," said O'Donoghue.

"Thanks," said the judge. "It's kind of you both to say that."

"Not at all; it's the simple truth. I look up to you a good deal in your capacity of judge. Judge of the King's Bench, I think?"

The judge nodded.

"In order to make my position quite plain," said Meldon, "and to prevent any possibility of your thinking that I'm meddling with your affairs in an unwarrantable manner, I may add that I recognise in you one of the pillars of society, a bulwark of our civil and religious liberty, a mainstay of law and order. So does O'Donoghue."

"I'm a Nationalist myself," said the doctor, who felt that he was being committed to sentiments which he could not entirely approve.

"I'm speaking of Sir Gilbert as an English judge," said Meldon, "and the law and order I refer to are, so far as Sir Gilbert is concerned, purely English. Nothing that I am saying now compromises you in the slightest either with regard to the land question or Home Rule."

"I didn't understand that at the time you spoke," said the doctor; "but if you don't mean any more than that I'm with you heart and soul."

"You hear what he says," said Meldon to the judge.

"I need scarcely say," replied Sir Gilbert, "that all this is immensely gratifying to me."

"It won't surprise you now," said Meldon, "to hear that we look upon your life as a most valuable one—too valuable to be risked unnecessarily."

"I should appreciate this entirely unsolicited testimonial," said the judge, "even more than I do already, if I knew exactly who was giving it to me."

"I don't suppose that you'd be much the wiser if I tell you that my name is Meldon—J. J. Meldon. I was at one time curate of Ballymoy."

"Thanks," said the judge. "Won't you go on with your luncheon? I'm afraid your chop will be cold."

"I have," said Meldon, "a duty to perform. I don't mind in the least if my chop does get cold. I wish to warn you that your life, your valuable life— and I never realised how valuable your life was until I read your summing-up in the case of Mrs. Lorimer. That was, if I may say so, masterly. Milton himself couldn't have done it better."

"Milton?" said the judge.

"I mentioned Milton," said Meldon, "because he was the most violent misogynist I ever heard of. Read what he says about Delilah in 'Samson Agonistes' and you'll see why I compare your remarks about Mrs. Lorimer to the sort of way he wrote."

"I've read it," said the judge, "and I think I recollect the passages you allude to. I don't quite see myself what connection there is between his views and the case of Mrs. Lorimer. Still, I'm greatly obliged to you for what you say about my summing-up. But you were speaking of my life just before you mentioned Milton."

"The connection is obvious enough," said Meldon; "and if you've really read the poem—"

"I have," said the judge.

"Then you ought to recognise that the strong anti-feminist bias which Milton displays is exactly similar to the spirit in which you attributed the worst possible motives to Mrs. Lorimer. I'm not now entering on a discussion of the question of whether you and Milton are right or wrong in your view of women. That would take too long, and, besides, it hasn't anything to do with the business on hand."

"That," said the judge, "as well as I recollect, is the danger of my losing my life."

"Your life," said Meldon, "will not be safe in Ballymoy. We met you at the station to-day in order to warn you to go straight home again."

"Really!" said the judge. "I travelled down from London with a Member of Parliament last night, and he gave me a description of the state of the country which bears out what you say. He mentioned anarchy and conspiracy as being rampant—or else rife; I forget for the moment which word he used. He said that the west of Ireland lay at the mercy of an organised system of terrorism, and that—"

"That must have been a Unionist," said Meldon.

"Damned lies," said O'Donoghue.

"He was a Unionist," said the judge. "But I met another man in the steamer, also an M.P., who said that, owing to the beneficent action of the Congested Districts Board, Connacht was rapidly becoming a happy and contented part of the empire; that the sympathy with Irish ideas displayed by the present Government was winning the hearts and affections of the people, and—"

"That," said Meldon, "must have been a Nationalist."

"More damned lies," said Dr. O'Donoghue.

"And now," said the judge, "I meet you two gentlemen, one of you a Nationalist and the other a Unionist—"

"Don't call me that," said Meldon; "I'm non-political. Nothing on earth would induce me to mix myself up with any party."

"And you," the judge went on, "after comparing me in the most flattering manner to the poet Milton, tell me that my life won't be safe in Ballymoy. I'm inclined to think that the best thing I can do is to go and find out the truth for myself."

"If it was simply a question of murder," said Meldon, "I should strongly advise you to go on and see the thing through; but what we have in mind is something infinitely worse. Isn't it, O'Donoghue?"

"It is," said the doctor; "far worse."

"Is it," said the judge, "high treason? That's the only crime I know which the law regards as more malignant than murder. The penalties are a little obsolete at present, for nobody has ventured to commit the crime for a great many years; but if you like I'll look the subject up when I go home and let you know."

"We're not talking about crime," said Meldon, "but drains. Doyle's drains."

"I beg your pardon," said the judge. "Did you say drains?"

"Yes," said Meldon distinctly. "Drains—Doyle's drains. The drains of the house you mean to stop in. I needn't tell you what drains mean. Blood-poisoning, typhoid, septic throats, breakings out in various parts of your body, and a very painful kind of death. For although O'Donoghue will do his best for you in the way of mitigating your sufferings he can't undertake to save your life."

"I'm pretty tough," said the judge, "and I'm paying a good price for my fishing. I think I'll face the drains."

"I don't expect that you quite realise how bad those drains are. Does he, O'Donoghue?"

"He does not," said the doctor.

"Then you tell him," said Meldon. "As a medical man you'll put it much more convincingly than I can."

O'Donoghue cleared his throat.

"I've no doubt," said the judge, "that you can make out a pretty bad case against those drains; but I'm going on to Ballymoy to catch salmon if they're twice as rotten as they are."

"It was only last winter," said Meldon, "that Mr. Simpkins wanted to prosecute Doyle on account of the condition of his drains. You probably don't know Simpkins; but if you did, you'd understand that he's not the kind of man to take drastic action unless the drains were pretty bad."

"And they're worse since," said O'Donoghue.

"It's extremely kind of you," said the judge, "to have come all this way to warn me, and of course if I knew Simpkins I might, as you say, act differently. But I think, on the whole, I'll go on and risk it. If I do get a septic throat or anything of the kind I shall send at once for Dr. O'Donoghue; and I shall ask you, Mr. Meldon, to write an obituary notice for the papers in case I succumb. I am sure you'd do it well, and you could put in all you said about Delilah and Mrs. Lorimer. I shan't mind once I'm buried."

"You won't be able to say afterwards," said Meldon, "that you were not fairly warned. We've done our duty whatever happens."

"You've done it in the most thorough way," said the judge, "and I hope I shall see a great deal of you while I'm in Ballymoy."

"I'll just finish this chop," said Meldon, "and then O'Donoghue and I must be off. We have a long ride before us. I'll tell Doyle to sprinkle some chloride of lime in your bedroom, and to damp the sheets with Condy's Fluid. I don't suppose it will be much use, but it's the best we can do if your mind is made up."

CHAPTER XIV

Meldon left the hotel and mounted his bicycle without speaking another word. He rode rapidly out of the town, followed at some distance by O'Donoghue, who was a cyclist of inferior strength and energy. For the first four miles the road to Ballymoy goes steadily up hill. Meldon, gripping his handle-bars tightly, rode at a fast rate. O'Donoghue was left further and further behind. At the top of the hill Meldon had a lead of a full quarter of a mile. Then the left pedal of his bicycle came off, and he was obliged to dismount. He was working at it with a spanner when O'Donoghue, breathless and in a bad temper, came up with him. Meldon greeted him cheerfully.

"Obstinate old swine the judge is," he said. "You would have thought a man like that whose business in life consists very largely in weighing evidence, and who has been specially trained to arrive at sound conclusions from the facts presented to him, would have seen the necessity of giving up this ridiculous expedition of his to Ballymoy."

"Why did you ride on like that and leave me behind?" said O'Donoghue shortly.

"If I were inclined to be captious and wanted to find fault," said Meldon, "I might say why did you lag behind and leave me to ride by myself? I don't want to ride by myself. I want to discuss the judge's conduct."

O'Donoghue also wanted to discuss the judge's conduct. He was even more anxious to find out, if he could, why Meldon disliked the idea of this particular judge paying a visit to Ballymoy. He recovered his temper with an effort.

"I don't think," he said, "that he believed a word you said about the drains."

"That's exactly what I'm complaining of. He ought to have believed us. According to all the rules of evidence, no stronger testimony could possibly have been offered than the statements of a clergyman and a doctor, neither of whom had any personal interest in the condition of the drains. Unless we'd brought a bottle of water out of Doyle's well, and shown him the bacilli swimming about in it, I don't see what more we could have done."

"I wish I knew," said O'Donoghue, "exactly why it is that you want to keep Sir Gilbert out of Ballymoy. What harm is there for him to do if he comes?"

"He won't do me any harm at all. In fact I shall be delighted to have him there. He struck me as a very intelligent and highly-educated man. You saw how he caught my point about 'Samson Agonistes' at once. Neither you nor Doyle, nor for the matter of that the Major, would have known in the least what I was talking about. A man like that about the place would be a great comfort to me. I should have some one to talk to. I wish I could get you all to understand that I'm acting in this whole business from purely disinterested and altruistic motives. I don't want to get rid of Simpkins. You and Doyle and the Major do."

"The thing I can't understand," said O'Donoghue, "is what the judge has to do with Simpkins. If I was clear about that— What I mean to say is if I could make out why—"

"Thank goodness," said Meldon, "I've got that beastly pedal fixed again. Come on, doctor. We haven't a minute to waste. I want to be in Ballymoy a clear hour before the judge arrives there."

He mounted the bicycle as he spoke, and rode off at full speed. The slope of the road was downwards from the place of the halt, and O'Donoghue was able to keep close to Meldon for some time. He made a number of breathless attempts to speak.

"If you'd only tell me," he panted, "why—"

Sometimes he got a little further than the "why."

He never succeeded in completely finishing his sentence. After a while he began to drop behind again. On a long level stretch of road Meldon drew rapidly ahead and might have reached Ballymoy a whole mile in front of O'Donoghue if the pedal of Doyle's bicycle had not failed him again. The accident gave the doctor his opportunity. He came up with Meldon and asked his question.

"What difference will the judge make to Simpkins? That's what I want to know, and I won't go on blindfold doing exactly what you tell me. If I saw my way it would be different."

"I can't explain the position fully to you," said Meldon, "without giving away a secret which isn't really mine; a secret which involves the honour of a lady. But when I tell you that my plan for getting rid of Simpkins permanently involves my marrying him to Miss King, you'll no doubt be able to make out for yourself why it is absolutely necessary to keep Sir

Gilbert Hawkesby out of Ballymoy. Any intelligent man, able to put two and two together, ought to see the whole thing, especially if he's been reading the newspapers."

O'Donoghue sat down on the bank at the side of the road and thought deeply. Meldon worked vehemently at the pedal.

"I can't see in the least what you're at," said O'Donoghue at last. "But it doesn't matter. If your plan of making Simpkins marry that lady depends on your keeping the judge out of the place, then, so far as I can see, it's done for. He's coming in spite of you."

"My plan will be all right," said Meldon, "if he doesn't stay; and I think he won't stay."

"He doesn't seem to mind drains a bit; and he'll mind them less when he sees them. They're bad, of course; but they're not near so bad as you made out. I don't expect a man that age will catch anything."

"I'm not now relying on the drains," said Meldon. "I quite give in that they've failed. I'm on my way back to make other arrangements which will have him out of Ballymoy in twenty-four hours."

"You mean the chloride of lime in his bedroom."

"That and other things. I'm convinced that we run a grave risk every hour he spends in Ballymoy, and so I shall naturally take pretty strong measures to get him out."

"Don't mix me up in them if you can help it. I backed you up about the drains, but for a man in my position it doesn't do to go too far, especially with a judge."

"All you have to do," said Meldon, "is to supply the chloride of lime and the Condy's Fluid. I shan't ask you to do anything else. You can't complain about a trifle like that. Most men would do a great deal more in order to get rid of Simpkins."

The pedal was fixed again. Meldon shook it violently to make sure that it was really firm.

"I hope," he said, "it will stick on this time. These delays are most exasperating when one's in a hurry. We shall have to buck up now, O'Donoghue, and ride really fast."

O'Donoghue groaned. He had been riding at the top of his speed since he left Donard, and there were still six miles between him and Ballymoy. Meldon led off at a racing speed, leaving the doctor to follow him through a choking cloud of dust. About three miles outside Ballymoy, O'Donoghue, having entirely lost sight of Meldon, sat down to rest on the side of the road. The pedal was holding to its place, and he had no hope of seeing his companion again.

Meldon propped his bicycle up outside the door of the hotel, walked into the hall, and shouted for Doyle.

"I could do," he said, "with a cup of tea, if you'll be so good as to tell Sabina Gallagher to make it for me."

"I'll do that," said Doyle. "I'd do more than that for you, Mr. Meldon. The tea will be laid out for you in the commercial room in five minutes if so be Sabina has the kettle on the boil, and it's what I'm always telling her she ought to see to."

"I don't want it set out in the commercial room," said Mr. Meldon, "nor yet in the drawing-room. I want to take it in the kitchen along with Sabina."

"Is it in the kitchen? Sure that's no place for a gentleman like yourself to be taking his tea."

"All the same it's there I mean to have it. The fact is, I have a word or two to say to Sabina privately."

Doyle opened a door at the end of the hall in which they stood, and shouted down a long passage:

"Sabina, Sabina Gallagher! Are you listening to me? Very well then. Will you wet some tea in the silver teapot which you'll find beyond in—"

"I'd prefer the brown one," said Meldon, "if it's all the same to you. I hate the taste of plate-powder. I don't think it's likely that Sabina has been wasting her time polishing your silver, but you never can tell what a girl like that would do."

"In the brown teapot," shouted Doyle. "And set out a cup and saucer on the kitchen table—"

"Two cups," said Meldon. "I want Sabina to join me, so that I'll be sure of getting her in a good temper."

"Two cups," shouted Doyle. "And when you have that done be off and clean yourself as quick as you can, for the Reverend Mr. Meldon will be down in a minute to take tea with you. If there isn't a pot of jam down below—and it's likely you have it ate if there is—go into the shop and ask for one. Is it strawberry you'd like, Mr. Meldon?"

"That or raspberry," said Meldon. "I don't care which. And now I want to say a word or two to you."

"Come inside," said Doyle. "There isn't a soul in the bar, and maybe you'd like a drop of something before your tea."

"I would not. You know very well, Doyle, that I never touch whisky before my meals, especially when I've any business to do; and you ought to be ashamed of yourself for offering it to me."

Doyle pushed forward a chair, selected another for himself, and sat down opposite Meldon.

"Is it about the judge that's coming this evening that you wanted to speak to me?"

"It is," said Meldon.

"I was thinking it might be. When you asked for the loan of my bicycle this morning, and told me that you and the doctor was off to Donard in a hurry, I made full sure it was him you were after. What have you done with the doctor?"

"He'll be here in a few minutes," said Meldon, "and when he comes he'll give you some chloride of lime and a bottle of Condy's Fluid. You're to sprinkle the lime on the floor of the judge's bedroom, and to damp the sheets on his bed with a solution of Condy's Fluid. O'Donoghue will give you exact directions about the quantities."

"And what would that be for?"

"The judge wants it done," said Meldon, "and that ought to be enough for you."

"I was reading a bit in the paper one day about what they call the Christian Science. I suppose, now, he'll be one of them?"

"No," said Meldon. "He's not. If you'd read a little more carefully you'd have understood that no Christian Scientist would walk on the same side of the street as a bottle of Condy's Fluid. The principal article of their creed is that there are no such things as germs, consequently it's mere waste of time trying to kill them. And as Condy's Fluid exists chiefly for the purpose of killing germs, it strikes the Christian Scientist as an immoral compound. I don't know exactly what religion your judge professes, but one thing is clear from his insisting on Condy's Fluid, he's not a Christian Scientist."

"It's as well he's not," said Doyle. "What I say, and always did say, is this: The Catholic religion is the right religion, meaning no offence to you, Mr. Meldon. And the Protestant religion is a good religion for them that's brought up to it. And if a man can't make up his mind to one or other of the two of them, it's better for him not to have a religion at all."

"Don't let your interest in theological controversy distract your attention from seeing after the thorough disinfection of the judge's bedroom."

"I will not," said Doyle; "but I'll see that your orders are carried out. It's a queer notion, so it is, to be sleeping in damp sheets. But a man like that ought to know what suits him."

"Right," said Meldon. "And now, if you'll excuse me, I'll be off to the kitchen and have my tea. You keep your eye lifting for the doctor, and get those things out of him as soon as you can."

Sabina Gallagher, blushing and embarrassed, with a clean apron on, stood with her back against the dresser when Meldon entered the kitchen. He shook hands with her, and noticed at once that she had obeyed her master's orders and made some effort to clean herself. Her hands were damp and cold.

"I'm glad to see you looking well," said Meldon, "Is the tea ready?"

"It is," said Sabina.

Meldon sat down and poured out two cups.

"Come along," he said, "and keep me company."

Sabina sidled towards the table.

"I'm just after my tea," she said, "and I'd be ashamed to be sitting down with a gentleman like yourself."

"Nonsense," said Meldon, "I want to talk to you, and I can't do that if you're standing there in the middle of the floor so as I'd get a crick in my neck trying to look at you. Sit down at once."

Sabina grinned sheepishly and sat down. Meldon drank off his cup of tea at a draught, and poured out a second.

"Have you taken the advice I gave you the other day about your cooking?" he asked.

"Is it making them things with olives?"

"It is."

"Well, I have not; for I wouldn't be fit."

"I'm glad to hear it," said Meldon. "Circumstances have arisen since I last saw you which render it desirable that you should cook as badly as possible during the next few days. There's a judge coming here this evening."

"I heard Mr. Doyle saying that same," said Sabina.

"And he'll be expecting some sort of a dinner to-night."

The Simpkins Plot | 121

"There's a chicken ready to go into the oven for him any minute."

"What you have to do," said Meldon, "is to see that he gets as bad a dinner as possible, and a worse breakfast to-morrow morning."

"Bad, is it?"

"Uneatable," said Meldon. "Serve him up food that a pig wouldn't look at. Can you do that, do you think?"

"I might, of course," said Sabina; "but—"

"Then do."

"Sure if I do he'll not be for stopping in the hotel."

"Exactly," said Meldon. "He's not wanted to stop."

"Mr. Doyle will lacerate me after, if the gentleman leaves, and the language he'll use will be what I wouldn't like to be listening to."

"Mr. Doyle," said Meldon, "may take that view at first. He's a short-sighted man, and is inclined to consider only the immediate present; but, in giving you the directions I am giving about the judge's food, I am acting in Mr. Doyle's best interests. I'm looking into the future, and doing what will be best for Mr. Doyle in the long run. After awhile he'll come to understand that, and then he'll be extremely pleased with you, and most probably he'll raise your wages."

"He'll not do that," said Sabina confidently.

"In any case," said Meldon, "whatever view he ultimately takes of your action, you will have the feeling that you are securing the greatest good of the greatest number, and that's a reward in itself—a much better reward than a few shillings extra wages."

"It might be," said Sabina; but she spoke without conviction.

"As to the exact method that you ought to pursue," said Meldon, "I don't lay down any hard and fast rules; but I should suggest that paraffin oil is a thing that has a most penetrating kind of taste, and I don't know that I ever met any one who liked it. I remember once a servant we had at home cleaned the inside of the coffee-pot with paraffin oil. I tasted the stuff for weeks afterwards, and I couldn't make out for a long time where the flavour came from."

"Would there be any fear," said Sabina, "but I might poison him?"

"Not a bit," said Meldon. "You'll do him good if he eats the things. You may not know it, but vaseline is made from paraffin oil, and it's well known that vaseline is an extraordinarily wholesome sort of stuff, good for almost anything in the way of a cut or a burn. Then there's a kind of emulsion made from petroleum—that's the same as paraffin—which cures consumption. For all we know this judge may be suffering from consumption, and a little paraffin may be the best thing in the world for him."

"I wouldn't like if he was to die on us."

"Nor would I; but he won't. You needn't be the least bit afraid of that. For one thing, the moment he smells the paraffin he'll stop eating the food. However, all this is only my idea. Better plans may suggest themselves. For instance, I have noticed that if you chop up an onion with a knife, and then spread butter with the same knife, the butter gets a most objectionable taste. You have onions about the house, I suppose."

"I have."

"Then you might try that. And there's a way of dealing with bacon. I'm not quite sure how it's done, but the taste all goes out of it, and it gets extremely tough. Then you fry it in such a way that it's quite limp, and sprinkle a little soot on it. I've often tried to eat bacon done that way—before I was married, of course—and I never could. I don't suppose the judge will be able to either. Boiled eggs are difficult things to tamper with, but you could always see that they were stale."

"I could not, then."

"You could, Sabina. Don't raise frivolous difficulties. Anybody could keep an egg until it was stale."

"Not in this house."

"And why not?"

"Because they'd be ate," said Sabina. "Whatever many eggs the hens might lay they'd be ate by some one before they were a day in the house, and I couldn't keep them. There was a little Plymouth Rock hen that was wanting to sit here last week, and it took me all I could do and more to get the eggs saved up for her, and at the latter end I had only nine."

"Is she sitting yet!"

"She is, of course."

"Then you might try the judge with the eggs that's under her."

"I will not, then. Is it after all the trouble I had with her, and the chickens will be out early next week. I never heard of the like."

"Well," said Meldon, "I'll have to leave the boiled eggs to you, Sabina, but I'll be disappointed in you if the judge eats them. Do you think now that you thoroughly understand what you've got to do?"

"I do. Why wouldn't I?"

"Then I'll say good-bye to you. I'm much obliged to you for the cup of tea. And remember, Sabina, this isn't any kind of a joke. It's serious business, and I mean every word I say. It's most important that the judge should leave Ballymoy as soon as possible."

"Is it persecuting the League boys he's after?" said Sabina. "For there's a cousin of my own that's in with them, and—"

"Brother of the red-haired girl at Mr. Simpkins?"

"He is; and I wouldn't like any harm would come to him."

"You act as I have told you, and no harm will come to him. But if the judge stays on here it's impossible to say what may happen. You know what judges are, Sabina."

"I've heard tell of them, and it's mighty little good is ever said of them or their like."

"Quite so," said Meldon. "So you do your best to get this one out of Ballymoy."

CHAPTER XV

Meldon, although he still kept Doyle's bicycle, did not arrive at Portsmouth Lodge until after eight o'clock. Major Kent had waited dinner for him, and was therefore, as even the best men are under such circumstances, in a very bad temper. When Meldon walked into the study he was sitting with *The Times* spread out on his knee.

"I have had," said Meldon, "a long and particularly exhausting kind of day. I didn't get much lunch with the judge at Donard, and although I had a cup of tea with Sabina Gallagher at the hotel, I had so much to say to her that I didn't eat much. I hope dinner's ready."

"Dinner," growled the Major, "has been ready for more than an hour."

"Good," said Meldon. "I'm certainly ready for it. Come on."

"I wish to goodness," said the Major, rising, "that you'd occasionally try to be in time for a meal."

"There's no use wishing that. I won't. It's a matter of principle with me. I regard punctuality as the vice of little minds. Time is meant to be the servant, not the master of—"

"Don't begin a tirade," said the Major, "but let us get at what's left of our dinner. There won't be much, and what there is will be charred."

"Wait a minute," said Meldon. "I don't deny that I'm hungry and tired, but I'd rather ride all the way back to Donard than sit down at table with you in the temper you're in at present."

"It'll be worse," said the Major, "if I'm kept waiting any longer. And I know what your tirades are. If you start on a vague sort of subject like time you'll be at it for an hour before you've finished."

"Very well," said Meldon. "As a matter of fact, what I wanted to say wouldn't have taken five minutes, and I could have said it while you were ladling out the soup. But if you'd rather gorge down your food like a wild beast in a cavern without the civilising accompaniment of intellectual conversation, you can. I shan't mind. I may perhaps say, however, that everybody doesn't share your tastes. Sir Gilbert Hawkesby welcomed what I had to say about Milton at lunch to-day, and showed that he'd not only read 'Samson Agonistes,' but—"

"The dinner is spoiled, any way," said the Major. "I suppose another hour won't make it any worse. Will you be able to finish that disquisition in an hour, do you think, J. J.?"

"I've finished now; so we can go in to our dinner and eat it. It may be, as you say, spoiled; but it can't be nearly so objectionable as what poor Sir Gilbert Hawkesby is trying to eat at the present moment. That ought to be some consolation to you."

"What's that you're saying about the judge's dinner?"

"Merely that it's in a much worse state than yours. A little too much cooking is all you have to complain of. His dinner is soaked in paraffin oil. But come along, Major; the thought of his sufferings needn't prevent our satisfying our appetites."

"What have you been doing, J. J.? Tell me, like a good fellow. I'd like to know the worst at once."

"Nothing would induce me," said Meldon, "to start another tirade while you're hungry. It wouldn't be fair to you."

"I shan't be able to eat comfortably, J. J., with the thought of what you may have been doing hanging over my head. I shall be imagining all the time that it's something even worse than it really is. What have you done to the judge?"

"A disquisition," said Meldon—"as well as I recollect disquisition was the second word you used—on that subject would certainly last an hour, and by that time your dinner would be almost, if not quite, in as bad a state as the judge's. I'm going into the dining-room. You can stay here if you like, but I advise you to come with me."

The Major rose with a sigh, and followed his guest into the dining-room. The soup was nearly cold. So, when they appeared a little later, were the potatoes and the spinach. The leg of mutton was hot but badly burned. Meldon ate heartily. The Major laid down his knife and fork with a sigh.

"You said you were hungry," said Meldon. "Why don't you eat?"

"My appetite is gone," said the Major. "I'm too nervous about you and that judge to care about food. Besides, look at that"—he prodded a piece of charred mutton with his fork as he spoke—"how can I eat that?"

"You'd like it even less if it tasted of paraffin oil. That's what the judge is having to put up with. I daresay he'd be glad enough to change places with you."

"Tell me what you did, J. J. You must have eaten enough of that mutton now."

"I've had," said Meldon, leaning back in his chair, "a long and exhausting day. It has also been a disappointing day. I haven't accomplished all I hoped."

"You never do."

"On the contrary, I always do—in the end. My first plan for keeping the judge out of Ballymoy failed. I frankly admit that. It failed because the judge turns out to be a pig-headed and obstinate man, who doesn't know what's good for him. I told him distinctly that if he came to Doyle's hotel he'd get typhoid fever and die. O'Donoghue backed me up. But we didn't produce the slightest effect on the judge. His attitude reminded me of that saying of Napoleon's about Englishmen being such fools that they don't know when they are beaten. This wretched judge thinks he can defy disease germs, which of course he can't."

"The fact being," said the Major, "that he recognised at a glance the kind of man you are, and knew that he needn't believe a word you said. I rather respect the judge."

"You like to put it that way," said Meldon; "but as a matter of fact it was I who recognised the sort of man he is. I see now—I saw before I had been a quarter of an hour in his company—that there is absolutely no use making any further appeal to his intellect. If I'd known that he was such a thorough Englishman as he turns out to be, I shouldn't have wasted my time in trying to reason with him. I should have gone straight to the only part of him which an Englishman really dislikes having touched—his stomach."

"Look here, J. J.," said the Major, "I don't mind your scoffing at Englishmen now and then. I know you don't really mean it, but you oughtn't to go too far. Remember I'm an Englishman myself by descent, and I have some feelings. Try not to be offensive. I'm not always saying nasty things about Irishmen to you."

"No," said Meldon; "your insults are more directly personal. A minute ago you called me a liar, which is much worse than anything I said about Englishmen. Besides which it isn't true, whereas what I'm saying about the English is an absolute fact. Take yourself, for example. What was it that upset your temper just now in the study? Was it an overwhelming love for the abstract quality of punctuality? I should have some respect for you if I thought it was, but I can't think that. Nobody who knows you could. You wouldn't care a pin if everybody in the world was late for every engagement they made for a whole year. What you do care about is your own miserable stomach. If it isn't filled at just exactly the usual moment you get savage, although you are usually a fairly good-tempered man. That demonstrates the truth of what I say. And if it's truth about you after all the years you've lived in this country, it is, of course, much more true about this judge. Therefore, to get back to what I was saying a minute ago—having failed in my appeal to his intellect—I fall back upon the one vulnerable part of him and try if I can influence him through that."

"Do tell me what you've done, J. J."

"I've told Sabina Gallagher—"

"Who is Sabina Gallagher?"

"She's Doyle's cook. She is, in the opinion of the judge, quite the most important person in the whole of Ballymoy."

"I don't expect he really thinks that," said the Major, "after seeing you. But what did you tell Sabina?"

"I told her that everything he got to eat was to taste of paraffin oil. That, I think, ought to drive him out of Ballymoy in twenty-four hours."

"It'll probably drive Sabina out of her job. Doyle will sack her to-morrow morning."

"No, he won't. *His* food won't taste of paraffin."

"In any case she won't do it," said the Major. "No girl would be so wicked."

"The only thing that will defeat her," said Meldon, "will be the case of a boiled egg. I don't myself see how she's to manage a boiled egg. I had to leave that to her own imagination. But she's a smart girl, and she may hit upon some way of doing it. In any case, the judge can hardly live entirely on boiled eggs. Everything else he gets will have more or less paraffin in it, except the butter, and it's to taste of onions. His bed will be damp, too—horribly damp—with Condy's Fluid."

"You'll probably kill the old man," said the Major.

"I don't think so. He'll leave before it comes to that. And in any case, I warned him that he'd endanger his life if he came to Doyle's hotel."

The dinner was, for the most part, difficult to eat; but the Major, who was really an abstemious man, succeeded in satisfying his appetite with biscuits and cheese; a tumbler of whisky and soda and a glass of port further cheered him. His anxiety was allayed, for he did not believe that Doyle's cook would venture to poison a judge, even at the request of Meldon. Therefore he was able to light his pipe in the study with a feeling of satisfaction. He settled down in his accustomed chair, and took up *The Times* again. This time he expected to be able to read it. Before dinner his irritation had prevented him from getting any good even out of the leading articles. Meldon sat down at the writing-table and wrote a letter to his wife, full of good advice about the management of the baby. When he had finished it he roused the Major.

"I told you," he said, "that I'd had a disappointing day. I don't think I mentioned to you that the judge's obstinacy was by no means the worst part of it."

"Oh! So you attacked some one else besides the judge."

"I don't know whether attacking is quite the right word to use. I called in on my way home at the gate lodge of Ballymoy House. That fellow Callaghan lives there, you know."

"Yes. Did you urge him to lie in wait for the judge and shoot at him?"

"No; I didn't. Callaghan has nothing to do with the judge one way or other. He has his own business to attend to. I wanted to hear from him how Simpkins and Miss King have been getting on."

"I may as well tell you," said the Major, "that I don't at all care for this plan of yours of setting servants to spy on people, especially on ladies. It doesn't strike me as honourable, and I wish you'd stop it. What did Callaghan tell you?"

"My dear Major, your scruples are perfectly ridiculous. I'm not asking Callaghan to report to me Miss King's private conversations, or to read her letters, or anything of that sort. I merely want to know whether Simpkins kisses her. There's nothing objectionable about that."

"I should say that supposing Simpkins did, and she let him, which is perfectly absurd, for Miss King isn't that sort at all, and it's grossly insulting to talk of her in that way— Besides, putting her out of the question, no woman that ever lived could bear—"

"Lots of women do. It's far commoner than you think. I should say that hardly a day passes but some woman somewhere lets—"

"Not Simpkins. He's such a horrid cad."

"When they are married she'll have to, though I daresay it will hasten Simpkins' end if he does it too often—always supposing that she agrees with you about him. I don't, as I've said several times. I think he's a decent enough sort of man, though he does show an extraordinary want of enterprise in this business."

"Any way," said the Major, "if anything of the sort happened—which is remotely unlikely—"

"It's absolutely certain," said Meldon, "even before they're married; repeatedly, I should say."

"If it did, there's nothing Miss King would dislike more than having it talked about. I should say that she, or any other woman, would be absolutely furious at the thought of her gardener creeping up behind a tree and spying on what, if it occurs at all, ought to be done in the most confidential way, and then going and reporting to you all—"

"Any how," said Meldon, "it hasn't happened yet, so far as Callaghan knows. That is why I say that my day has been such a bitter disappointment. Callaghan tells me that the miserable beast Simpkins hasn't been near the place, or even seen her, since yesterday, when we had them both out in the *Spindrift*. I can't imagine why he won't make use of his opportunities. I told him distinctly that he couldn't expect her to run after him, however anxious she was to marry him."

"Perhaps he doesn't want to marry her."

"He wants to all right, but he's such a wretchedly inefficient beast that he won't turn to and do it. I've no patience with that sort of dilly-dallying. I shall go down to-morrow and speak to him about it again."

"Take care the judge doesn't catch sight of you."

"I don't mind in the least if he does," said Meldon. "That won't matter. What I have got to take care about is that he doesn't catch sight of either Miss King or Simpkins. I don't know whether you quite realise, Major, that as long as that judge is in Ballymoy we are living on the edge of a volcano. The smallest spark might set the thing off and cause an alarming explosion."

"Do sparks set off volcanoes?"

"That, I suppose, is the kind of remark that you consider clever. As a matter of fact, it is simply an evidence of your mental sluggishness. My thoughts had passed on, by a perfectly natural transition, from volcanoes to powder magazines, which are things that sparks do set off. Any one with even a moderate amount of what I may call mental agility would have followed me without any difficulty, and refrained from asking your very foolish question. But it is difficult to be literal enough to please you. What I ought to have said, what I would have said if I had realised at the moment that I was talking to you, is this. We are living the kind of life comparable to that of the people whose cottages are built round the edge of the crater of an active volcano, liable to erupt at any moment; or, to change the metaphor, our position bears a certain resemblance to that of the careless workman who smokes a pipe on the top of a barrel of blasting powder, and if we're not extremely careful we'll find ourselves scattered about in little bits, like the boy who stood on the burning deck. Have you any fault to find with that way of expressing my thought? or would you like to have it still further amplified?"

"What I suppose you mean," said the Major, "is that this judge of yours may possibly recognise Miss King as Mrs. Lorimer."

"Precisely."

"Well, he won't. So you can make your mind easy about that. And if he did—"

"Have you any reasons to adduce in support of your assertion," said Meldon; "or are you simply contradicting me for the sake of being disagreeable?"

"I have one good reason."

"Then trot it out. I shall be delighted to hear it, if it really is a good reason. Nothing appeals to me more strongly than a convincing argument. But don't waste my time and your own with some foolish theory which wouldn't carry conviction to an audience of politicians at an election meeting."

"Mine is a good reason, the best possible. It is—"

"It must be very good indeed if it is to get over the fact that Mrs. Lorimer's features are burned into that judge's brain, owing to his having been obliged to stare at her for ten whole days."

"It's this," said the Major. "He can't recognise Miss King as Mrs. Lorimer, because she isn't Mrs. Lorimer. I'm convinced of that."

"I'm trying," said Meldon, "to be as patient with you as I can. Many men would throw something heavy at your head for saying that. I don't. In spite of the fact that I spent hours proving to you by absolutely irrefragable evidence that Miss King is Mrs. Lorimer, I am still prepared to listen quietly to what you have to say. What convinces you that Miss King isn't Mrs. Lorimer?"

"The woman herself. I know she isn't a murderess. She can't possibly be, and no amount of evidence will make me think she is."

"You've seen her twice," said Meldon; "once on Sunday afternoon when she had just been to church, and was in a chastened and gentle mood owing to the effect of my sermon on her, when the lethal side of her character was temporarily in abeyance. You couldn't form much of an opinion about her real character at a time like that. The other occasion on which you saw her was when she was sea-sick, and no woman is her true self when she's profoundly humiliated. Yet, on the strength of these two interviews, you are apparently prepared to contradict the result of a careful induction of mine and the lady's own express statement. I don't know how you manage to work yourself into a frame of mind in which that is possible."

"As a matter of fact," said the Major, "I've seen her three times."

"Twice."

"No; three times. The third time—" He paused.

"Well?"

"I spent the afternoon with her to-day," said the Major sheepishly, "while you were at Donard with the judge."

"I don't wonder," said Meldon, "that you're ashamed of yourself. I begin to see now why Simpkins has behaved in the extraordinary way he has. I was inclined to blame him at first. In fact, I'm afraid I said rather hard things about him. I admit now that I was wrong. Simpkins couldn't and wouldn't go near her while you were there. It would have been no use if he had. I must say, Major, you are a most difficult man to work with. Here I've been sacrificing the whole of my short holiday to carrying through a difficult negotiation for your benefit, and all you do is to balk me at every turn, to fling obstacles in my way, to foul every rope I'm trying to get a pull on. How can I marry Simpkins to Miss King if you won't let him go near her?"

"She won't marry him, J. J.; so you may put the idea out of your head once for all. She doesn't like him."

"I suppose," said Meldon, "that you spent the afternoon crabbing him; saying all the evil you could think of about him. But you've wasted your time. Miss King's views of marriage are entirely unconventional. She doesn't marry her husbands with the intention of living with them. The less she likes a man the more willing she is to marry him, because she'll feel less compunction afterwards if she thoroughly detests her husband to start with."

"She won't marry Simpkins, any how," said the Major obstinately.

"Did she tell you so?"

"Not in plain words. I gathered that she wouldn't from the way she spoke of him."

"You've gathered, as you call it, so many entirely wrong things from the way Miss King speaks, that you can place absolutely no reliance on this impression of yours. You gathered, for instance, that she isn't Mrs. Lorimer."

"I did."

"And you are wrong about that, so the chances are that you're wrong about this too. I see no reason to alter my opinion that she will marry and afterwards kill Simpkins as soon as ever she gets the chance."

CHAPTER XVI

Major Kent, who was at heart a very kindly man, and had besides a genuine affection for Meldon, repented during the night of his fit of bad temper. He was sorry that he had grumbled about the spoiling of his dinner. While he was shaving in the morning he made up his mind to enter as sympathetically as possible into Meldon's plans, whatever they might be.

"What are you thinking of doing with yourself to-day?" he asked at breakfast. "If you want to go into Ballymoy to rag that judge again I can let you have the cob."

"Thanks," said Meldon, "but I think the judge may be left alone for the present. The wisest line for me to take in this case is to allow the paraffin oil to soak in. I hardly think it will be necessary for me to see him again. He'll probably leave by the mid-day train. The fact is, I'm thinking of taking a half-holiday."

"Do," said the Major. "After what you went through yesterday you must want—"

"No, I don't. And I'm not the kind of man who pretends that he takes holidays because he finds them necessary for his health. I take them simply because I enjoy them."

"We might," said the Major, "have a day in the *Spindrift*."

"I said a half-holiday," said Meldon. "In the afternoon I must go in and explain to Simpkins that you don't really mean anything by your rather pronounced attentions to Miss King."

The Major sighed. He had no doubt that Meldon would do exactly as he said, and he foresaw fresh complications of a most embarrassing kind. Still, a half-holiday was something to be thankful for.

"We might," he said, "have a sail in the morning and come back for lunch."

"No," said Meldon, "we can't do that. There's not a breath of wind. But, without actual sailing, we might spend a pleasant and restful morning on board the yacht."

"Do you mean simply to sit on deck while she's at anchor?"

"I rather contemplated lying down," said Meldon, "with my head on a life-buoy."

"I don't think I'd care for that. It strikes me as rather waste of time."

"It would be for you, Major, and I don't advise you to do it. My time won't be wasted, for I shall use it profitably. I shall take a quantity of tobacco and a tin of biscuits. You can let me have some biscuits, I suppose?"

"Certainly. And you'll find a bottle of beer on board, which Simpkins couldn't drink at luncheon the other day, but I must say that, if that's your idea of a profitable use of your time—"

"It isn't. The tobacco and the biscuits are mere accessories. What I really mean to devote my morning to is meditation. One of the greatest mistakes we make nowadays is not giving sufficient time to quiet thought. We go hustling along through life doing things which ought not to be done in a hurry, and when physical exhaustion forces us to pause for a moment, we run our eyes over printed matter of some kind—newspapers, magazines, or books—and never give a single hour from one year's end to another to meditation."

"What do you intend to meditate about, J. J.? That German philosopher of yours, I suppose."

"I haven't settled that yet," said Meldon. "If there's any affair of yours, either practical, or an intellectual difficulty, which you want to have carefully thought out, now is your time. I'll devote myself to it with pleasure."

"Thanks," said the Major, "but there isn't."

"Are you quite sure? A chance like this doesn't occur every day."

"Quite sure; thanks."

"In that case I shall first of all meditate on Simpkins, Miss King, and the judge. Say an hour and a half for them. Then I shall consider the subject of my little daughter's education. Now that the various professions are opening their doors to women, it's most important to have a reasoned out scheme of education for a girl, and you can't get at it too soon. These two subjects, I think, will make a tolerably complete programme for the morning. If you ring a bell outside the door at one o'clock, I shall row in to luncheon. I shall be pretty hungry by that time, I expect, in spite of the biscuits."

Meldon carried out his plan successfully for the first part of the morning. He arranged the biscuits, his tobacco pouch, and a box of matches in convenient places; laid down a life-buoy as a pillow, and stretched himself at full length on the deck. After a time he shut his eyes, so that no insistent vision of the *Spindrift's* rigging should interrupt the working of his thought. At half-past eleven he was hailed from the shore. He raised himself slightly, and, leaning on his elbow, looked over the gunwale of the yacht. Major Kent stood on the beach.

"Anything wrong?" shouted Meldon.

"No. Nothing, except that Doyle is up at the house wanting to see you, and he seems to be in an uncommonly bad temper."

"I'm not going to drag myself all the way up to the house to gratify some whim of Doyle's. If he thinks he has a grievance, let him come down to the shore and I'll pacify him."

"Very well," said the Major. "I'll bring him. You row ashore and be ready when he comes."

"I shall do nothing of the sort. I can shout at him from here. He can't possibly have any business of a confidential kind. He merely wants to be soothed down about some trifle, and that can be done just as well from a distance."

A quarter of an hour later Major Kent hailed Meldon again; this time he had Doyle with him on the shore. Meldon sat up on his life-buoy, and leaned both elbows on the boom.

"That's right, Major," he shouted. "You've brought him down. Just stay where you are. I won't keep you long. Now then, Doyle! I understand that you are in an abominably bad temper about something, and have come down here with the intention of working it off on me. I may tell you that I don't at all care for being interrupted while I'm meditating; and as a general rule I simply refuse to do any business until I've finished. However, as you're an old friend, I'm making an exception in your case. Can you hear what I say?"

"I cannot," shouted Doyle, "nor nobody could."

"You can," said Meldon. "If you couldn't, how did you answer me?"

"We can't," said the Major, shaking his head vigorously.

Meldon pulled the punt alongside the yacht, got into her and rowed towards the shore. When he was within about ten yards of it, he swung the punt round and rested on his oars facing Doyle and Major Kent.

"Now," he said, "trot out your grievance; but speak briefly and to the point. I can't and won't have my morning wasted. If you meander in your statements, I shall simply row back again to the yacht and leave you there."

"It's a curious thing," said Doyle, "that a gentleman like you would find a pleasure in preventing a poor man from earning his living."

He spoke truculently. He was evidently very angry indeed.

"Don't," said Meldon, "wander off into generalities and silly speculations about things which aren't facts. So far from taking a pleasure in preventing poor men from living, I'm always particularly anxious to help them when I can."

"You didn't help me then with your damned tricks, the like of which no gentleman ought to play."

"If you refer to yourself as a poor man," said Meldon, "you're simply telling a lie. You're rich, nobody knows how rich, but rich enough to buy up every other man in the town of Ballymoy."

"And if I was itself, is that any reason why them that would be staying in my hotel should be hunted out of it?"

"Are you talking about Sir Gilbert Hawkesby?"

"I am," said Doyle. "Who else would I have in my mind?"

"And is he gone?"

"He is not gone yet? but he's going without something would be done to stop him."

"I'm glad to hear it. I hardly hoped it would have happened so soon. I told you, Major, that I was appealing to him in the right way."

"It's a loss of three pounds a week to me," said Doyle, "without reckoning what he might take to drink. I'll be expecting you to make that good to me—you and the Major between you."

"It was the cooking did it, I suppose," said Meldon.

"That and the state his bed was in," said Doyle. "It was close on eleven o'clock last night, and I was sitting smoking quiet and easy along with the doctor, when there came a noise like as if some one would be ringing a bell, and him in a hurry. It was the doctor drew my attention to it first; but I told him he'd better sit where he was, for it was Sabina's business to go up to any one that would ring a bell. Well, the ringing went on terrible strong, for maybe ten minutes, and—"

"Sabina funked it, I suppose," said Meldon.

"She did be in dread," said Doyle, "on account of the way the bell was going, not knowing what there might be at the other end of it. That's what she said any way, and I believe her. The doctor spoke to her, encouraging her, the way she'd go and see whatever it might be, and we'd be at peace again. But for all he said to her she wouldn't move an inch. Then I told the doctor that maybe he'd better go himself, for it could be that the gentleman was ill. 'It's hardly ever,' I said, 'that a man would ring a bell the way that one's being rung without there'd be some kind of a sickness on him. It'll be a pound into your pocket, doctor, and maybe more,' I said, 'if you get at him at once before the pain leaves him.'"

"I should think O'Donoghue jumped at that," said Meldon.

"He did not then, but he sat there looking kind of frightened, the same as Sabina did; like as if there might be something that the judge would want to be blaming on him. At the latter end I had to go myself. It was in his bedroom he was, and devil such a state ever you saw as he had the place in. The sheets and the blankets was off the bed, scattered here and there about the floor, and the pillow along with them. It was like as if they'd been holding a meeting about the land, and the police were after interfering with it, such a scatteration as there was. I hadn't the door hardly opened before he was at me. 'You detestable villain,' says he, 'what do you mean by asking me to sleep in a bed like that? Isn't it enough for you to have me near poisoned with paraffin oil without—' 'If there's hell raised on the bed,' said I, 'and I don't deny but there is, it's yourself riz it. The bed was nice enough before you started on it. I had the sheets damped with the stuff the doctor give me—'"

"Did you say that?" asked Meldon, pushing the punt a little nearer to the shore.

"I did, and if he was mad before he was madder after. I offered to fetch the doctor up to him, but he wouldn't listen to a word I said. It was twelve o'clock and more before I got him quietened down, and I wouldn't say he was what you'd call properly pacified then. He was growling like a dog would when I left him, and saying he'd have it out with me in the morning."

"I daresay," said Meldon, "he was worse after he got his breakfast."

"He was," said Doyle. "It was Sabina he got a hold of then; for, thanks be to God, I was out in the yard seeing after the car that was to drive him up to the liver. He went down into the kitchen after Sabina, and he asked her what the devil she meant by upsetting one lamp over his dinner and another over his breakfast. Sabina up and told him straight to his face that it was you done it."

"What a liar that girl is!" said Meldon.

"J. J." said the Major, "did you do it?"

"No. I didn't. How could I possibly have been upsetting lamps in Doyle's hotel when I was sitting in your house talking to you? Don't lose your head, Major."

"Sabina told me after," said Doyle, "that it was by your orders she did it."

"That's more like the truth," said Meldon. "If she'd confined herself to that statement when she was talking to the judge, I shouldn't have complained. I didn't exactly tell her that she was to upset the lamp, but I did say that she was to flavour everything the judge got to eat with paraffin oil."

"It's a queer thing that you'd do the like," said Doyle, "knowing well all the time that no man would stay where he couldn't get a bite to eat, and that I'd be losing three pounds a week by his going."

"If you understood the circumstances thoroughly," said Meldon, "you would joyfully sacrifice not only three pounds, but if necessary thirty pounds, a week to get rid of that judge."

"I would not," said Doyle confidently. "I wouldn't turn away any man that was paying me, not if he was down here with orders from the Government to put me in jail on account of some meeting that the League would be having."

"Do you or do you not," said Meldon, "want to get rid of Simpkins?"

"I do, of course. Sure, everybody does."

"Very well. In order to secure the death of Simpkins it was necessary to hunt away that judge. I can't explain the whole ins-and-outs of the business to you. It's rather complicated, and I doubt if you'd understand it. In any case, I can't go into it without betraying a lady's confidence, and that's a thing I never do. But you may take my word for it that it's absolutely necessary to remove the judge if you are to have the pleasure of burying Simpkins. If you don't believe what I say ask the Major. He knows all about it."

"No; I don't," said Major Kent.

"You do," said Meldon. "What's the use of denying it when I told you the whole plan myself?"

"Any way," said the Major, "I won't be dragged into it. I've nothing whatever to do with it, and I've always disapproved of it from the start. You and Doyle must settle it between you without appealing to me."

"You can see from the way he speaks," said Meldon to Doyle, "that he knows just as well as I do that we must get the judge out of Ballymoy."

"Out of Ballymoy?" said Doyle.

"Yes," said Meldon, "clear away from the place altogether. Back to England if possible."

"Well, then, he's not gone," said Doyle. "So if it's that you want you're as badly off this minute as I am myself. He's not gone, and what's more he won't go."

"You told me this minute that he was gone. What on earth do you mean by coming up here and pouring out lamentations in gallons about the loss of your three pounds a week if he hasn't gone? What do you mean by representing to me that the judge used bad language about his food if he didn't? I don't see what you're at, Doyle; and, to be quite candid, I don't think you know yourself. Go home and think the whole business over, and I'll see you about it in the afternoon."

"Every word I told you is the truth."

"Either the judge is gone," said Meldon, "or he isn't gone. What do you mean?"

"What I said was, that he isn't gone yet but he's going, without something's done to stop him."

"That's the same thing," said Meldon, "for nothing will be done."

"But he'll not go from Ballymoy? Why would he when he has the fishing took?"

"He'll have to go out of Ballymoy if he leaves your hotel. He may think he'll get lodgings somewhere else, but he won't. Or he may expect to find some other hotel, but there isn't one. If he has left you it's the same thing as leaving Ballymoy."

"It is not," said Doyle, "and I'll tell you why it's not."

"Has he a tent with him?" said Meldon. "He doesn't look like a man who would care for camping out, but of course he might try it."

"He has no tent that I seen," said Doyle. "But I'll tell you what happened. As soon as ever he'd finished cursing Sabina he said the car was to come round, because he was going off out. Well, it came; for I was in the yard myself, as I told you this minute, and I seen to it that it came round in double quick time, hoping that maybe I'd pacify him that way."

"With my cushions on it?" said the Major.

"He took no notice of the cushions. In the temper he was in at the time he wouldn't have said a civil word if you'd set him down on cushions stuffed full of golden sovereigns. He just took a lep on to the car—I was watching him from round the corner of the yard gate to see how he would conduct himself—and—"

"Wait a minute," said Meldon. "Had he his luggage with him?"

"He had not."

"Well then he can't have been going to the train."

"He was not. But—"

"Had he his rod?"

"He had not. But—"

"He'd hardly have gone fishing without his rod, however bad his temper was. I wonder now where on earth he did go."

"It's what I'm trying to tell you," said Doyle, "if you'd let me speak."

"If you know where he went," said Meldon, "say so at once. What's the use of leaving me to waste time and energy trying to discover by inductive reasoning a thing that you know perfectly well all the time?"

"It's what I'm trying to do is to tell you."

"Stop trying then," said Meldon, "and do it."

"He took a lep on the car," said Doyle, "the same as it might be a man that was in a mighty hurry to be off, and says he to the driver, 'Is there a place here called Ballymoy House?' 'There is, of course,' said Patsy Flaherty, for it was him that was driving the car."

"Ballymoy House!" said Meldon. "Nonsense. He couldn't have asked for Ballymoy House."

"It's what he said. And what's more: 'Is it there that a young lady stops by the name of Miss King?' said he. 'It is,' said Patsy Flaherty, 'and a fine young lady she is, thanks be to God.' 'Then drive there,' says he, 'as fast as ever you can go, and if you have such a thing as a bottle of paraffin oil in the well of the car,' says he, 'throw it out before you start.' Well, of course, there was no oil in the car. Why would there?"

"If Mr. Meldon had seen Patsy Flaherty last night," said the Major, "there probably would have been."

"Do you mean to say," said Meldon, "that he drove straight off to see Miss King?"

"It's where he told the driver to go, any way," said Doyle, "and it's there he went without he changed his mind on the way. What I was thinking was that maybe he's acquainted with Miss King."

"He is," said Meldon. "I know that. I don't believe that he's ever spoken to her except in public, but he certainly knows who she is."

"What I'm thinking," said Doyle, "is that he intended asking if he might go up to the big house and stay there along with her for such time as he might be in Ballymoy."

"He can't have done that," said Meldon. "There are reasons which the Major understands, though you don't, which render that idea quite impossible. Speaking on the spur of the moment, and without thinking the matter out thoroughly, I am inclined to suppose that he connects Miss King with the condition of his bed last night and the persistent flavour of paraffin oil in his food. He's probably gone up to speak to her about that."

"He couldn't," said Doyle, "for Sabina Gallagher told him it was you."

"He wouldn't believe Sabina," said Meldon, "and he has every reason to suspect Miss King of wanting to score off him. I think I may tell you, Doyle, without any breach of confidence, that Miss King has a stone up her sleeve to throw at that judge. He tried to do her a bad turn some weeks ago, and she's just the woman to resent it."

"But the young lady was never in the inside of my house, and never set eyes on Sabina. How could it be that she—"

"I know what you're going to say," said Meldon. "She couldn't have had anything to do with the Condy's Fluid or the paraffin oil. That's true, of course. But my point is that the judge, puzzled by an extraordinary combination of circumstances, all tending to make him uncomfortable, would naturally think Miss King was at the bottom of them. The one thing I don't quite understand is how he came to know she was in Ballymoy. I'll find that out later on. In the meanwhile I think I'd better go into Ballymoy after all. It's a nuisance, for I was extremely comfortable on the yacht, but I can't leave things in the muddle they're in now, and there's nobody else about the place I could trust to clear them up."

CHAPTER XVII

"You may as well drive me into Ballymoy, Doyle," said Meldon, as they walked up together from the shore. "You've your trap with you, I suppose?"

"I have, and I'll drive you of course, but I'll be expecting that you'll do something when we get there the way the judge won't be leaving the hotel altogether."

"You may put that out of your head at once," said Meldon, "for I'll do nothing of the sort. I've already explained to you at some length that my chief object at present is to chase away the judge, not only from your hotel but from Ballymoy."

Doyle relapsed into a sulky silence. He did not speak again until he and Meldon were half way into Ballymoy. Then he broke out suddenly.

"Any way," he said, "Sabina Gallagher won't spend another night under my roof. She'll be off back to her mother as soon as ever she can get her clothes packed. I'll give her a lesson that will cure her of playing off tricks on the gentlemen that stops in my hotel."

"If you take that kind of revenge on Sabina," said Meldon, "you will be doing an act of gross injustice for which you will be sorry up to the day of your death."

"I will not, but I'll be serving her out the way she deserves."

"She has been acting all through," said Meldon, "in your interests, though you can't see it; and you'll make a kind of dog Gelert of her if you sack her now. You know all about the dog Gelert, I suppose, Doyle?"

"I do not," said Doyle, "and what's more I don't care if there was fifty dogs in it. Sabina'll go. Dogs! What has dogs got to do with Sabina and myself? It's not dogs I'm thinking of now."

"You evidently don't know anything about the dog I'm speaking of," said Meldon. "He belonged to a Welsh king whose name at this moment I forget. The king also happened to have a baby which slept, as many babies do, in a cradle. You're listening to me, I suppose, Doyle?"

"I am not," said Doyle. "It's little good I, or any other body, would get by listening to you. Sabina Gallagher listened to you, and look at the way she is now. It's my belief that the less anybody listens to you the better off he'll be."

"All the same, I expect you are listening," said Meldon. "In any case, as I'm speaking distinctly, and you can't get away, you're bound to hear, so I'll go on with the story. One day the king came in and found the dog close to the cradle with his mouth all covered with blood. He leaped to the conclusion that he'd eaten the baby."

"He was a damned fool if he thought that," said Doyle. "Who ever heard of a dog eating a baby?"

"You are listening to me," said Meldon. "I thought you would when the story began to get interesting. And you're perfectly right. The king was a fool. He was such a fool that he killed the dog. Afterwards it turned out that the dog had really been behaving in the most noble way possible—had, in fact, been fighting a wolf which wanted to eat the baby. Then the king was sorry, frightfully sorry, because he saw that through his own hasty and ill-considered action he had killed his best friend, a friend who all along had been acting in his interests. You see the point of that story, don't you? You'll be exactly in the position of the king, and you'll suffer endless remorse just as he did if you go and sack Sabina."

Doyle meditated on the story. It produced a certain effect on his mind, for he said,—

"If so be it wasn't Sabina that put the paraffin oil into the judge's dinner, but some other one coming in unbeknown to her, and Sabina maybe doing her best to stop it, then of course there wouldn't be another word said about it; though as soon as ever I found out who it was—"

"You mustn't push the parable to those extremes," said Meldon. "No parable would stand it. Sabina did pour in the paraffin oil. I'm not pretending that a wolf or any animal of that sort came in and meddled with the judge's food. I'm merely trying to explain to you that later on, when you understand all the circumstances, you'll find yourself tearing out your hair, and rubbing sack-cloth and ashes into your skin, just as the king did when he realised what he had done in the case of the dog Gelert. As well as I recollect the poor man never got over it."

"Dogs or no dogs," said Doyle, "Sabina Gallagher will have the wages due to her paid, and then off with her out of my house. For conduct the like of hers is what I won't stand, and what nobody in a hotel would stand."

"Very well," said Meldon; "I've told you what the consequences of your action will be. If you choose to face them you can. I've done my best to save you. But you are evidently bent on going your own way. I daresay you may be quite right in supposing that you won't suffer much, even when you find out that you have committed a gross injustice. After all, it requires a man to have some sort of a conscience to suffer in that sort of way, and you apparently have none. But there's another consideration altogether that I'd like to bring under your notice. I've had some talk with Sabina during the last few days, and I've come to the conclusion that she's a young woman with a talent for cooking of a very rare and high kind. There's nothing that girl couldn't do if she got a little encouragement. Give her the smallest hint and she acts on it at once."

"I wish to God then," said Doyle, "that you'd held off from giving her hints, as you call it. Only for you I don't believe she'd ever have thought—"

"I'm not speaking now of the paraffin oil business. You mustn't allow that to become an obsession with you, Doyle. There are other things in the world besides that judge's meals. As it happens, I was giving Sabina a short lecture on the art of cookery some days before I heard of the judge's arrival. I was speaking to her about the advisability of knocking together an occasional omelette for you, or a nice little savoury made of olives and hard-boiled eggs. I found her unusually receptive, and quite prepared to follow up the ideas I put before her. There was just one thing stood in her way—"

"Who'd eat the like of them things?" said Doyle.

"You would," said Meldon, "if you got them. But you won't, not from Sabina Gallagher, because you're determined to sack her. And not from any other cook as long as you pay the perfectly miserable wages you do at present. You can't expect first-rate results when you sweat your employees. That's a well-known maxim in every business, and the sooner you get it into your head the better. You set yourself up here in Ballymoy as a sort of pioneer of every kind of progress. You're the president of as many leagues and things as would sink a large boat. There isn't hardly a week in the year but you make a speech of some sort. Ah! here we are at the hotel. Remind me some time again to finish what I was saying to you. I must find out now what has happened to the judge."

He leaped out of the trap and walked straight through the hotel to the kitchen. He found Sabina there.

"Good morning, Sabina Gallagher," he said. "I hear you did exactly as I told you. You're a good girl, Mr. Doyle is angry just at present, and you'd better keep out of his way."

"He'll hunt me," said Sabina.

"He will not," said Meldon. "If you have the sense to keep out of his way until he has cooled down a bit, and cook him decent dinners in the meanwhile. I've spoken to him very strongly about you, and I don't think he'll dare to push matters to extremities, although he may grumble a bit. If he catches you, and you find his temper particularly bad, just mention the dog Gelert to him. I told him the story this morning and it produced a great impression on his mind."

"He'll hunt me," said Sabina tearfully. "Whatever dog I might talk to him about he'll hunt me."

"If he does," said Meldon, "I'll engage you myself. We'll be wanting a girl as soon as ever we go home, to look after the baby a bit and do the cooking and washing, and keep the whole place clean generally. You'd like to come and live in the house with me, wouldn't you, Sabina?"

"I'm not sure would I."

"You would. There's no doubt about it. But we need not discuss that yet, for I don't expect Mr. Doyle will sack you. What I really want to talk to you about is that judge. Where is the judge?"

"He's gone," said Sabina.

"I know that," said Meldon. "But he'll come back all right. He must come back for his luggage."

"He will not then. It's not an hour ago since Patsy Flaherty, the same that does be driving the car, came in and said he had orders to take all the luggage there was and the fishing-rods, and the rest of whatever there might be in the place belonging to the gentleman."

"He was not taking them to the train, I suppose?"

"He was not then, but up to Ballymoy House."

"Nonsense! He couldn't possibly have been taking them up to Ballymoy House."

"It's what he said any way, for I asked him. And he told me that the gentleman had it made up with the young lady that does be stopping there beyond, the way he'd go and live with her."

"This," said Meldon, "is perfectly monstrous. I must go and see about it at once. He has evidently been bullying that unfortunate Miss King, coercing her with threats until she has agreed to board and lodge him. I can't have that sort of thing going on under my very eyes. You'll excuse me,

Sabina, if I run away from you. It's absolutely necessary that I should go up to Ballymoy House at once. I'll borrow Mr. Doyle's bicycle again."

He went out through the back door into the yard, and found Doyle stabling his pony.

"I suppose," he said, "that I can have your bicycle again. Affairs have taken a turn which I'm bound to say I did not foresee. I have to get at that judge as soon as possible. He seems to have been ill-treating Miss King. I expected that he'd go for her over that paraffin oil affair, but—"

"Amn't I telling you," said Doyle, "that she'd neither act nor part—"

"I know that; but the judge thinks she had, and he's— You'd hardly believe it, Doyle, but he's had the unparalleled insolence to go and quarter himself on her in Ballymoy House."

"It's what I said he'd do," said Doyle, "and I'm not surprised."

"If you understood the peculiar and delicate relations which exist between that judge and Miss King—but of course you don't, and I, unfortunately, can't explain them to you. If you did, you'd see at once that the judge must simply have forced himself on Miss King, using, I have no doubt, the most unchivalrous and despicable threats to achieve his end. Considering that he's getting his board and lodging out of her he might very well be prosecuted for blackmail. Just conceive to yourself, Doyle— But I can't talk about it. Where's the bicycle?"

"You took it out with you to Portsmouth Lodge last night," said Doyle, "and so far as I know you didn't bring it back again. But there's an old one in the stable belonging to Patsy Flaherty, and you can take that if you like."

"It can't be worse than yours," said Meldon, "with that loose pedal. Just you wheel it round to the door for me, and pump up the tyres if they want it. There's something I forgot to ask Sabina. I'll go through the kitchen, and meet you by the time you have the machine ready."

He darted into the kitchen, leaving Doyle to tie up his pony and pump the bicycle.

"Is that you back?" said Sabina. "I thought you were gone. Didn't you tell me there was a hurry on you?"

"I'm just going," said Meldon; "but before I start I want to ask you how you managed the boiled egg. I suppose the judge had a boiled egg for breakfast. Did you put paraffin into it?"

"I did."

"How? I'm most anxious to know how it was done."

"It's what the gentleman asked me himself," said Sabina, "and I told him the truth."

"Then tell it to me."

"I'm not sure will I. The gentleman was terrible upset when he heard it, worse than you'd think; for he had the egg ate."

"There can't have been much paraffin in it, then."

"There was not; but there was some."

"And how did you get it there?"

"It was with a hairpin I did it."

"Do you mean to say that you took a hairpin out of your head, and—"

"I did, of course. Where else would I get one?"

"And dipped it in paraffin, and then stuck it through the egg. I declare I could find it in my heart to be sorry for that judge. Only that he deserves all that he's got on account of the way he has behaved to Miss King, I'd go and apologise to him. You're a smart girl, Sabina. I always said you were, and now you've proved that I was perfectly right in my estimate of your abilities. Good-bye again. This time I really must be off."

He seized Sabina's hand, and greatly to her surprise shook it heartily. Then he left the kitchen and slammed the door behind him. Doyle was waiting for him with Patsy Flaherty's bicycle. Meldon jumped on it and rode off, ringing his bell as he went along the street. Doyle watched him disappear, and then turned and walked into the kitchen. Sabina, forgetful of his wrath and her own threatened fate, broke out when she saw him.

"Well now, did any one ever see the like? Many's the queer one I've come across since I entered this house, but never the equal of him for goings on. Anybody would think he was—"

"It's not drink," said Doyle. "Nobody ever saw the sign of it on him."

He was angry, angry with Sabina Gallagher, and perhaps more angry with Meldon; but he had a sense of justice, and was loyal to the man who had once been his friend. He thought that Sabina was going to make an accusation which might be natural enough, but was certainly false. As a matter of fact, she had not meant to say anything of the sort, and disclaimed the suggestion hotly.

"I wasn't saying it was drink. I know well it couldn't be, for he's a simple, innocent kind of gentleman that wouldn't do the like. But I'd say he was one that liked a bit of sport, and didn't care what foolishness he might be after so long as he got it."

She smiled amiably at Doyle, as she spoke; but he was not a man to be diverted from his purpose by smiles, or lulled into forgetfulness by the charm of general conversation.

"You'll go upstairs this minute, Sabina Gallagher," he said, "and you'll pack up whatever clothes you have—and that's not many—and as soon as you have that done you'll go off home, for I'll not have you in this house another night."

"I was thinking," said Sabina, "that you'd likely be saying that."

"I'd say more," said Doyle, "only if I did I might say what I'd be sorry for after."

"You might surely."

"Though I wouldn't say more than you deserve whatever I said. What in the name of all that's holy did you mean by poisoning the gentleman that came here to stop in the hotel, and would have paid me three pounds a week and maybe more?

"It was Mr. Meldon told me," said Sabina, "and how was I to know but you sent a message to me by him, the way I'd be doing what it was you wanted done?"

"Is it likely I'd send him to you on a message? Oughtn't you to have more sense than to think I'd trust that one with a message? And wouldn't anybody that wasn't a born fool know that I didn't want the lamp upset over the dinner?"

"It was you told me to put the stuff the doctor was after giving you on the sheets of the gentleman's bed, and after the like of that was done on him, it wouldn't make much matter what other devilment he'd have to put up with. Sure there's nothing in the world worse on a man than a damp bed, and me after airing them sheets at the kitchen fire for the best part of the morning, so as no one would have it to say that they wasn't dry. If you didn't want him hunted out of the house, why did you bid me do that?"

Doyle felt the force of the argument; felt it more acutely than Sabina could guess. He himself, at the bidding of Meldon, had done much to make an honoured and profitable guest uncomfortable. Could he fairly blame Sabina for acting in a similar way with precisely the same excuse? He felt the necessity for speaking very sternly.

"Will you get out of this?" he said, "for I'm in dread but I might raise my hand to you if you stand there talking to me any more. You'd provoke the patience of a saint; but I wouldn't like to have it cast up to me after that ever I struck you."

"I'm going. You needn't think I'm wanting to stay. There's plenty will be glad to get me, and pay me more wages than ever you done."

Doyle recognised the truth of this. He had got Sabina cheap—cheap even by the standard of wages which prevails in Connacht. He felt half inclined to reconsider his determination. The judge was gone. The dismissal of Sabina, though a pleasant and satisfying form of vengeance, would not bring the lost three pounds back again; while there might be a good deal of trouble in getting another cook.

"Before I go," said Sabina, who did not want to go, and was watching Doyle's face for signs of relenting, "before I go I've a message to give you from Mr. Meldon."

"I seen him myself this morning," said Doyle, "and I don't know what there could be in the way of a message for me that he wouldn't have told me himself."

"What he bid me tell you was this—" Sabina paused. "Well now," she said, "if I haven't gone and forgot the name of the dog!"

"Was it a dog that a king killed one time," said Doyle, "on account of his thinking it had his baby ate?"

"It might," said Sabina. "It was a queer name he had on it, and I disremember what it was."

"I disremember it myself," said Doyle, "but it was likely the same dog as he was telling me about when I was driving him in. He always did have a liking for dogs, that same Meldon."

"It might be that one or it might be another. Any way, he thought a deal of it, for he said to me no later than this minute that if I mentioned the name of it to you, you wouldn't hunt me."

"Listen to me now, Sabina Gallagher. I'll let you stay on here, though it's a deal more than you deserve—I'll let you stay on and do the cooking the same as you used to, on account of the respect I have for your mother, who is a decent woman, and your father that's dead—I'll let you stay on if you'll tell me this: What had the dog to do one way or the other with the paraffin oil you put on the judge's dinner?"

"I never seen the dog; and I don't know that I ever heard tell of any dog doing the like."

"Then what are you talking to me about the dog for if it didn't do something, be the same less or more, in the way of helping you to destroy the judge's dinner?"

"It was Mr. Meldon told me to mention the name of the dog to you. And I would, I'd do it this minute, only I disremember it."

"Will you ask him the next time he's here, and tell me after, what it was the dog had to do with the matter?"

"I will, of course, if it's pleasing to you."

"Then you may stay on a bit yet, Sabina. You may stay on till you learn enough about cooking to be able to better yourself; and it's what you should be able to do soon with the opportunities that you have in this house. But I'd like if you could find out about the dog, for Mr. Meldon was saying a lot about him this morning, and I'd be thankful if I knew what sort of a dog he was."

CHAPTER XVIII

Meldon rode rapidly westwards out of the town, in the direction of Ballymoy House. He swept round the sharp corner and through the entrance gate at high speed, leaning over sideways at so impressive an angle that the six Callaghan children, who were standing in the porch of the gate lodge, cheered enthusiastically. He disappeared from their view before their shouts subsided, and rushed up the avenue. He reached the gravel sweep in front of the house, pressed on both brakes with all his force, brought the bicycle to an abrupt standstill, and dismounted amid a whirling cloud of dust and small stones. He rang the door bell furiously. Finding that the door was not immediately opened he rang again, and then a third time, leaving less than half a minute between the peals. Then a maid, breathless, and in a very bad temper, opened the door and asked him what he wanted.

"I must see Miss King at once," said Meldon, "on most important business."

"Miss King is out, sir," said the maid.

"Where is she? When did she go out? When will she be home?"

The servant could have answered two of the three questions without difficulty. She knew when Miss King went out. She also knew where she had gone to. She could have guessed at the hour of her return; but seeing that Meldon appeared to be in a hurry she took her revenge for the violent ringing of the bell which had disturbed her.

"I'll go and enquire, sir," she said.

She spent nearly ten minutes making enquiries. Then she returned with the information that Miss King had gone out immediately after luncheon. She had accompanied Sir Gilbert Hawkesby to the river where he intended to fish.

"She's gone with Sir Gilbert Hawkesby!" said Meldon.

"Yes, sir."

Meldon turned away and walked slowly down the avenue. When he reached the tennis court he propped his bicycle up against a tree and took out his pipe. Miss King's brilliant hammock was still hanging between the two trees to which Callaghan had attached it on the morning after her arrival. Meldon lit his pipe and lay down in the hammock. He was puzzled. Miss King's conduct was unaccountable. The judge's was strange. But Meldon held a belief that there is no problem so difficult but will yield its solution to patient thought and tobacco. He drew in and expelled rich clouds of smoke; and set himself to think hard. The judge had recognised the impossibility of living in Doyle's hotel. That was a plain and intelligible point from which to start. He had gone straight to Ballymoy House, knowing that he would find Miss King there. It was difficult to guess where he got his information; but mere speculation on points of that kind was obviously useless. The judge did know, and had made up his mind to settle down in Ballymoy as Miss King's guest. Miss King had apparently received him; had even gone out fishing with him. Meldon could find no explanation of the facts except one, and it was extremely unsatisfactory. The judge must have imposed himself on Miss King, and induced her to receive him by means of threats. Such things have, no doubt, been done occasionally; though rarely by judges. People, especially women with doubtful pasts, are always open to threats of exposure, and may be induced to submit to blackmail. Sir Gilbert Hawkesby was evidently—Meldon had ample evidence of this—determined to fish. He was, according to Doyle and Sabina Gallagher, in a bad temper, and therefore, for the time, unscrupulous. He had spent a most uncomfortable night. He was also extremely hungry. It was just possible that he had forced himself upon Miss King. Meldon sighed. This adjustment of the facts was not satisfactory, but there was no other. He knocked the ashes out of his pipe and stood up. Then he became aware that Callaghan was watching him from the far end of the lawn. Meldon walked over to him.

"If it's news about Mr. Simpkins you want," said Callaghan, "there's none, for he hasn't been near the place since the last day I was talking to you."

"For the immediate present," said Meldon, "I'm not so much interested in Mr. Simpkins as in another gentleman that came here to-day."

"Is it him they call Sir Gilbert Hawkesby?"

"It is," said Meldon, "that very man. Did you see him?"

"I did. It was half past ten o'clock, or maybe a little later, and the young lady was just after coming out with a terrible big lot of papers along with her. She sat herself down there in the little bed where you were lying this minute, and 'Good morning to you, Callaghan,' she says when she saw me."

"What were you doing there?" said Meldon.

"I was looking at her. Wasn't that what you told me to do? I was watching out the same as I've been doing this last week, the way Simpkins wouldn't come on her unawares, and me maybe somewhere else and not seeing him."

"All right," said Meldon. "I haven't the least doubt that's exactly what you were doing. I put the wrong question to you. What I ought to have asked you was this: What did Miss King think you were doing? What were you pretending to do?"

"I was making as if I was scuffling the walk with a hoe, and the Lord knows it wants scuffling, for the way the weeds grow on it is what you'd hardly believe."

"Well, and after she said good morning to you what happened?"

"There wasn't anything happened then," said Callaghan, "unless it would be some talk there was between us about the weather, me saying it was seasonable for the time of year, and—"

"You needn't go into details about the weather," said Meldon. "I suppose, sooner or later, something else happened?"

"There did then."

"And what was it?"

"There came a car up along the avenue with a gentleman on it, and it was Patsy Flaherty that was driving it; and him lacing the old mare with the whip the same as if the gentleman might be in a hurry."

"He was in a hurry," said Meldon. "As a matter of fact, he hadn't had a bite to eat since the middle of the day yesterday, and not much then. Any man would be in a hurry if he was as hungry as that judge."

"That may be. Any way, whatever the reason of it was, he had Patsy Flaherty leathering the mare like the devil. Then, as soon as ever Miss King set eyes on him, she was up out of the little bed where she was, and the papers threw down on the ground, and her running as fast as ever she could leg it across the grass."

"Poor thing!" said Meldon. "It must have been a shock to her to catch sight of him like that. Where did she run to?"

"To meet him, of course," said Callaghan.

"To meet him! Be careful what you're saying now, Callaghan. It's more likely she ran the other way."

"Amn't I telling you it was to meet him? And, what's more, you'd say by the way she was running that she was thinking it a long time till she got to him."

"You're mistaken about that," said Meldon. "Unless she completely lost her head through sheer nervousness; it must have been away from him she ran."

"It was not, but to him. And then as soon as ever he seen her coming he put out his hand, and gripped a hold of Patsy Flaherty by the arm, and 'Stop, ye divil,' says he. 'Haven't ye had enough of battering that old screw for one day?' says he, 'and don't you see the young lady that's coming across the lawn there and her lepping like a two-year-old, so as the sight of her would make you supple and you crippled with the rheumatics?'"

"I know now," said Meldon, "that you're telling me a pack of lies from start to finish. There's not a judge in the world would say the words you're putting into that one's mouth. It isn't the way judges talk, nor the least like it. You oughtn't to try and invent things, Callaghan. You can't do it. You haven't got any faculty for dramatic probability in characterisation. That story of yours wouldn't go down with Major Kent, and what's the good of your offering it to me? You may not know it, Callaghan, but I'm something of an expert in textual criticism. I can separate up the Book of Genesis into its component documents as well as any man living, and I'm quite capable of telling by internal evidence, that is to say by considerations of style and matter, whether any particular verse is written by the same man that wrote the verse before. Now in both respects, matter and style, I recognise in your story the strongest possible evidence of fabrication. Any literary critic who knew his business would agree with me. In the first place, Miss King wouldn't have run to meet that judge. She'd have run away from him if she ran at all."

"It was to him she did run," said Callaghan, "and what's more—"

"In the second place," said Meldon, "the judge wouldn't have spoken that way to Patsy Flaherty. If he'd wanted to have the car stopped he'd have said, 'Pull up for a minute, my good man,' or words to that effect."

"Well," said Callaghan, "it might have been that he said. How was I to hear what passed between them when I was half ways across the lawn at the time scuffling the path with my hoe?"

"And if you couldn't hear," said Meldon, "what on earth do you mean by pretending to repeat to me the exact words the judge used?"

"I told you the best I could. If them wasn't the words he said he looked mighty like as if they were. Any way Patsy Flaherty gave over lambasting the old mare, and she stood still, the way you'd think she was glad of the rest. Then the gentleman took a lep down off the car, and away with him to meet the lady."

"Well?"

"She was mighty glad to see him," said Callaghan, "for she kissed him twice."

"Nonsense," said Meldon, "she couldn't possibly have kissed him. And, listen to me now, Callaghan. You set up to be mighty particular about moral conduct, and the day I first talked to you about Miss King you said a lot about disliking any kind of impropriety. But you don't hesitate to tell me a grossly scandalous story about a lady who never did you any harm. I don't think you ought to do it."

"There was no impropriety of conduct about it."

"There was. How can you possibly say there wasn't? What could be more improper, judged by any conceivable standard of conduct, than for a young lady to go rushing and tearing across a lawn—and I declare I don't like to repeat the thing you said."

"There was no impropriety of conduct," said Callaghan, "because the gentleman was her uncle."

"Do you mean to tell me," said Meldon, "that Sir Gilbert Hawkesby is Miss King's uncle?"

"He is. I might have guessed it when I saw her kissing him. And I partly did guess there must be something of the sort in it; for I have a respect for Miss King, and I know well that she's not the sort that would do the like of that without the gentleman would be a near friend of her own. But the way I'd make sure I went and asked the young lady within in the kitchen."

"Do you mean the cook?"

"I do," said Callaghan. "It might have been an hour after or maybe more when I was taking in a dish of peas for the dinner. 'Miss Hodge,' says I, speaking respectful—for the girls that does be in it thinks a lot of themselves on account of their coming over here all the way from London—'Miss Hodge,' says I, 'that's a mighty fine gentleman that's come to see the mistress to-day.' 'The devil a much credit it is to you to find that out,' says she, 'for—'"

"She didn't," said Meldon. "Nobody of the name of Hodge who came from London would or could say 'the devil a much credit' under any circumstances."

"It's what she meant," said Callaghan, "and what's more, she told me about his being a high-up gentleman, and a judge, no less. 'Do you tell me that now?' says I. 'I'm glad of it, for, if you believe me, it's the first time ever I set eyes on one of them.' 'You'll see plenty of him,' says she, 'for he'll be stopping here along with Miss King till he's done fishing.' 'Will he then? And what could he be doing that for?' 'It's on account of the way them murdering villains down in the hotel—'"

"I wish," said Meldon, "that you wouldn't try to repeat the cook's exact words. You're getting them wrong every time and making it more and more difficult for me to believe your story."

"It's the truth I'm telling you whether or no," said Callaghan, "and what she said was that he was coming up here to stay on account of the way they had him poisoned down in the hotel, which is what I was sorry to hear her say, for Sabina Gallagher's a friend of my own, her sister being married to my wife's cousin, and I wouldn't like to hear of the girl getting a bad name. Any way, 'it's that way it is,' said Miss Hodge, 'and where would he come to if it wasn't—?'"

"You're at it again," said Meldon. "Why can't you tell what you have to tell without spoiling what might be a good story by insisting on making the cook talk in that unnatural way?"

"What she said was," said Callaghan, "that it was no more than right and proper that he'd come to the house of his own niece."

"You're absolutely certain she said that?"

"I am; for it wasn't once nor twice she said it, but more; like as if she was proud of being along with a lady that was niece to a judge."

"If the facts are as you state them," said Meldon, "a good many things become clear to me, and the general situation is by no means so desperate as I was inclined to think."

"Would you say now, your reverence," said Callaghan, "that it's true what she was after telling me about Sabina doing the best she could to poison the judge with paraffin oil?"

"There's a foundation of truth in the statement," said Meldon, "but it has been very much exaggerated."

"It's what I didn't think Sabina would do, for she was always a quiet, decent girl, with no harm in her."

"Don't run away with the idea that Sabina has done anything wrong," said Meldon, "for she hasn't. I can't stop here to explain the whole circumstances to you, for I have other things to do, and in any case you wouldn't be able to understand. But I would like to fix this fact firmly in your mind: Sabina is in no way to blame."

"Is there any fear now," said Callaghan, "that she might be took by the police?"

"Not the slightest."

"Him being a judge and all?"

"That doesn't make the least difference. If Sabina had poisoned anybody—she hasn't, but if she had—or even if she'd tried to, she'd be had up for it whether her victim was a judge or a corner boy. It's worse, I believe, if you poison the king; but short of that it's the same thing exactly. The law doesn't set a bit more value on a judge's life than on any one else's, and Sir Gilbert Hawkesby would be the first man to tell you that. You can ask him if you like. But the point isn't really of any importance, because, as I said before, Sabina has neither poisoned nor tried to poison anybody. She has simply done her duty."

CHAPTER XIX

"On the whole," said Meldon, "things are turning out better than I expected. They developed in a way that at first a little surprised me. In fact, for an hour or two I was rattled, and hardly knew what to say or do; but on thinking the whole affair over quietly, after an interview I had with Callaghan, I have every reason to feel fairly well satisfied."

He and Major Kent sat together at afternoon tea on the verandah of Portsmouth Lodge. The Major was evidently nervous and uncomfortable. The teaspoon tinkled in the saucer as he handed a cup to his friend, and he forgot to help himself to a lump of sugar.

"I took Doyle quite the right way," said Meldon, "and I don't think he'll sack Sabina. I should have been sorry if Sabina had got into serious trouble—"

"What about the judge?" said the Major.

"I'm talking about Sabina Gallagher at present, I'll come to the judge later on. As a matter of fact he's perfectly well able to look after himself. Sabina isn't, and it is my practice—it ought to be yours, Major, but of course it isn't—it is my practice to look after the poor and helpless, especially when they happen to be women, before I do anything for those who are rich and powerful. You, I regret to say, go upon a different plan. Because Sabina happens to be a friendless servant, with no one to take her part, you don't care a pin what happens to her. You are interested only in this judge, who is well off and has the whole force of the British constitution at his back if any one attempts to do him any harm."

The Major accepted the rebuke meekly.

"I only meant," he said, "that I'd like to hear about the judge now I know that Sabina is all right. And after all, J. J., the British constitution isn't much use to a man when you are set on ragging him."

"Of course not," said Meldon. "In fact, the British constitution is a greatly over-rated thing. It didn't save poor Lorimer from his untimely end. It wouldn't save this judge if I had determined to make him miserable. It won't save Simpkins when his time comes. However, as things turn out, I don't want to harry the judge. There's no particular point in it. I don't much mind now even if he goes back to Doyle's hotel."

"He really left then?"

"Yes. Doyle was rather upset about it. It's a serious loss to him, and I'm sorry it occurred, for it turns out now that it was quite unnecessary. I couldn't possibly be expected to guess; but, as a matter of fact, I needn't have worried about that judge at all. He won't do us any harm. In fact, I expect he'll turn out to be a most valuable ally. I shall see him to-morrow and try to enlist his sympathies for our Simpkins plot. I expect he'll simply jump at it."

"I thought you said he'd gone."

"He has gone from the hotel, but not from Ballymoy. He's at present staying with his niece."

"I didn't know he had a niece."

"Miss King, or, to be quite accurate, Mrs. Lorimer, is his niece, and he's staying with her."

Major Kent started and laid down his teacup. Then a look of relief came into his face, and he smiled.

"You'll give up that absurd theory of yours now, I suppose," he said, "and admit that Miss King isn't a murderess. I always knew she wasn't, though I couldn't convince you."

"I don't see," said Meldon, "that anything has happened to invalidate the evidence on which we originally concluded that Miss King is Mrs. Lorimer."

"Don't be an ass, J. J. You say she's the judge's niece; so of course she can't—"

"You apparently think," said Meldon, "that a judge's niece, merely because her uncle happens to occupy a position of legal eminence, couldn't possibly commit a crime. You're entirely wrong. Some of the greatest women criminals the world has ever seen have been the nieces of men of high position. Look at Lucrezia Borgia, for instance. Her uncle was a Pope; and whatever our religious opinions may be we must admit that a Pope is a bigger man than an ordinary judge, and yet Lucrezia is famous for some of the most remarkable crimes in all history. I could quote other instances, but that one ought to be sufficient to convince you that relationship to a judge is no safeguard—"

"That wasn't what I meant, J. J. You say that this judge tried Mrs. Lorimer. Now if—"

"Do you mean to suggest," said Meldon, "that a judge wouldn't try his own niece for murder?"

"Of course he wouldn't. How could he?"

"You're entirely wrong," said Meldon. "As a matter of fact any right-minded and really upright judge, such as we have every reason to suppose this Sir Gilbert Hawkesby is, would take a special pride in trying his own niece. He'd like to hang her if he could, always supposing that he felt sure that she was guilty. If there's one thing judges are more determined about than another it's their independence of all considerations of private friendship in the discharge of their duties. There are several recorded instances of judges hanging their own sons. The expression, 'A Roman father,' arises, as well as I recollect, from an incident of the sort, and the men who have done that kind of thing have always been regarded as the brightest examples of incorruptibility. Every lawyer is brought up in the tradition that he can't do a finer action, if he becomes a judge—and they all expect to become judges in the end—than to hang a relative of his own. Sir Gilbert saw his opportunity when Miss King was brought up before him, and the moment he became convinced of her guilt he summed up against her in the most determined way."

"You may talk as you like, J. J., but no judge would do it."

"You have evidently a very low opinion of judges," said Meldon. "So has Doyle. He thinks that they are all influenced by political prejudices, and are ready to condemn a man who belongs to any League, without waiting to find out whether he has committed a crime or not. That's bad enough; but what you charge them with is infinitely worse. You say that they are habitually guilty of nepotism—that is to say of partiality to their own nieces, which is one of the worst crimes there is in a judge, as bad as simony would be in a bishop."

"I don't say anything of the sort. I say—"

"Either you say that Miss King isn't his niece or you say that he wouldn't try her for murder. You must be saying one or the other, though you don't express yourself very distinctly, because there's nothing else you could say."

"I don't, of course, agree with you," said the Major, after a pause. "In fact, I think you're talking downright nonsense, but I'm not going to argue with you. I'm—"

"I wish you'd always take up that attitude," said Meldon. "Your arguments waste a lot of time."

"I'm just going to ask you one question. Supposing Miss King is Mrs. Lorimer—"

"She is. There's no supposition about it."

"And supposing the judge tried her as you say—"

"That's in all the papers. There's no use attempting to deny that, whatever else you deny."

"And supposing she's his niece—"

"Callaghan says the cook told him she was," said Meldon, "and it appears that she kissed him when they met, which she'd hardly have done if they weren't relations."

"Then," said the Major triumphantly, "how can you account for his going to stay with her as if she hadn't done anything wrong?"

"I don't quite catch your point, Major."

"Is it likely that, knowing his niece to be a murderess, or at all events believing her to be a murderess, a judge—a judge, mind you, J. J.—would go and stay in the house with her, and kiss her?"

"It was she who kissed him," said Meldon, "but that's a minor point. I see your difficulty now, Major, and I quite admit there's something in it, or appears to be something in it to a man like you who doesn't understand the legal point of view."

"No point of view can alter facts," said the Major, "supposing they are facts, which of course they're not."

"Yes, it can," said Meldon. "To the legal mind a fact ceases to be a fact the moment a properly qualified court has decided the other way. The judge may be, in this particular case he is, as we know, absolutely convinced that his niece is a murderess. But a jury says she isn't, and so from a legal point of view she's a perfectly innocent and upright woman. The judge can't hang her. He can't even warn her not to do it again. He is bound, whatever his private feelings and convictions are, to accept the jury's verdict at its face value, and to treat his niece exactly as he did before all the unpleasantness arose."

"He needn't kiss her," said the Major.

"If he's a consistently just man and was on what we may call kissing terms with her before," said Meldon, "he'll of course kiss her again afterwards. He can't do anything else. In the eye of the law—that's what I mean by the legal standpoint—she's an innocent woman. Now the judge's whole position in society and even his income depends on his keeping up the theory that the law is infallible. Whatever you and I as private individuals may do, a judge has only one course open to him. He must take the view that the law takes. That's why I say that it's quite natural for Sir Gilbert to go and stop with his niece and kiss her, though, as I said before, it was really she who kissed him. If he didn't, he'd be admitting publicly that the law was wrong, and he can't do that without giving himself and his whole position away hopelessly."

"It doesn't strike me as a bit natural," said the Major. "In fact, it's quite impossible. That's why I say—"

"I can understand your feeling," said Meldon. "Indeed I was a good deal surprised at first; but when I came to think it all out, and to realise the sort of way the judge would look at it, I saw, as you'll probably be able to see some time tomorrow—"

"No. I won't. I'll never see that. It's absurd to suppose—"

"I don't deny," said Meldon, "that when we consider Sir Gilbert Hawkesby as a private individual, separating for a moment the man from the judge, we must credit him with the feeling that Miss King is rather a—what the French would call a *mauvais sujet*."

"A what?"

"A black sheep," said Meldon, "a disgrace to the family. The sort of relation whom one is inclined to keep in the background as much as possible. I am relying on that feeling to secure the help of the judge."

"For what?"

"To marry Miss King to Simpkins, of course. The thing we've been at all along."

"He won't do that. No man living would marry his niece to Simpkins."

"That depends on the nature of the niece. There are nieces—there's no use denying it, Major, because it's unfortunately true. There are nieces that a man would be glad to see married to any one. And there's a great deal to be said in favour of the Simpkins alliance in this particular case."

"No, there isn't. The man is a cad."

"I don't think nearly so badly of Simpkins as you do, Major. I've told you that before. But, even granting what you say is true, the judge probably argues that Miss King with her record can't expect anything better. He'll be glad enough to get Simpkins for her. He'll recollect that Ballymoy is a frightfully out-of-the-way place, and that if Miss King is married to a man who lives here none of her friends will ever see any more of her. That's exactly what he wants; and so I confidently expect that, once the position is explained to him, he'll simply jump at the chance."

"Do you mean to say," said the Major—"I am now supposing that all your ridiculous ideas are true, and that Miss King will really—"

He hesitated.

"Kill Simpkins?" said Meldon. "That's what you want done, isn't it?"

"Do you mean to say that you think the judge will go out of his way to encourage her to commit another crime?"

"It's not the business of a judge to prevent crime," said Meldon. "You mustn't mix him up with the police. The police have to see that people don't do what's wrong. Judges have to punish them afterwards for what the police fail to stop them from doing. The judge won't step out of his proper sphere and start doing police work. If he did there'd be endless confusion. And besides that, I don't expect the judge will think that she means to kill Simpkins. He doesn't understand as we do that she is acting in the interests of her art. She probably, in fact certainly, hasn't told him what she told me— that she has come to Ballymoy with the intention of going on with her work. He'll think that the narrow shave she had over the Lorimer affair will have given her a lesson, and that from now on she'll want to settle down and live a quiet, affectionate kind of life. When she kissed him in that spontaneous way this morning, what do you suppose was passing through his mind? What was he thinking? Remember that he hadn't seen her since the day of the trial, and then ask yourself what thoughts those two kisses would suggest to him."

"I don't know. That she was glad to see him, I suppose."

"A great deal more than that. A judge doesn't stop short at those superficial views of things. He looks deep down into the more recondite emotions of the human heart. As soon as he felt those kisses he said to himself: 'Here is a poor girl who's really sorry for what she's done—'"

"I thought you said he didn't believe she'd done it. I certainly don't."

"As a judge he doesn't; but I'm speaking of him now as an uncle, a simple unofficial uncle. As an uncle he can't help recollecting poor Lorimer, but he'll want to give his niece every possible fair play, and as soon as she showed signs of penitence—her kisses were a pretty convincing sign of penitence, considering the way he summed up against her—he'd be all for burying the past and letting her get a fresh start in life if she could."

"Of course I don't attach the smallest importance to anything you've said. I don't believe, in the first place, that Miss King is Mrs. Lorimer. I don't believe any judge would try to hang his own niece. I don't believe, if he had tried her, he'd go and stop in the house with her afterwards, and I'm perfectly certain he wouldn't kiss her. But you apparently like to pretend to me that you do believe all the rot you've been talking, and that being so, I'd rather like to know what you intend to do next."

"It doesn't in the least matter to you what I do," said Meldon. "If I'm the kind of drivelling idiot you make out, my actions are of no importance, either to you or to any one else."

"All the same, I'd like to know what they're going to be."

"Why?"

"So that I can do my best to prevent their doing any irreparable mischief, if possible; though I don't expect it is possible."

"I shall do no irreparable mischief to any one," said Meldon; "except Simpkins; and you always said you wanted him poisoned."

"I never said such a thing."

"Keep cool, Major. There's no use losing your temper. You and Doyle and O'Donoghue all said you'd be glad to gloat over Simpkins' corpse. If you hadn't said so I shouldn't be taking all this trouble. If I didn't still believe that you hate Simpkins I should drop the matter at once. After all, it's no business of mine."

"Then do drop it. Like a good man, J. J., leave Miss King alone, and let the judge fish in peace."

"No; I won't. I'll see the thing through now I'm this far, and within easy reach of success. I don't want to have you reproaching me afterwards for going back on my word."

"I won't reproach you. I promise not to."

"You'd mean not to; but when the present flurry is over, and when Simpkins begins to annoy you again about the fishing and other things, you won't be able to help reproaching me. Even if you refrain from actual words I shall see it in your eye. I can't go through life, Major, haunted by your eye with a mute, unspoken reproach in it."

Major Kent sighed heavily.

"Then what do you mean to do?" he asked.

"I shall see the judge to-morrow," said Meldon, "and—"

"I advise you not to. He's sure to have found out about the paraffin oil by that time."

"I'm prepared for that. There may be some slight temporary unpleasantness, but that will pass away at once when the judge hears the proposal that I have to make."

"What's that?"

"That he should encourage the marriage between Simpkins and his niece. I shall explain to him that it is very much to his own interest to do so, and of course he'll see the force of what I say at once. I shan't mention the ultimate fate of Simpkins. I don't suppose he'd care much if I did. He can't be particularly keen on preserving Simpkins' life, for he doesn't know him. Still it is best to avoid all risks, and I shall treat the marriage as the ordinary conventional love-match, without hinting at any connection between it and Miss King's peculiar art. When I've settled things up with him—that'll be about twelve or one o'clock, if I get at him before he starts fishing for the day—I shall go down to the village and get a hold of Simpkins. He'll be in his office, I expect. I shall lunch with him, and then lead him up and lay him at Miss King's feet."

"Will he go for you? He hasn't shown any great eagerness for the match so far."

"I shan't give him much choice," said Meldon. "I shall tell him that the thing has got to be done at once. Very few men are able to stand up to me when I take a really determined tone with them, and I shall speak in the strongest way to Simpkins. When I have, so to speak, deposited him in front of Miss King—"

"On his knees?" said the Major.

"Very probably. In these matters of detail I must of course be guided by circumstances; but when I have put him down, either on his knees or in some other posture, I shall slip away unobtrusively—"

"I should like to see you doing that. I don't think you could. You're generally more obtrusive than any one else I've ever met."

"Leaving them together," said Meldon, "with Callaghan watching from behind a tree, so as to be able to report to me exactly what happens. In the meanwhile I shall stroll up the river and find the judge. If he isn't actually into a fish at the moment, I shall bring him straight down to the house and let him hear the result at once. If he has a salmon hooked, I shall of course wait till it's landed, and then bring him down. Afterwards I shall take Simpkins up to the rectory and make arrangements about the licence. We ought, bar accidents, to have the whole thing finished in the inside of a fortnight from now. After that I must leave it in the hands of O'Donoghue. He'll have to be careful how he treats Simpkins when he's called in. It won't do to make mistakes and go curing him accidentally."

"I suppose," said the Major bitterly, "that you'll employ Sabina Gallagher to make the wedding-cake. She might begin the poisoning."

"Certainly not," said Meldon. "Sabina couldn't make a wedding-cake, and in any case Simpkins won't eat enough of his own wedding-cake to do him any harm, whatever it's made of. If you were accustomed to weddings, Major, you'd know that the whole cake is invariably eaten by the postoffice officials—a most deserving class, whom nobody wants to poison. Besides, in a case like this, it will be better to avoid all publicity and show. It wouldn't do to have the newspapers getting hold of the fact that Mrs. Lorimer is being married again so soon. There'd be paragraphs, and the suspicions of Simpkins would be excited. On the whole, I don't think we'll have a wedding cake, or bridesmaids, or anything of that sort. But you can be best man if you like."

"I know you don't mean a word you're saying, J. J., and that you won't really do anything."

"Wait and see."

"But if I thought you meant to cause Miss King the slightest uneasiness or discomfort, I should simply turn you straight out of my house. I wouldn't be a party for a single moment to any plan for insulting a really nice woman like Miss King."

"Don't fret about that," said Meldon. "What I'm doing is exactly what Miss King wants done. She told me so herself."

CHAPTER XX

Sir Gilbert Hawkesby was, on the whole, a good-tempered man; but he was liable to sudden outbursts of anger of a violent kind. Lady Hawkesby knew this, and always bowed meekly to the storm. His butler knew it, and felt no resentment when he was called an incompetent fool. The barristers who practised their art in his court knew it, and always gave up pressing objectionable points on his notice when they recognised the early signs of approaching indignation. The butler and the barristers, not Lady Hawkesby, admitted that the judge's anger was invariably justified. He never lost control of himself without some good excuse. Therefore they suffered patiently, knowing that they suffered justly, and knowing also that they would not suffer long; for the judge's outbursts were as brief as they were fierce, and he bore no malice afterwards. Doyle unfortunately did not know Sir Gilbert's peculiarities, and so he was depressed and unhappy. Sabina Gallagher did not know them either, and the judge had not spared her. He had no hesitation, as Lady Hawkesby, the butler, and the barristers knew, in attacking the most defenceless people when the mood was on him, and he had used exceptionally strong language to Sabina Gallagher. It took him on this occasion longer than usual to recover his self-possession. He gave no kiss in response to his niece's affectionate salutation. He ate the really excellent luncheon which she had prepared for him in gloomy silence and without a sign of appreciation. The gilly, who accompanied him up the river in the afternoon, came in for the last gusts of the expiring storm.

At about four o'clock Sir Gilbert hooked a fine salmon and landed him successfully. The gilly, who was a man of tact, greatly over-estimated the weight of the fish, and paid a rich compliment to the judge's skill. Miss King said all the most appropriate things in tones of warm conviction. Sir Gilbert began to feel that life was not altogether an intolerable affliction. An hour later, in a pool strongly recommended by the gilly, another fish was caught. It was inferior to the first in size, but it was a very satisfactory creature to look at. The judge's temper was quite normal when he sat down at dinner. When, at Miss King's request, he lit his cigar in the drawing-room afterwards, he began to take a humorous view of the misfortunes of the morning.

"I ought to have accepted your invitation at once, Milly, and not attempted to live at the local hotel. I never came across such a place in my life, though I have knocked about a good deal and am pretty well accustomed to roughing it. My bedroom reeked of abominable disinfectants. The floor was half an inch deep in chloride of lime. The sheets were soaked with— By the way, what is the name of the local parson?"

"I don't know," said Miss King. "He's an old man, and, I fancy, delicate. I've never seen him. He wasn't in church last Sunday."

"Has he a curate?"

"Yes; I believe so. But the curate is away on his holiday. Somebody—I forget who; very likely Callaghan the gardener—told me so. At all events, I've not seen anything of him. But what do you want with the local clergy?"

"I only want one of them," said the judge; "but I want him rather badly. The man I mean can't be a Roman Catholic priest. He has a bright red moustache. I wonder if you've come across him."

"That must be Mr. Meldon. He has a parish somewhere in England, I believe. He's over here on his holiday. I travelled in the carriage with him from Dublin. He is staying with a Major Kent."

"He's apparently quite mad," said the judge, "and ought to be shut up. He's dangerous to society."

"He's certainly eccentric. We had a long talk in the train, and he told me a lot about his baby, which had been keeping him awake at night. I was out yachting one day with him and Major Kent."

"Don't go again," said the judge. "Your life wouldn't be safe. Is Major Kent mad too?"

"Not at all. He struck me as a very pleasant man, most considerate and kind."

"He must be very unusually kind if he tolerates Meldon. Of all the objectionable lunatics I ever met, that parson is out and away the worst."

"I shouldn't have said he was actually mad. In some ways I think he's rather clever. He preached quite a remarkable sermon last Sunday, the sort of sermon you can't help listening to."

"I can easily believe that," said the judge. "He preached me a sermon yesterday which I'm not at all likely to forget."

"Where did you meet him, Uncle Gilbert?"

"I didn't meet him. He met me. I shouldn't have dreamed of meeting him. He met me at the railway station at Donard, and invited himself to luncheon with me. He also brought a doctor whom he had along with him. Then he warned me that my life wouldn't be safe in Ballymoy. I thought he was the usual sort of fool with scare ideas about leagues and boycotting. But it wasn't that at all. He thought he'd frighten me off with stories about bad drains; said I'd be sure to die if I stayed at the hotel. He was quite right there, I must say. I should have died if I hadn't left at once."

"Were they very bad?"

"Were what very bad? Oh, the drains. Not at all. At least I daresay they were bad enough. I wasn't there long enough to find out. But I shouldn't have died of the drains in any case. I'm not the kind of man who catches diseases."

Sir Gilbert's chest swelled a little as he spoke, and he slowly puffed out a large cloud of smoke. He was justly proud of his physical health, and was accustomed to hurl defiance at microbes and to heap contempt on the doctor's art.

"I'm sure you're not," said Miss King dutifully.

"What I should have died of," said the judge, "if I had died, would have been starvation. You'll hardly believe me when I tell you that every scrap of food I got, even the boiled egg which I ordered for breakfast, thinking it would be safe—"

Miss King had heard all about the paraffin oil before. She had indeed heard about it more than once. She did not want to hear of it again, because she feared that a repetition of the story might put her uncle into another bad temper.

"I can't understand it," she said. "How any one could be so careless as—"

"It wasn't carelessness," said the judge. "If it had been I might have given the place another trial. It was done on purpose."

"Surely not."

"I pursued the cook," said the judge, "into the fastnesses of her kitchen. She fled before me, but I ran her to earth at last in the scullery. A filthier hole I never saw. I went for her straight, and expected to be told a story about somebody or other upsetting a lamp over all her pots and pans. Instead of that, she answered me, without a sign of hesitation and said— Now what do you think she said?"

"I can't guess. Not that she thought you'd like the flavour?"

"No. She hadn't quite the effrontery to say that. She told me that Mr. Meldon, this parson of yours who takes you out yachting, had given orders before I came that all my food was to be soaked with paraffin oil."

"Oh! But that's too absurd."

"So you'd think. So I thought at the moment. I didn't believe her. I thought that she was putting up an unusual line of defence to excuse her own gross carelessness. But I was evidently wrong. The girl seems to have been telling the truth. I think I mentioned to you the state in which I found my bed last night."

"You said it was damp."

"Damp! I never said damp. Soaking is the word I used; or at all events ought to have used. It was soaking with Condy's Fluid, as it turned out, though I didn't know at the time what the stuff was. I had an interview with the hotelkeeper himself, a ruffian of the name of Doyle, about that. I had very nearly to break the bell before I could get any one to come to me. It's a very odd thing, but he told me practically the same story; said that this man Meldon, whoever he is, had given orders to have Condy's Fluid poured all over my bed and chloride of lime shovelled on to the floor. I did not believe him at the time any more than I believed that miserable slut of a cook the next morning. I was in such a temper when I left that I didn't think of putting their two stories together; but going over the whole thing this afternoon in my mind it struck me as rather peculiar that they should both have hit on such a grotesque sort of a lie, if it was a lie."

"Surely you don't think that Mr. Meldon—he's rather eccentric, I know, but I can scarcely believe that he'd—"

"I'm not at all sure what I ought to think. It seems unlikely that any clergyman, unless he is quite mad, and you say he's not mad—"

"No; he's not mad. He's peculiar. But he is certainly not mad. Major Kent has the highest opinion of him, and Major Kent is quite sane."

The judge threw the end of his cigar into the fire and sat silent for a minute or two. His mind was working on the curious series of events which had followed his arrival in Ballymoy. He became very much interested.

"Milly," he said at last, "I'll take your word for it that the man's not mad. But how on earth am I to explain his actions? For I really have no doubt that he's at the bottom of all I've been through. First of all, he met me at the station at Donard, having travelled twenty miles for the express purpose of trying to prevent my coming on here. Now why did he do that?"

"Perhaps he really thought you'd be uncomfortable at the hotel."

"He seems to have done his best to make me uncomfortable, anyhow."

"And succeeded," said Miss King with a smile.

"And succeeded brilliantly. I don't in the least wish to deny that. I never was more uncomfortable in my life. But what I want to know is, what possible motive he had for doing it. Unless he's an absolute lunatic, and you say he's not that—"

"No. He's sane, though I think he's decidedly eccentric."

"Then he must have had a motive of some sort. He plainly doesn't want to have me here in Ballymoy. Now why not? That's what's puzzling me. Why not? I never saw the man in my life till yesterday. I never heard of him. What on earth can it matter to him whether I spend a fortnight here or not?"

"There was some dispute about the fishing before you came," said Miss King. "I heard about it from Callaghan the gardener. Mr. Meldon's friend, Major Kent, thought he had a right to fish in some part of the river—"

"But what difference would my being here make? I'm not the owner of the fishing. Major Kent may be right or wrong. But there's no use his disputing with me. He wouldn't be in a bit better position if I had turned round and gone home."

"I suppose not."

"So we may rule that explanation out of court. And yet the man must have had a motive of some sort. No one would take all the trouble that he has taken unless he saw his way to gain something by it." The judge paused again, thinking deeply. Then he smiled suddenly. "Look here, Milly. You don't mind my asking you rather a personal question, do you?"

"Not a bit. My conscience is quite easy. I didn't bribe the cook to put paraffin oil in your dinner, and I should never have thought of pouring Condy's Fluid over your bed."

"Has that curate, Meldon, I mean—"

"He's not a curate," said Miss King. "He's a vicar at least."

"I shouldn't wonder if he turned out to be an archdeacon. But has he— It's rather an awkward question to ask; but you're not a child, Milly. You know that you're a very attractive young woman, and you have what would seem to some people quite a good fortune, besides what you earn by your writing. Has this man been trying to make love to you?"

Miss King laughed aloud. The cheerful ring of her obviously spontaneous mirth shattered the theory which the judge was building up.

"No," she said; "he has not. Quite the contrary. Oh, Uncle Gilbert, I must tell you. It's too funny. He warned me in the most solemn way that I wasn't to attempt to make love to him."

"In spite of all you say, Milly, he must be stark mad."

"No. He thought, he really did think, that I wanted to flirt with him, and he told me not to. He said he couldn't have it. I was awfully angry with him at the time. No one ever said such a thing to me before. It was the first day he called here."

"Does he often call here?"

"Nearly every day. He was here this afternoon while we were up the river. He said he wanted to see me on most important business."

"I wish I'd seen him."

"You will soon. He's sure to come to-morrow."

"If he does," said the judge, "I'll take the opportunity of having a talk with him. But tell me more about that curious incident, Milly. Are you sure he doesn't want to make love to you?"

"Quite. I couldn't possibly be mistaken. Besides, he's married. He told me that in the most insulting way, so as to prevent my making any attempt to marry him myself."

"Of course that settles it," said the judge. "I thought for a moment that he might possibly have some wild idea of marrying you. That would account for his making the desperate efforts he has made to keep me out of the place. He'd know that I wouldn't like you to marry a mad parson. But if it wasn't that, Milly, and after all you've told me it clearly can't be, what on earth is the idea at the back of his mind? Why has he arranged for this systematic persecution of me?"

"Are you sure the fishing dispute has nothing to do with it. I can't think of anything else."

"Unless he's a fool," said the judge, "he can't suppose that my giving up the fishing would make it any easier for his friend to poach."

"Major Kent wouldn't poach," said Miss King warmly. "He's a gentleman. If you knew him, Uncle Gilbert, you wouldn't say such things about him."

"You seem to know him very well," said the judge. "Oh yes! You told me you had been out yachting. Does *he* often call here?"

"He was here on Sunday afternoon. Yes, and on Tuesday, now I come to think of it."

"And you were out yachting with him on the Monday in between. That's not bad for three days, eh, Milly?"

He looked at her keenly as he spoke, and a half smile flickered on his lips. Miss King blushed slightly, and then, being very angry with herself for blushing, grew quite red in the face. The judge's smile broadened.

"From what you've seen of this man Meldon," he said, "would you suppose that he's a very altruistic sort of person?"

"What do you mean?"

"Is he the sort of man who'd put himself about a great deal and take a lot of trouble for the sake of doing a good turn to a friend? Do you think, for instance, that he'd indulge in all sorts of elaborate practical jokes with a view to frightening me out of Ballymoy, if he thought my presence here was likely to interfere with any plan that his friend Major Kent might have very much at heart?"

Miss King looked at the judge in some surprise. Then she suddenly blushed again.

"Uncle Gilbert," she said, "you're too bad. I know what you're thinking about. But why do you suppose that any of these men should want to marry me?"

"You're a very attractive young woman, my dear," said the judge. "I can quite understand— What sort of a man is this Major Kent?"

"I won't talk about him," said Miss King. "It's not nice of you to cross-question me in that way. I hate being treated as if I did nothing but go about hunting for a husband; as if I never spoke to a man without wondering in my own mind whether he'd be likely to marry me. That's the way you always treat us, and I won't stand it. If there are such women, and I don't think there are many, I'm not one of them."

"No," said the judge; "you're not. If you had been you'd have been married long ago. But in this case it seems that the possible husband is hunting you with some vigour. He has certainly done his best to get rid of me, regarding me, no doubt, as a possible obstacle in his way."

"I'm sure Major Kent had nothing to do with that. He's not at all the kind of man who'd make plans and schemes. But the whole thing is utterly absurd. What's the good of talking about it?"

"It is utterly absurd. It's the most absurd thing I ever heard of in my life. I simply wouldn't have believed it possible if it hadn't actually happened, that this red-haired parson—the man has a perfectly diabolical imagination. I wonder what he'll do next. I feel certain he won't give up. Could he possibly get at your cook, Milly?"

"I'm sure he couldn't. Hodge has the greatest contempt for all the Irish. She regards them as savages, and is rather surprised to find that they wear clothes."

"That's a comfort. I can face almost anything if I get my food properly. But I must keep a careful look out. Meldon seems to me the kind of man who wouldn't stick at a trifle, and he's evidently determined to get rid of me."

"Perhaps he'll ask you out yachting and—"

"And maroon me on a desert island?"

"No, but make you— Oh! I forgot, you don't get sea-sick."

"No. There's not a bit of use his trying to get the better of me in that way. I should simply laugh at the worst ground swell he can produce. I hope he will ask me out yachting. I should like to have a nice long day alone with Mr. Meldon. He's a man worth knowing."

The conversation drifted on to other topics. The judge, after the manner of fishermen, rehearsed the capture of his two salmon, compared them to similar fish caught elsewhere, and made enquiries about the netting at the mouth of the river. At about ten o'clock he lit a fresh cigar and returned to the subject of Meldon.

"You say," he said, "that he's likely to call here to-morrow morning."

"He's almost certain to. Except the day when he went to meet you at Donard he has never missed paying me a visit."

"About four o'clock, I suppose, is his regular hour?"

"He has no regular hour," said Miss King. "He's quite unconventional. He may drop in for breakfast, or he may turn up suddenly while we're dressing for dinner."

"I hope he'll do one or the other. I don't want to sit waiting for him all day. If he comes while I'm fishing you must bring him up the river after me. By the way, how is your novel getting on, Milly? Have you finished it off?"

"I've hardly done a stroke of work since I came here. I'm dissatisfied with the whole thing. I'm thinking of beginning it again."

"If you do," said the judge, "put Meldon into it."

"I should like to."

"Do. Tell the story of his bribing the cook to poison me, and I'll buy two hundred copies straight away. I've always wanted to be put into a novel, and I should like to go down to posterity side by side with Meldon."

"I wish I could."

"There's no difficulty that I can see. He'll do equally well for a hero or a villain."

"I'm afraid all the other characters would look like fools. That's the difficulty."

"They would," said the judge. "I'm very much afraid they would. Perhaps after all you'd better not put me in. Let him poison some one else. I shouldn't be an attractive figure if I were posed as one of Meldon's victims."

"Perhaps," said Miss King, "I might work out the plot in such a way that you'd get the better of him in the end."

"I fully intend to. I shall see him to-morrow, and if the thing is possible at all, I shall make him thoroughly ashamed of himself."

"Then I'll wait till after to-morrow," said Miss King, "before I decide on my plot. It will be much easier for me if I get the whole thing ready-made."

Sir Gilbert Hawkesby finished his cigar and went to bed. He was tolerably well satisfied with himself. He understood, so he believed, the motives which had induced Meldon to make his life in Ballymoy uncomfortable. He was sure that Miss King was able to manage her own affairs, and he was not anxious to make objections to her marrying Major Kent, or any other tolerably respectable man whom she happened to like. He knew, too, that Lady Hawkesby would be pleased to have her niece settled in life in any way which would put a stop to the growing notoriety of the novels she wrote.

CHAPTER XXI

At breakfast the next morning Major Kent spoke to Meldon in a gentle, rather hopeless tone. It was as if he had no great expectation of his words producing any effect.

"I suppose," he said, "that nothing I can say will prevent your thrusting yourself into the company of this judge to-day."

"If you refer," said Meldon, "to my intention of calling civilly on Sir Gilbert Hawkesby, nothing you say will alter my view that it is a very proper thing to do, considering that the man is a stranger in the locality."

"Then I beg of you, J. J., to be careful. Don't say anything insulting about Miss King. Remember that she's his niece, and he won't like to hear her abused. Besides, he'll tell her what you say afterwards, and it would be very painful to her to hear the sort of accusations you've been bringing against her since she came to Ballymoy."

"Major," said Meldon, "we've been intimate friends for years, and you ought to know that, whatever else I may be, I'm always a gentleman. Is it likely I'd go out of my way to insult a helpless woman?"

"You wouldn't mean to, J. J., but you might do it. Your ideas of what is insulting are so peculiar. Believing the sort of things you do believe about her, you might say something very offensive without meaning any harm. Do be careful."

"I shall not allude to her past, if that's what you are thinking of. I never have alluded to her past to any one but you, except on the one occasion on which she brought up the subject herself. Nothing could possibly be in worse taste than to fling that story in the judge's face."

"I wish," said the Major, "that I could persuade you not to be quite so cock-sure about what you call her past. You ought to try and realise that you may possibly be mistaken."

"That," said Meldon, "is practically what Oliver Cromwell said to the Scotch Presbyterian ministers. It may have been a sound remark from his point of view, but I'm rather surprised to hear you quoting and endorsing it. I always thought you were a Conservative."

"I am. But what has that got to do with your theories about—?"

"If you are a Conservative you ought not to be backing up Oliver Cromwell. He was a revolutionary of an extreme kind. You ought to be ashamed of giving your adherence to any sentiment of his. You might just as well propose to cut off the king's head."

"I don't quite see why I'm bound to believe in your infallibility because I happen to be a Conservative. All I suggested was that you might possibly be mistaken."

"In putting your suggestion in the way you did," said Meldon, "you proclaimed yourself a disciple and admirer of Oliver Cromwell. I've no particular objection to that. I'm not a prejudiced man in political matters, and Cromwell is a long time dead. If you choose to proclaim yourself a regicide, I shan't quarrel with you. All I want you to understand is that you can't have it both ways. No man can quote Oliver Cromwell with approval and still go on calling himself a loyalist."

"All the same, you may be mistaken about Miss King."

"I may," said Meldon; "any man may be mistaken, unless he happens to be a Pope, who of course never is, *ex officio*; but as a matter of fact I very seldom am, and in this particular case I'm demonstrably right."

"Well, don't air your theory to the judge; that's all I care about."

"Not being a perfect fool, I won't. I have a considerable natural talent for diplomacy, as I daresay you've observed, and I'm not the least likely to start off by putting up that judge's back. My game is to pacify and soothe him in such a way that he will become our active ally."

"You'll find that difficult after the paraffin oil."

"If necessary," said Meldon, "I shall apologise for the paraffin, but I scarcely expect it will be necessary. The judge is a sensible man. He knows that we have to take the rough with the smooth in life. He'll regard that as a mere incident, a more or less humorous incident."

"He'll be a queer sort of man if he does."

"And now," said Meldon, "I must be off. It's nearly ten o'clock, thanks to your lazy habit of not breakfasting till after nine. Fortunately, I've still got Doyle's bicycle. Not that it's at all a dependable machine. The pedal will probably come off once at least on my way in. However, at worst, I'll be there by eleven."

The pedal on this occasion held to its place, and Meldon reached Ballymoy House at a quarter to eleven. The door was opened to him by

Miss King, who had seen him coming up the avenue. She greeted him with a smile, and, in reply to his enquiry, told him that the judge had gone up the river.

"I promised," said Miss King, "to send him word if you called. I think he wants to see you. Won't you come in? I'll send Callaghan to look for him."

"Thanks," said Meldon. "I think I'll go and look for him myself. I should rather like the walk, and I might be some use to him in showing him the pools. I used to fish this river a good deal myself at one time. By the way, did he say what he wants to see me about?"

"He didn't go into details," said Miss King, "but I rather think he wants to ask you some questions about—"

"Did he mention the subject of paraffin oil?"

Miss King smiled.

"I'm sorry that's weighing on his mind," said Meldon. "I thought he might have got over it by this time. However, it won't take long to explain it. I won't say good-bye, Miss King. I shall probably see you again this afternoon."

"Won't you come back for luncheon? It will be ready at half-past one."

"No, thanks. I can't. The fact is I'm thinking of dropping in on Mr. Simpkins about that time. He may be coming up here with me in the afternoon. He has something he wants to say to you."

"About the fishing?"

"No. The fact is—but I'd better let the poor fellow explain himself. I'll run off now and hunt about for Sir Gilbert. If he's had any luck at all this morning he'll have forgotten about the paraffin oil before I get to him. Good-morning, Miss King. Don't believe all the Major says about Mr. Simpkins. There's no one I know who's fairer-minded in a general way than the Major. But in the case of Mr. Simpkins he's regularly warped, and you ought not to take any notice of what he may have said."

Sir Gilbert Hawkesby was up to his knees in the river when Meldon came upon him. He was throwing a fly over a most likely pool and had already been rewarded by a rise. On the bank lay a remarkably fine salmon, at least twenty pounds in weight, which he had caught. He was in a very cheerful mood, and felt kindly towards every one in the world.

"Don't let me interrupt you," said Meldon. "You're at one of the best spots on the whole river. I'll sit down here and wait till you've finished."

But the judge, though a very keen fisherman, was evidently more eager to talk to Meldon than to catch another salmon. He waded ashore at once and laid down his rod.

"I'm very glad to meet you, Mr. Meldon," he said. "There are one or two questions I'd like to ask you."

"I thought there very likely were," said Meldon, "and I need scarcely say that I'm perfectly ready to answer them, so far as I can with proper consideration for your peace of mind."

"My peace of mind!"

"Yes. I shan't, of course, say anything which would be liable to upset you. I know you're here on a holiday, and nothing spoils a holiday so much as worry of any sort. I have the greatest respect and liking for you."

"That's what you said when you were telling me that cock-and-bull story about the drains."

"Doyle's drains are bad," said Meldon. "I hardly exaggerated at all about that. You ask Simpkins. He wanted— By the way, have you met Simpkins yet?"

"No; I haven't. But it isn't about Simpkins I want to talk now."

"That's a pity. I enjoy talking about Simpkins. He's not a bad fellow at all, though the Major doesn't care for him. But I expect you'll meet him this afternoon."

"Thanks," said the judge. "I shall be glad of the chance of forming my own estimate of Simpkins' character. I am sure it will agree with yours. But to get back to what I was saying about the drains. Would you mind telling me why you went all the way to Donard to warn me about the drains?"

"To be perfectly frank—by the way, do you want me to be perfectly frank?"

"Certainly. Even at the expense of my peace of mind."

"I don't think what I'm going to say now will affect your peace of mind. The fact is, I thought at that time that it would be better for you not to come to Ballymoy. I hope you don't mind my saying so. I need scarcely tell you that it wasn't a personal matter. There's nothing I should enjoy more than having you here permanently."

"I suppose that the Condy's Fluid and the paraffin oil were—?"

"Means to the same end," said Meldon. "They were kindly meant. If they caused you any serious inconvenience—"

"They did."

"Then I apologise, frankly and unreservedly. The fact is, I acted under a complete misapprehension. If I had known then what I know now I should have welcomed you, and done my best to make your stay here pleasant. That's what I intend to do now; so if any one annoys you in the slightest just let me know, and I'll put a stop to the performance at once."

"Thanks; and now perhaps, as we've gone so far, you'll satisfy my curiosity a little further by explaining why you object to my presence here."

"I don't object to it in the least. I did once, as I said; but I don't now."

"What has happened to change your views?"

"Now that is a question I can hardly answer without going into some very private and delicate matters which I am sure you would not care to discuss. It wouldn't be pleasant for you if I talked about them. You'd be sorry afterwards."

"Would my peace of mind be affected?"

"Seriously. That's the reason I won't go into the matter."

"All the same," said the judge, "I think I'll hazard a guess about it. Are these mysterious affairs you allude to in any way connected with Miss King?"

"I see," said Meldon, "that you've been talking it all over with her, and that's she given you a hint, so I need say no more."

"Miss King's only idea," said the judge, "is that you think I'm likely to make myself objectionable in some way about the fishing. It appears that there has been a dispute—"

"That miserable business between Simpkins and the Major. I know all about that, and I may say at once that it had nothing whatever to do with my attempt to keep you out of Ballymoy."

"I thought not. I merely mentioned it to show you that my niece is quite in the dark about your real reason, and that I got no hint from her."

"She may not be quite as much in the dark," said Meldon, "as she pretends when she's talking to you. The subject would naturally be an awkward one for her to discuss. It's awkward enough for us. I think we'd better drop it at once."

"I suppose," said the judge boldly, "that your friend thought he'd have a better chance if I were not here to interfere with him."

"I don't like that way of putting the case," said Meldon. "Why not say that Miss King would have had a better chance?"

"Considering that Miss King is my niece," said the judge, "you will understand that I rather object to your way of putting it. It's scarcely respectful to her. Whatever the facts may be in any particular case, there's a well-established convention in these matters. We don't, any of us, talk as if it were the lady who is, so to speak, the aggressor."

"I see your point, though in this particular case I can't help feeling— But why should we go on? It's far better to drop the subject."

"But I don't see yet why you first of all wanted to keep me out of Ballymoy, and then suddenly changed your mind. What happened in the interval?"

"If you're quite determined to thrash the matter out," said Meldon, "the best way will be to get at the main point at once. Everything will come easier to us after we have that settled. Have you any objection to our proposal?"

"What proposal?"

"Come now. I know that it's quite the correct thing for judges to ask ridiculous and silly questions, affecting not to know what everybody in the world knows quite well. There was one the other day—I don't think it was you—who inquired quite solemnly what a 'bike' was; and I recollect another—it was in a horse-racing case—who pretended not to know the meaning of the phrase 'two to one on.' I don't profess to understand why you all do that kind of thing, but I'm willing to suppose that there's some good reason for it. I daresay it's what's called a legal fiction, and is an essential part of the machinery by which justice is administered. If so, it's all right in its proper place; but what on earth is the good of keeping it up out of court? Sitting here on the bank of a west of Ireland river, with a large salmon lying dead at our feet, it really is rather absurd to ask me what proposal."

"I merely wanted," said the judge, "to make quite sure—"

"You were quite sure. You couldn't have had the slightest doubt in your mind. You yourself began the discussion about Miss King's chances of marrying—"

"I said your friend's chances of marrying Miss King."

"It doesn't in the least matter which you said. The point just now is that you knew perfectly well what I meant when I spoke of the proposal at present under discussion."

"Has he proposed yet?"

"No, but he will this afternoon; and what I want to get at is whether you're going to put a stop to the marriage or not."

"I, really— Miss King is, I think, quite able to manage her own affairs; and I shouldn't in any case care to interfere, beyond offering advice in case your friend should turn out to be an obviously unsuitable person."

"That's all right. I can't expect you to say more than that. I knew all along that you didn't want to have the thing put to you at the point of the bayonet. You'll recollect that I had no wish to force it on you."

"You mustn't suppose," said the judge, "that I'm in any way committed to a definite support—"

"Certainly not," said Meldon. "A man in your position couldn't. I thoroughly understand that. And I hope you don't think that I've been in any way disrespectful to you. I didn't mean to be. I have the highest possible regard for all judges, and what I said just now about legal fictions was simply meant to avoid prolonging a discussion which can't have been pleasant for you. And after all, you know, it was rather absurd your trying to come the judge over me, considering what we were talking about. You wouldn't have done it, I'm sure, if you'd stopped for a moment to consider the peculiar and rather delicate circumstances under which we are carrying on this negotiation. I expect the habit of talking in that judicial way was too strong for you. You forgot for the moment what it was we were speaking about, and thought it was some ordinary law case. The force of habit is a wonderful thing. Have you ever noticed—"

"So far as I have been able to discover up to the present," said the judge, "you are greatly interested in bringing about a marriage between your friend and my niece."

"Interested is a dubious sort of word to use, and I don't like it. Let us be quite clear about what we mean. In one sense I am interested; in another sense I am entirely disinterested—which is the exact opposite. You catch my point, don't you? It is a very instructive thing to reflect on the curious ambiguity of words. But I am sure you can tell me more about that than I can possibly tell you. With your legal experience you must have come across scores of instances of the extraordinarily deceptive nature of words."

"You thought apparently that I should be likely to object to the marriage, and therefore you tried to keep me out of Ballymoy, using means which might be described as unscrupulous."

"I've already apologised for the paraffin oil," said Meldon. "A full and ample apology, such as I have offered, is generally considered to close an incident of that kind. In the old duelling days, when men used to go out at early dawn to shoot at each other with pistols, the one who had shied the wine glass at the other the night before often used to apologise; and when he did the pistols were put up into their case, and both parties went back comfortably to breakfast. I've often wondered that men of your profession—judges, I mean—didn't do something effective to put a stop to duelling. It was always against the law, and yet we had to wait for the slow growth of public opinion—"

"Then," said the judge, "you changed your mind, and came to the conclusion that my presence here wasn't likely to interfere with your friend's plans. Now will you tell me why—"

"I've made three distinct and separate efforts," said Meldon, "to change the subject of conversation. I tried to start you off on habits, a subject on which almost every man living can talk more or less. I thought you'd have taken that opportunity of telling the story about the horse which always stopped at the door of a certain public house, even after the temperance reformer had bought him. I'm sure you'd have liked to tell that story. Everybody does."

"I don't.".

"So it appears. You're an exceptional man. Recognising that, I started the subject of words, which is more philosophical. You might quite easily have got off on the degradation of the English language owing to the spread of slang. Then we could have spent an agreeable half-hour."

"But I didn't want to talk about words. I—"

"I saw that; so I gave you another chance. Starting on the annals of your profession, I proposed a question to you which ought to have aroused in you a desire to defend the public utility of the great legal luminaries of the past. I practically denied that judges are any good at all. Instead of showing me, as you very easily might have, that it was the judges who created the public opinion which put a stop to duelling, and not public opinion which goaded the judges on to hang the duellists, you—"

"I wanted to know, and I still want to know, why you changed your mind."

"If you can't think that out for yourself," said Meldon, "I'm not going to do it for you. A man like you ought to be able to follow a perfectly simple line of thought like that. If you can't see the plain and obvious mental process which led to my change of opinion, I don't see how you can expect to track the obscure workings of the criminal mind. The criminal, as of course you know, is always more or less demented, and consequently doesn't reason in the obvious and straightforward way in which I do. His mentality—"

"I suppose you're changing the conversation again," said the judge.

"I'm trying to; but it doesn't seem to be much use."

"I'll talk to you on any subject you choose to select with pleasure," said the judge, "if you'll tell me what it was that led to your change of mind about my probable action in this matter of your friend's proposal to marry my niece."

"There's just one fact which I haven't mentioned. You ought to have; you perfectly well might have guessed it. But as you haven't, I'll tell it to you. When I first heard of your coming to Ballymoy, I didn't know that you were Miss King's uncle. I only found that out yesterday."

"That makes things worse than ever," said the judge. "I was beginning dimly to understand some of your actions before you told me that. Now I'm utterly and completely at sea. Why you should have tried to stop me coming to Ballymoy if you didn't know I was Miss King's uncle is beyond me altogether."

"I really can't go into that," said Meldon. "You must understand it perfectly well, and in any case I'm bound to respect Miss King's confidence. I can't possibly repeat to you things she has said to me in a strictly private way."

"Of course if my niece—but that puzzles me even more. She hasn't said a word to me about any private understanding with you."

"She wouldn't," said Meldon, "and I daresay I ought not to have mentioned that such a thing exists. However, in the end, of course, you'll know all about it."

"In the end?"

"Yes. After the marriage. Shortly after."

"If she really is to be married," said the judge, "I wish she'd hurry up about it. I hate these mysteries."

"You can't hate them more than I do," said Meldon, "and you can rely upon me to bring things to their crisis, their preliminary crisis—the actual marriage can't take place for a fortnight—as soon as possible."

"Do. By the preliminary crisis I suppose you mean the engagement."

"Certainly. I shall use every effort to bring that off this afternoon. Now that I know you're as keen on it as I am myself, I think I may pledge you my word that it will come off this afternoon. But, if so, I must leave you now. Good-bye."

CHAPTER XXII

It was nearly twelve o'clock when Meldon left Sir Gilbert Hawkesby. He walked rapidly down to Ballymoy House, and seized his bicycle. Miss King, who had been watching for him, ran out and invited him to stay for luncheon. Meldon excused himself briefly on the plea of really urgent business.

"But can't you spare us even an hour?" said Miss King persuasively.

Meldon sprang into the saddle. It was his custom to mount from the pedal, and on this occasion the pedal came off.

"Now," said Miss King, "your bicycle is broken and you must stay."

"It's Doyle's bicycle," he said. "I wouldn't own a machine like this. My temper would wear thin in a week if I did."

He turned the bicycle upside down, and set to work vigorously with a wrench.

"If," said Meldon, "my business were my own—that's to say, if I were acting in my private capacity for my own interests—I should let the whole thing slide at once." He screwed hard at a nut as he spoke. "But what I have to do concerns the whole community here. It is also of the greatest importance to you, Miss King."

"To me?"

"And my action has, I may add, the warmest approval of the judge. There! Thank goodness, that wretched thing is stuck on again. Good-bye for the present, Miss King."

"But— Oh, do wait for a moment! You really must explain—"

Meldon mounted and rode away while she spoke. Just before he disappeared from view, he turned his head and shouted back,—

"You'll know all about it this afternoon, Miss King."

He rode rapidly down to the village, and dismounted at the door of Simpkins' office. It was shut. Meldon knocked loudly several times, but received no answer. He mounted his bicycle again and rode off at high speed to Simpkins' house. Here the door was opened to him by the red-haired servant.

"I want to see Mr. Simpkins at once," said Meldon.

"It'll fail you to do that," said the girl, "for he isn't within."

"Tell me this, now," said Meldon. "Aren't you a cousin of Sabina Gallagher's?"

"I am, of course."

"Very well. I'm a friend of Sabina's. I'm the chief, if not the only friend Sabina has in Ballymoy, I daresay she's told you that herself."

"She has not then; for I didn't see her this last week only the once."

"Well, you must take my word for it that I am. Now, recollecting that fact, I expect you to show a proper family feeling and to treat the friends of your near relations as if they were your own. Is Mr. Simpkins really out, or is he simply in bed and ashamed to confess it?"

"He is not in bed. Nor he wasn't in it since nine o'clock this morning. It's away off he is ever since he had his breakfast; and if you don't believe what I'm telling you, you can go upstairs and see for yourself."

"I do believe you," said Meldon. "Where has he gone to?"

"How would I know? Barring that he took a packet of sandwiches with him, I don't know where he is no more than yourself."

"Sandwiches! That looks as if he won't be back for luncheon."

"He will not then, for he told me so."

"Did he go on his bicycle?"

"It could be that he did, for it's not within in the house."

"Then we may assume that he did," said Meldon, "and it follows from that that he intended to go some distance. Now tell me this, what direction did he start in?"

"How would I know? As soon as ever I had the sandwiches made for him I went to feed the fowl, and by reason of the way the white hen has of rambling and her chickens along with her—"

"Thanks," said Meldon. "If it wasn't that I have to find Mr. Simpkins at once, I'd stay and hear about the white hen. But under the circumstances I can't. Good-bye."

He rode down to the hotel and found Doyle, who was sitting on the window-sill of the commercial room reading a newspaper.

"Doyle," he said, "where's Simpkins gone?"

"I don't know," said Doyle, "that he's gone anywhere; though I'd be glad if he did, and that to a good, far-off kind of a place."

"Did you see him this morning?"

"I did. I seen him. It might have been half-past ten or maybe eleven o'clock—"

"On his bicycle?"

"He was on his bicycle."

"Where was he going?"

"I don't know where he was going, for I didn't ask, not caring; unless it might be to some place that he wouldn't get back from too easy."

"It is of the utmost possible importance," said Meldon, "that I should know where he's gone. I am pledged to produce him at Ballymoy House this afternoon. Unless I do, our whole plan for getting rid of him is likely to miscarry."

"I'm sorry to hear that," said Doyle. "But I couldn't tell you where he went, not if it was to have him hanged when you caught him."

"I am not going to have him hanged," said Meldon. "I can't; for he hasn't done anything, so far as I know, that any court would condemn him for. What I want is to get him married."

"Married, is it?"

"Yes, to Miss King."

"But— What you said at the first go-off, the day you was within talking to me and the doctor, was that you'd—"

"I can't possibly enter into a long explanation now," said Meldon; "but if you want to get rid of Simpkins permanently, you'll rack your brains and help me to find out where he's gone to-day."

Doyle thought deeply for a couple of minutes.

"Where he's gone," he said at last, "is beyond me. But I took notice of the trousers he had on him when he was starting. I'm not sure will it be any use to you to know it, but they was white."

"Good," said Meldon. "As it happens, that fact does throw a great deal of light on the problem. No man wears white trousers unless he's going boating on a fine day, or going to play cricket, or going to play lawn tennis. We may cross off the boating at once. Simpkins wouldn't go in a boat voluntarily, even on the finest day. We may also exclude cricket; because there's no cricket within fifty miles of Ballymoy in any direction. There only remains tennis; so we may take it as certain that it is lawn tennis which Simpkins has gone to play. You follow me so far, I suppose, Doyle."

"It might be what they call golf."

"No, it couldn't. You don't understand these things, Doyle; but, as a matter of fact, no one plays golf in white trousers. It wouldn't be considered proper, and so we may be perfectly certain that Simpkins wouldn't do it."

"I wouldn't say," said Doyle, "that you're much nearer knowing where he's gone to."

"Not much, but I am a little. I happen to know—Sabina's red-haired cousin told me—that he has taken a packet of sandwiches with him and doesn't expect to be home till late. It follows from that that he's not playing tennis in this immediate neighbourhood. It also follows that he isn't going to any friend's house. Nobody ever brings sandwiches to a private tennis party. Therefore Simpkins must have gone to play at some sort of club."

"Unless it would be at Donard," said Doyle, "I don't know where there'd be a thing of the kind."

"Right," said Meldon. "And, as a matter of fact, there is a club at Donard. I know that, because I was once invited to play there in a tournament. I think we may feel tolerably certain that Simpkins is there. Let me see now. It's not quite one o'clock. If I ride fast—I'll borrow the doctor's bicycle. I can't stand this loose pedal of yours any more. If I ride fast I'll be there by half-past two. Say twenty minutes to three. Allowing for twenty minutes in which to persuade Simpkins to start home at once, I ought to be on my way back by three. I'll hustle him along a bit, and there's no reason that I can see why he shouldn't be at Ballymoy House by half-past five."

"You'll never do all that," said Doyle. "Is it likely he'll go with you?"

"It's not exactly likely, but he will. I shall speak to him in such a way that he practically must. Get me the doctor's bicycle at once."

"If it's that you want," said Doyle, "you haven't far to go to look for it. It's within in the hall this minute, for he left it here last night, saying he'd be round for it this morning."

"Good. I'll take it at once and be off."

The grounds of the Donard tennis club are pleasantly situated about a mile outside the town on the Ballymoy road. Meldon reached them well before the time he had arranged, passing through the gate at a quarter past two o'clock. The annual tennis tournament was in full swing. All three courts were occupied by players, and an eager crowd of spectators stood round watching the progress of the matches. Simpkins was perched on top of a step ladder, acting as umpire for two ladies. His position rendered him very conspicuous, and Meldon caught sight of him at once. He took a short cut through a court where a mixed double was in progress and seized Simpkins by the leg.

"Simpkins," he said, "get off that ladder at once."

Simpkins was surprised. So were the two ladies who were playing tennis. They stopped their game and stared at Meldon. Then they glanced at Simpkins with puzzled suspicion. Men, as every one is aware, even men with reputations for respectability, are sometimes arrested suddenly in the most unlikely places for crimes of which no one ever suspected them. It is true that they are very rarely arrested by clergymen, but it is on record of the most famous of all detectives that he once assumed the dress of a clergyman as a disguise. The lady who was serving when Meldon interrupted the game had read the history of that detective's life. She looked at Simpkins with awed horror. Simpkins wriggled uncomfortably on his ladder. He was conscious of being placed in a very unpleasant position, and was anxious, if possible, to divert the attention of the ladies.

"Forty-fifteen," he said loudly, but erroneously, for the score was thirty all. Then he turned to Meldon and added in a whisper: "Go away at once, please."

He hoped that the ladies would go on with their game. They did not. He had given their score wrongly, and they became more suspicious than ever. Nor did Meldon stir.

"Come down off that ladder at once," said Meldon. "I don't want to make a very unpleasant affair public property; but if you don't come down, I'll speak out, and there's a small crowd gathering round us."

This was true. The lady who had been serving dropped the two balls she held in her hand and sidled up towards the step ladder. A number of people, who had been watching an exciting match in the next court, left it, and approached Meldon to find out what was going on. Simpkins' conscience was quite at ease. He had done nothing wrong. He was not, as far as he was aware, mixed up in anything unpleasant. His innocence, though it did not make him feel comfortable, gave him courage to attempt an argument with Meldon.

"Why should I come down?" he said. "I'm umpiring in this match, and I see no reason for leaving it in the middle."

"Very well," said Meldon. "If you choose to take up that sort of attitude you'll only have yourself to thank for the unpleasantness which will follow.

Still, I've always had a regard for you, although you're not what I'd call popular with the people of Ballymoy, so I won't say more than I can help at first. Have you forgotten Miss King?"

"No," said Simpkins, "I haven't. Why should I? I mean to say, there's nothing particular for me to remember about Miss King."

The secretary of the tennis club pushed his way through the crowd. He was in an excited and irritated condition. Every single competitor had complained that the handicapping was disgracefully done. Some were angry because their skill was reckoned too cheaply; others thought that their chances of winning were unduly prejudiced. They had all expressed their opinions freely to the secretary. It was also becoming more and more evident that the tournament could not possibly be finished in the time allotted to it. The secretary had spent the morning urging the players not to waste time. It particularly annoyed him to see that Simpkins' two ladies had stopped playing.

"What's the matter?" he said. "Why the—I mean to say, why on earth don't you go on with your game?"

"I'm sorry to interrupt the proceedings," said Meldon, "but it is imperatively necessary for me to have a few words in private with Simpkins."

The secretary turned on Simpkins at once. He was one of the people who had grumbled most loudly and continuously about his handicap. He had also wasted time by raising obscure points of law on two occasions. The secretary had conceived a strong dislike for him.

"Why don't you go," he said, "and hear what this gentleman has to say? I'll get another umpire."

"He hasn't anything to say to me," said Simpkins.

"He says he has," said the secretary, "and he ought to know."

"Quite right," said Meldon. "I'm the only person who does know. Simpkins can't be really certain that I haven't until he comes and listens."

"Go at once," said the secretary.

Simpkins looked round him for sympathy, but got none. Public opinion was dead against him. The mention of Miss King, whom nobody knew, suggested the possibility of some horrible and deeply interesting scandal. Simpkins got down from his ladder. Meldon at once took him by the arm and led him away.

"Where's your bicycle?" he said.

"What on earth do you want with me?" said Simpkins. "It's quite intolerable—"

"Miss King is waiting for you," said Meldon. "She expects you this afternoon, and if you start at once you'll just be there in time."

"But I've no engagement with Miss King."

"You have not," said Meldon, "at present. But you soon will have an engagement of the most solemn and enduring kind."

"What on earth do you mean?"

"Look here," said Meldon. "There's no use beating about the bush when we haven't a moment to spare. You gave me to understand that you wanted to marry Miss King."

"I didn't. All I said was—"

"That won't do," said Meldon. "You may think that you can play fast and loose with a poor girl's affections in that sort of way, and so you might if she was lonely and unprotected. But as it happens that judge who came to Ballymoy the other day turned out to be Miss King's uncle, and he's quite determined to see this business through. I was telling him about it this morning. I pledged my word to have you on the spot this afternoon, and to get the whole thing settled before dinner."

"But this is utterly ridiculous. I've only spoken to the woman three times in my life."

"A good deal can be done in three interviews," said Meldon. "In this case it appears that a good deal has been done. I don't profess to know exactly what you said to Miss King—"

"I never said anything to her."

"Do you mean to assert that you went through three interviews without uttering a single word."

"Of course not. What I mean to say is—"

"Now you're beginning to hedge," said Meldon, "and that's a bad sign, an uncommonly bad sign. No man hedges in that sort of way unless he has something to conceal. It's perfectly plain to me that you said a good deal to Miss King. Anyhow, she evidently thinks you did. She told the whole story to the judge last night, and he spoke to me about it this morning."

"Told what story?"

"Your story. And the upshot of it was that I promised to bring you there this afternoon. It's all arranged. Miss King is to be at home. The judge will be up the river. I shall leave you with Miss King, and then join the judge. We shall give you a clear hour, and when we come back we shall expect to hear that the whole thing is settled."

"I never heard of such an absurd entanglement in my life."

"There is no entanglement about it. It's perfectly simple, plain, and straightforward. Where's your bicycle?"

Simpkins wavered.

"Perhaps," he said, "I'd better go and explain. It's an infernal nuisance—"

"I don't quite know what you mean by explaining," said Meldon. "There seems to me only one thing for you to do, and that is to go at once and offer to marry Miss King. Where's your bicycle?"

"It's behind the tent; but I must tell the secretary that I'm going. I'm afraid he'll be angry."

"If that bald-headed man with the white moustache is the secretary," said Meldon, "I should say from the way he spoke just now that he'll be extremely glad. If you tell him the whole story you'll find that he'll quite agree with me about what your duty is."

"I shan't tell him, and I hope you won't."

"I certainly won't," said Meldon. "I have too high a sense of the value of time to waste it telling stories to that secretary. Come along and get your bicycle."

"It's just as well," said Meldon a few minutes later, when he and Simpkins had mounted their bicycles—"it's just as well that you have on those white trousers and a cool sort of shirt. We've got to ride pretty fast, and it wouldn't do for you to arrive in a state of reeking heat."

"I want you to understand clearly," said Simpkins, "that I'm not going to do anything more than explain to Miss King that some absurd mistake has arisen; explain, and apologise."

"If you like to call it explaining, you can. But I strongly recommend you to do it thoroughly. I may tell you that I have Callaghan posted behind a tree to watch you, and if you don't offer Miss King proper tokens of affection, I shall hear of it, and so will the judge. It's scarcely necessary for me to tell you, Simpkins, that the judge isn't a man to be trifled with."

"Tokens of affection! Do you mean that I—?"

"I do," said Meldon. "I mean that exactly. And you're to do it as if you liked it. You very probably will like it, once you've broken the ice."

For a few minutes they rode on in silence. Then Simpkins spoke again, —

"Do you mean that I should — that I should hold her hand and kiss her?"

"After you've proposed to her," said Meldon, "not before. It would be what Callaghan calls impropriety of conduct if you did it before, and he'd probably interrupt you. He doesn't like that sort of thing. I shouldn't like it myself either, and I don't think the judge would, although he's evidently a liberal-minded man."

"I couldn't possibly do that," said Simpkins. "I've only spoken to her three times."

"You'll have to," said Meldon, "after she's accepted you. It's the usual thing. Miss King will be angry, quite rightly angry and insulted, if you don't. You read any novel you like, and you'll find that as soon as ever the hero has proposed to the heroine, often without waiting for her answer, he rains passionate kisses on some part of her, generally her hair. I don't ask you to go as far as that; but one or two kisses — you can begin with her hand if you like, and work on gradually."

"Of course I shall do nothing of the sort," said Simpkins. "I shall simply explain to Miss King that owing to some sort of muddle —"

"If I were you, Simpkins, I shouldn't talk too much. From the gaspy sort of way you're speaking now, I imagine you're not in particularly good training, and you have a long ride before you. It will be most unfortunate if, when I've planted you down in front of Miss King, you are unable to do anything except pant. No girl would stand that. By far the best plan for you is to breathe entirely through your nose, and sit well back in your saddle, so that your chest and lungs are kept properly expanded."

Simpkins spoke no more for some time. He may have considered the advice good. He may have felt an increasing difficulty in talking when riding very rapidly. When they reached Ballymoy there were signs of unusual excitement in the street. Doyle and O'Donoghue were standing on the steps of the hotel. A small crowd had gathered on the road in front of them. Most of the shopkeepers were at the doors of their shops. A considerable number of women were looking out of the upper windows of the houses. A cheer arose as the two bicyclists passed through the town. Meldon took off his hat and waved it.

"Musha, good luck to you," shouted a woman's voice.

"That," said Meldon, "is almost certainly Sabina Gallagher. She's naturally greatly interested on account of her cousin."

"Interested in what?" gasped Simpkins.

"Your marriage," said Meldon. "I mentioned it to Doyle this morning, and he has evidently told every one about the place."

Simpkins stopped abruptly and got off his bicycle.

"I'm damned," he said, "if I'm going to stand this."

Meldon also dismounted.

"Get up at once, Simpkins," he said. "We are late enough as it is."

"I'm going straight home," said Simpkins.

"From the look of Doyle and O'Donoghue and the crowd there was in the street," said Meldon, "I should say that they'll probably mob you if you go back now. You're not over and above popular in the place as things stand; and, if the people think that you're behaving badly to Miss King, they'll very likely kill you. From what I've heard since I've been here I don't expect the police will interfere to save you."

"I'm not going to be made a public laughing stock."

"You'll be that and worse if you turn back. There isn't a woman or a girl about the place but will be making jokes about you if you funk it now. Come on."

Simpkins looked back at the street he had just left. The people were standing together gazing after him curiously. He mounted his bicycle and rode on, followed by Meldon.

"I shall explain to Miss King," he said, "that the unpleasant situation in which we find ourselves placed is in no way my fault."

"You can try that if you like," said Meldon. "But I don't expect she'll be at all satisfied."

CHAPTER XXIII

In spite of the fact that his trousers were white instead of black, and that he wore a shirt with a soft collar attached to it, Simpkins looked hotter and more dishevelled than Meldon when they arrived together at the gate of Ballymoy House. They had ridden fast, and it was only a little after five o'clock when they turned off the highroad into the shady avenue.

"Now," said Meldon, "you can dismount if you like, and walk up under the trees to cool yourself. I quite admit that an appearance of breathless eagerness is suitable enough under the circumstances. Every woman likes to feel that a man would come to her at the top of his speed. Still, it's quite possible to overdo it, and I think you'd be better this minute of being a little less purple in the face. Are you very thirsty?"

"I am," said Simpkins. "Anybody would be."

He spoke rather sulkily. He resented the way in which Meldon had forced him to ride, and he did not like paying a visit to a lady, even though he did not intend to propose to marry her, when he was covered from head to foot with dust.

"You're not too thirsty to speak, anyhow," said Meldon. "I was afraid you might be. It wouldn't have done if your mouth had been all parched up like the Ancient Mariner's, just before he bit his arm and sucked the blood. Recollect that you have to speak distinctly and slowly, as well as persuasively. You can't expect Miss King to do all the talking in this case. Her business is to blush and hang back."

"I've told you already," said Simpkins, "that I'm simply—"

"Don't start an argument; but take a wisp of grass and wipe as much dust off your shoes as you can. I don't object to dusty shoes for myself in the least, but they don't suit your style."

Simpkins did as he was told, for he did not share Meldon's indifference to dust. He also wiped his face carefully with a pocket handkerchief, giving it a streaky look.

"I don't think," said Meldon, "that you've improved your appearance much by that last performance. You were better before. But never mind. Miss King has seen you at your best, the Sunday afternoon I brought you up to call, and she'll recollect what you looked like then. In any case, nothing you can do will make you as ghastly as you were that day on the yacht. If she put up with you then, she won't mind you now. Come on."

They left their bicycles near the gate, and walked up together along the avenue.

"Pull yourself together now, Simpkins," said Meldon. "The crisis of your life is almost on you. When we turn the next corner you'll see Miss King seated on a wicker chair on the lawn, waiting for you. At first she'll pretend not to see us; though, of course, she will see us out of the corner of her eye. When we get quite close, so close that she can't possibly ignore us any longer, she will look up suddenly, cast down her eyes again with a blush, and exhibit every sign of pleasurable embarrassment. That will be your opportunity. Step forward and fling yourself at her feet, if that's the way you have determined to do it. I shall slip quietly away, and be out of sight almost at once.... Hullo!"

The exclamation was one of extreme surprise. The scene, when he turned the corner, was not exactly as he had described it to Simpkins. Miss King, indeed, was there, seated in a wicker chair, very much as he had expected. Beside her was a table littered with tea things. At her feet, on a rug, sat Major Kent, in an awkward attitude, with a peculiarly silly look on his face. Sir Gilbert Hawkesby sat upright, at a little distance, in another chair. He appeared to be delivering some kind of an address to Miss King and Major Kent.

"This," said Meldon, "is awkward, uncommonly awkward. You see the result of being late, Simpkins. The judge has evidently given you up, and come down from the river. What the Major is doing here, I can't say. He's the sort of man who will blunder, if blundering is possible."

"I think," said Simpkins, "that we'd better turn back. I can call to-morrow instead."

"Certainly not," said Meldon. "It'll be all right. The judge knows what is expected of him, and will disappear at once, making a plausible excuse, so as not to embarrass Miss King unnecessarily. I shall deal with the Major. It won't take me five minutes."

"Still," said Simpkins, "it might be better—"

"You can't run away now, in any case," said Meldon. "They've seen us.—Hullo, Miss King! Here we are at last. I'm sure you thought we were never coming."

He dragged Simpkins forward by the arm. Miss King, blushing deeply, to Meldon's great delight, rose from her chair and came forward to meet them. The judge, a broad smile on his face, followed her. The Major hung about in the background, and appeared to be nervous.

"You'd like some tea, I'm sure," said Miss King.

"Not for me," said Meldon; "but Mr. Simpkins will be delighted to get a cup."

"Oh! but you must have some," said Miss King. "You look so hot."

"Mr. Simpkins is hot. I'm not in the least. In fact, what I'd like most would be a short stroll up the river with Sir Gilbert and the Major."

"Certainly," said the judge. "I've had my tea, and I'm quite ready for a walk."

"Come along, Major," said Meldon.

Major Kent showed no sign of moving. He had established himself behind Miss King's chair, and was eyeing Simpkins with an expression of hostility and distrust.

"Never mind the Major," said the judge. "He's all right where he is."

He took Meldon's arm as he spoke and strolled off across the lawn. Meldon turned and winked angrily at the Major. The judge began an account of the capture of his last salmon, holding fast to Meldon's arm.

"Excuse me one moment," said Meldon. "I must give the Major a hint. He's one of those men who, though extremely kind and sympathetic, is often a little wanting in tact."

"He's all right," said the judge. "He's quite happy."

"I daresay he is," said Meldon. "My point is that Simpkins isn't. How can he possibly—?"

"Now that we're out of earshot," said the judge, "I hope that you'll allow me to congratulate you on the success of your plan. Your management of the details was admirable."

Meldon was susceptible to this kind of flattery, and he felt that he deserved a little praise. It had been no easy matter to track Simpkins to Donard, and very difficult to bring him back to Ballymoy. He forgot the Major for a moment and went willingly with the judge.

"I had rather a job of it," he said. "I had to go the whole way to Donard to get him."

The judge seemed surprised.

"Really!" he said. "I should hardly have thought there's been time for you to go and come back."

"I ride pretty fast," said Meldon, with an air of satisfaction.

"And the Major never said a word about it."

"The Major didn't know. I don't tell the Major all the details of my plans. You scarcely know him yet, Sir Gilbert. When you do you'll understand that he isn't the kind of man to whom any one would confide the working out of a delicate negotiation. He's a thorough gentleman, quite the best type of military officer; a man who might be trusted to run absolutely straight under any circumstances. But he has the defects of his qualities. He's rather thick-headed, and he takes an extraordinary delight in arguing."

"I'm glad to hear you speak so well of him," said the judge, "now that he's—"

"I think I'll go back and get him now," said Meldon. "He has a very strong dislike for Simpkins, and I wouldn't like him to break out in any way before Miss King. It might be awkward for her."

"He won't," said the judge. "In his present temper he won't break out against any one. He's almost idiotically happy. You might have seen it in his face."

"He had a sheepish look," said Meldon. "It's a curious thing, isn't it, Sir Gilbert, that when a man is really satisfied with himself he gets to look like a sheep. I daresay you've noticed it, or perhaps you haven't. In your particular line of life you come more into contact with people who are extremely dissatisfied. Still, occasionally you must have had a chance of seeing some one who had just had an unusual stroke of good luck. Mrs. Lorimer, for instance"—Meldon winked at the judge—"when the jury brought in its verdict of 'Not Guilty.' But I really must run back for the Major."

The judge seemed disinclined to discuss Mrs. Lorimer, but he held fast to Meldon's arm.

"After what you said to me this morning," he said, "the events of the afternoon were not altogether a surprise, though I confess I didn't know that my niece cared as much as she does."

"Oh, she's very keen on it."

"So it appears; but would you mind telling me how you knew that?"

"She told me so herself."

"She— Oh!"

The judge looked Meldon straight in the face. He was surprised, and evidently sceptical.

"If you don't believe me," said Meldon, "ask Miss King."

"Anyhow," said the judge, "however you knew it, you were perfectly right. I don't like to go into details, but when I came down from the river this afternoon the position of affairs was quite plain to me."

"She was looking eager, I suppose, and perhaps a little anxious."

"I should hardly say anxious. The fact is that they—"

"Was the Major there then?"

"Of course he was," said the judge.

"I don't see any 'of course' about it. He might have come afterwards."

"If you'd seen what I saw," said the judge—"a mere glimpse, of course I coughed at once. But if you'd been there you'd know that he couldn't have come afterwards. He must have been there for some time."

"I don't know what you mean," said Meldon.

"If you will have it in plain language," said the judge, "the whole thing was settled, and the usual accompaniments were in full swing."

"Do you mean to suggest that my friend Major Kent was kissing Miss King?"

"As well as I could see, he was."

"After proposing to her?"

"Certainly. He wouldn't do it before."

"There's been some frightful mistake," said Meldon. "I must go back and set things straight at once."

"Wait a minute. Surely this is what you wanted all along?"

"No. It isn't. What I arranged—what do you suppose I brought Simpkins here for?"

"I don't know in the least. To tell you the truth, Simpkins strikes me as *de trop*. What did you bring him for?"

"I brought him to marry Miss King, of course."

"I must have misunderstood you this morning," said the judge. "I thought Major Kent was the man you were backing."

"You can't have thought that," said Meldon. "I spoke quite plainly."

"My niece seems to have made the same mistake," said the judge. "I'm sure she was quite prepared to take the man you recommended, whoever he was, and she has taken Major Kent. You can't have spoken as plainly as you thought you did. We both took you up wrong."

"Who brought the Major here?"

"Till just this minute" said the judge, "I thought you did."

"I didn't. How could I possibly have brought him when I was on at Donard kidnapping that idiot Simpkins, and carrying him off from the middle of a tennis tournament. It ought to have been perfectly obvious that I couldn't have brought the Major here. Even you, with your extraordinary faculty for making mistakes about perfectly simple things, must be able to see that."

"If you didn't bring him," said the judge, "I suppose he came by himself. Very likely he fell into the same mistake that my niece and I did. He may have thought you wanted him to marry her."

"He can't possibly have thought anything of the sort. I've told him all along—in fact, it was really his plan."

"That Simpkins should marry my niece?"

"Yes. We've talked it over a dozen times at least."

"Of the two," said the judge, "I'd rather have the Major for a nephew. I scarcely know him, and I don't know Simpkins at all; but judging simply by appearances, I should say that the Major is the better man."

"He is, decidedly. Simpkins is in every way his inferior. The fact is—I don't want to say anything to hurt your feelings."

"Don't mind my feelings. They're accustomed to laceration."

"Well, I think the Major is too good a man to—"

"You can't expect me to agree with you there," said the judge. "But I appreciate your point of view, and I respect your feeling of affection for your friend."

"There's no use beating about the bush in this way," said Meldon. "If you think I'm going to remain passively indifferent while my unfortunate friend allows himself to be entrapped by a woman like Mrs. Lorimer—"

"Good Heavens!" said the judge. "Mrs. Lorimer! What on earth has Mrs. Lorimer—?"

"There's no use your pretending to be ignorant of the facts," said Meldon. "You must know them."

He wrenched his arm from the judge's grip as he spoke, and started at a rapid pace towards the lawn. Sir Gilbert Hawkesby hesitated for a moment with a look of bewilderment on his face. Then he ran after Meldon, and caught him by the arm again.

"Hold on a minute," he said. "Something has just occurred to me. Before you do anything rash let me tell you a little story."

"I can't wait," said Meldon. "Every moment increases the Major's danger. Further endearments—"

"We needn't be afraid of that," said the judge, "while Simpkins is there, and I really do want to tell you my story. It may, I think it will, alter your whole view of the situation."

"I'll give you two minutes," said Meldon, taking out his watch.

"One will do," said the judge, speaking rapidly. "All I have to say is this. I met Mrs. Lorimer on the platform of Euston Station on the evening of her acquittal, and I mistook her for my niece who was travelling in the same train."

Meldon put his watch into his pocket and stared at the judge.

"It was quite an excusable mistake," said Sir Gilbert soothingly. "Any one might have made it. The likeness is extraordinary."

"The thing to do now," said Meldon after a long pause, "is to get Simpkins out of this as quickly as possible. He's no use here."

"None," said the judge. "Why did you bring him?"

"I brought him to marry your niece," said Meldon. "I told you that before."

"Marry!— Oh yes, while you thought she was— Do you dislike Simpkins very much?"

"No; I don't. But everybody else, including the Major, does."

"I'm beginning to understand things a little," said the judge, "and I agree with you that the first thing to be done is to remove Simpkins. We shall have a good deal to talk over, and his presence—"

"When you speak of talking things over," said Meldon, "I hope you've no intention of alluding to Mrs. Lorimer in your niece's company. After all, we ought to recollect that we're gentlemen. I've always done my best to spare her feelings, and I hope that nothing—"

"I shan't mention the subject."

Meldon and Sir Gilbert walked back together. They found the group on the lawn in a state of obvious discomfort. Major Kent was standing behind Miss King's chair, looking like a policeman on guard over some specially valuable life threatened by a murderer. His face wore an expression of suspicious watchfulness. Simpkins sat on the chair previously occupied by Sir Gilbert, and looked ill at ease. He had a cup of tea balanced on his knee. His eyes wandered restlessly from Miss King to Major Kent, and then back again. He did not see his way to making his apology or offering his explanation while Major Kent was present. At the same time he dreaded being left alone with Miss King. Now that he was face to face with her he felt a great difficulty in giving any account of himself. Miss King was doing her best to keep up a friendly conversation with him, but the Major refused to speak a word, and she felt the awkwardness of the situation.

"I suppose, Simpkins," said Meldon, "that your tournament would be over by the time you got back to Donard, even if you started at once."

Simpkins rose to his feet with alacrity. He did not like being hunted about the country by Meldon, and he had no intention of going back to Donard; but he welcomed any prospect of escape from the horrible situation in which he found himself.

"Won't you finish your tea?" said Miss King.

"He has finished it," said Meldon; "and he'd better not have any more if he means to ride back to Donard. He's not in good training, and another chunk of that rich cake of yours, Miss King, might upset him. Good-bye, Simpkins."

"I'd like," said Simpkins, trying to assert himself, "to speak a word to you, Mr. Meldon."

"So you shall," said Meldon, "but not now. The day after to-morrow you shall say all you want to. Just at present I haven't time to listen to you."

"Perhaps," said Simpkins, turning to Miss King, "I'd better say good-bye."

He shook hands with her and Sir Gilbert, absolutely ignored Meldon and Major Kent, and walked across the lawn. Meldon ran after him.

"I hope, Simpkins," he said, "that this will be a lesson to you. Owing to your miserable procrastination, the Major has stepped in before you and secured Miss King. You might just mention that to Doyle and O'Donoghue as you pass the hotel. They'll be anxious to hear the news."

CHAPTER XXIV

Major Kent and Meldon dined at Ballymoy House, and spent a very pleasant evening. At eleven o'clock they started on their drive home.

"I'm sorry—" said the Major, and then paused.

"I hope not," said Meldon. "You ought not to be."

"I'm not," said the Major. "I merely meant that I'm afraid this rather unexpected—"

"Go on," said Meldon. "I'd like to get at your exact feelings if I can."

"Isn't this rather—rather an upset for you, J.J.?"

"For me?"

"Yes. On account of that plan of yours—Simpkins, you know. I was afraid all the time you would feel disappointed."

"My plan," said Meldon, "is perfectly sound, and is working out admirably."

"But you said that you meant—"

"You're making one of your usual mistakes, Major. You're confusing the end I had in view with the means I adopted to bring it about. What I originally undertook to do was to remove Simpkins from Ballymoy. In that I have been entirely successful. He can't, simply can't, spend another week in the place. I mentioned to Doyle this morning that Simpkins intended to marry Miss King. Doyle evidently told several other people, for half the town was out to cheer us as we passed through on our way from Donard. When Simpkins sneaked back at about six o'clock this evening, looking like a whipped dog, there was sure to have been a large crowd to meet him. I said he was to tell Doyle the result as he passed; but whether he did or not, Doyle is sure to have found it out before night. How do you suppose Simpkins will be feeling?"

The Major chuckled.

"And what do you suppose will happen?" said Meldon.

"I don't know. They'll laugh at him, I expect."

"Laugh isn't the word," said Meldon. "They'll get out the town band and play tunes under his window half the night. He won't be able to put his nose outside the door without being met by a tribe of small boys grinning. There isn't a woman or a girl in the place, from Sabina Gallagher up, but will be making fun of him. Doyle and O'Donoghue and all the police will call round to condole with him. No man could stand it for a week. He'll go to-morrow, and have his luggage sent after him. That's the way my plan has worked out with regard to Simpkins, and I've no reason to be ashamed of it."

"I'm glad you look at it that way, J. J. I was afraid perhaps—"

"You needn't have been. I'm not one of those small-minded men who allow themselves to be tied to details, and are irritated because things don't go exactly as they expect. I look to the real object, the great ultimate end which I hope to achieve. As long as that comes off all right I don't worry myself about trifles. In this case I consider—and everybody who takes a large view will also consider—that I have been entirely successful. And now let's talk of something else. I'll marry you, of course."

"We both hope you will," said the Major.

"Right. That's settled. What about bridesmaids?"

"We haven't gone into that yet."

"You must have bridesmaids, of course. And I don't think you could do better than your own god-daughter. She'll be over the whooping-cough by that time, I hope."

"I'd like that very much," said the Major. "But isn't she rather small?"

"Not at all. She can be led up the aisle immediately behind the bride. Sabina Gallagher can lead her. I'm going to engage Sabina as nurse and general servant. Now that Simpkins is going, Doyle can get that red-haired girl, Sabina's cousin. She'll do him quite well for all he wants. And he never properly appreciated Sabina. Shall we regard that as settled?"

"I suppose it will be all right."

"Quite," said Meldon. "You may safely leave it in my hands. And now, Major, since everything has worked out in such a satisfactory way for you, I hope you'll try and feel more kindly towards poor Simpkins. He'll suffer a lot as it is; and I don't think you ought to make any further attempt on his life. I always thought you were going too far in your resentment."

"J. J., I really—"

"The judge will let you fish anywhere you like; so that you haven't a ghost of a grievance left."

"I'll ask Simpkins to the wedding if you like."

"That," said Meldon, "would be a refinement of cruelty, and I won't consent to its being done. Wanting to kill the man was bad enough. I never liked it. But what you propose now is infinitely worse. Why can't you forgive the wretched creature, and then forget all about him?"

It was half-past twelve o'clock. Major Kent, in spite of the excitement of the afternoon, was sound asleep when he was roused by a sharp knocking at his door. He sat up in bed and struck a match.

"Good gracious, J. J.," he said, "what on earth do you want at this time of night? Why aren't you asleep?"

"I couldn't sleep," said Meldon, "with the feeling on my mind that I had been doing a wrong—quite without malice and under circumstances which excuse it, but still doing a wrong to Miss King."

"You mean in mistaking her—"

"Quite so."

"That'll be all right, J. J. Don't worry about it. Go back to bed again."

"I'm not worrying in the least," said Meldon. "I never worry; but when I've done a wrong to anybody, I like to make amends at once."

"You can't do anything to-night. It's too late. Do go back to bed."

"I have done something. I've made amends, and here they are. I want you to give them to her to-morrow morning."

He held out a sheet of paper as he spoke.

"If that's a written apology," said the Major, "it's quite unnecessary. But you can leave it on the dressing-table. It's nice of you to think of making it."

"It's not an apology," said Meldon. "Apologies are futile things. This is something that will be of some use and real value to Miss King. It's the end of a novel."

"What are you talking about?"

"I've always understood," said Meldon, "that the last few paragraphs of a novel are by far the most difficult part to write. Now that I've found out what Miss King's art really is, I think the best thing I can do, by way of making amends for my unfortunate mistake, is to hand over to her the conclusion of a novel, ready written. I've been at it ever since you went to bed. Here it is. I'll just read it out to you, and then you can give it to her with my compliments to-morrow morning."

"'The evening closed slowly, a glory still lingering on the shining waters of the bay, as if day were indeed loth to leave the scene it had found so fair. A solitary figure breasted the long hill above the little town, striding steadily along the grey road, which wound eastwards into the gloom.'"

"It may perhaps be better to mention to you, Major, though Miss King will recognise the fact at once for herself, that the solitary figure is Simpkins."

"'At the crown of the hill, just where the road begins to dip again, at the spot where the last view of the town and the bay is obtained, the lonely traveller paused. He turned round, and for a while stood gazing wistfully at the scene he had left behind. The hum of the town's life, the sudden shoutings of the children at their play, even, as he fancied, the eternal pathos of the ocean's murmuring, were borne upwards to him on the evening breeze. Far off, among the trees, twinkled a solitary light. A great sob shook his frame suddenly. There, in the warm glow of the lamp, whose rays reached him like those of some infinitely distant star, sat the woman whom he loved, who might have been his, who was— Ah me! He set his teeth. His lips, bloodless now as the very lips of death, were pressed tight together. He turned again, and, still walking bravely, descended the hill into the gloom.

"'So life deals with us. To one is given, and he hath abundance. From another is taken away even that which he hath. Yet, who knows? It was towards the east he travelled. The sun had set indeed; but it would rise again. And it is always in the east that suns rise.'"

"Thanks, J. J.," said the Major sleepily. "It's awfully fine. If you wouldn't mind putting it on the dressing-table under my brush, it will be quite safe till morning."